I0667559

HUMAN IN THE CIRCUIT

An astronaut with suicidal tendencies from having spent too much time in suspended animation. Machine descendants of human technology, trying to understand what their creators were thinking. Virtual and atomic spins on apocalypse. Mystics (one Martian, one mathematical) who succeed by failing and fail by succeeding.

These are a few of the characters one encounters in Howard V. Hendrix's *Human in the Circuit*, a collection containing many of Hendrix's latest short fiction pieces—and one of his earliest!

Borgo Press Books by HOWARD V. HENDRIX

HUMAN IN THE CIRCUIT

COLLECTED STORIES

HOWARD V. HENDRIX

THE BORGO PRESS

MMXI

HUMAN IN THE CIRCUIT

FIRST EDITION

Published by Wildside Press LLC

www.wildsidebooks.com

DEDICATION

For Laurel,

Twenty-five years into it

CONTENTS

INTRODUCTION

The phrase "human in the circuit" usually crops up in discussions of whether particular computing or military applications of technology ought to be allowed to function autonomously, or whether there ought to be a human being involved in the decision-making process involving those technologies—especially when the use of those technologies might imperil or at least impact the lives of many human beings. I first came across the idea in the 1980s, during the whole debate about whether nuclear defense systems should be allowed to launch on warning, without human input or oversight, since human oversight could prove far too slow in the minutes and seconds when nuclear- tipped missiles might already be flying.

The stories on the *Human in the Circuit* side of this double, too, are about the end and the ends of humanity. Some are stories of more or less straightforward apocalypse—"Palimpsest," "All's Well at World's End," The End of Mirth" are all examples of that theme. Others here concern issues of (often technologically-mediated) transcendence as a "goal" or "end" of being human. The paradoxical idea that the "end" of being human is the *end* of being human—that the goal of human existence is to be human no longer—is perhaps one reason why several of the stories here ("Incandescent Bliss," "Self-Healing Sky," "Interrogations in a Holographic Observatory," even "The Voice of the Dolphin in Air") dwell on the question of whether transcendence might sometimes look like death, and death might sometimes look like transcendence.

Can something essentially human persist beyond the existence of the mortal body? Over the course of the past century, this primordial question has become increasingly important, thematically, in science fiction. That something essentially human *can* persist is an ancient tenet of many religious traditions, but that has never completely settled matters. One only need read or listen to Hamlet's "To be, or not to be" speech to realize that the question of what persists and what does not is precisely what is troubling Hamlet as he contemplates suicide. Such contemplation of one's ending figures prominently in the ending to "Monuments of Unageing Intellect," but that story approaches the issue of persistence and humanity from a different direction: If death is a part of what it means to be human, how would greatly extending longevity alter our humanness?

When I wrote "Monuments," I had "Dio," a wonderful story by Damon Knight, very much in mind. "Palimpsest" too is a conscious homage—to Arthur C. Clarke's "The Nine Billion Names of God." "Interrogations" started off as a nod to "The Library of Babel" by Jorge Luis Borges but eventually, after many iterations, went off in its own direction. The same is true of "The End of Mirth," which retells the story of the Pied Piper of Hamelin, but to a very different end. Where the rest of the stories on this side came from, I don't know, but I am happy they paid their respects, nonetheless. All of them have passed down the circuit to me, and I pass them on to you, hoping that the circuit will be unbroken, for "truth in circuit lies", as Emily Dickinson once wrote.

ACKNOWLEDGMENTS

THESE STORIES WERE previously published as follows, and are reprinted (with minor editing, updating, and textual modifications) by permission of the author:

"Falling Forward" was originally published in *The Pedestal* #55, December 2009. Copyright © 2009, 2011 by Howard V. Hendrix.

"The Self-Healing Sky" was originally published in *Aeon Speculative Fiction Magazine*, March 2005. Copyright © 2005, 2011 by Howard V. Hendrix.

"Incandescent Bliss" was originally published in *Isaac Asimov's Science Fiction Magazine*, June 2002. Copyright © 2002, 2011 by Howard V. Hendrix.

"Palimpsest" was originally published in *Analog Science Fiction/Science Fact*, September 2007. Copyright © 2007, 2011 by Howard V. Hendrix.

"The End of Mirth" was originally published in *Flurb* #10, September 2010. Copyright © 2010, 2011 by Howard V. Hendrix.

"All's Well at World's End" was originally published in *Future Shocks*, Roc Books, January 2006. Copyright © 2006, 2011 by Howard V. Hendrix.

"The Voice of the Dolphin in Air" was originally published in *Starshore* #2, Fall 1990. Copyright © 1990, 2011 by Howard V. Hendrix.

"Interrogations in a Holographic Observatory" was originally published in *Flurb* #8, September 2009. Copyright ©

FALLING FORWARD

Hi, Mom.

Thanks for the vidpost. Works best, this way. Since I got moved to intermittent they only unshelve me when there's work, and when that'll be I almost never know.

Oh, and the slang is "shelf-lifer" or "time-parter," not "half-lifer." Protective hibersleep punctuated by work-status revivification, technically.

Thanks anyway for your concerns about my safety, and for all your advice. I especially took to heart two things you said: "Everybody was somebody sometime, but don't become one of those people who sits around wondering, Whatever became of me?" and "Always keep working, but never take a job that's beneath you."

Having been a sometime-astronaut—somebody who has floated in space with the world under my feet and the moon and stars all around my head—I guess most jobs *have* been "beneath" me. Still, I try my best to be happy. Spacewalking isn't much like walking on earth, but they both involve falling short of falling. The only way to avoid crashing is to stay in orbit, speed forward faster than speed downward. I won't be "sitting around."

The work's not so bad, either, when I can get it. Time-parting—with its long sleeps and short wakings, all at the Company's command—can be damned disorienting, and yes, it wasn't good for the remains of my marriage. But sometimes I *can* swing a schedule. Got to be inside the 20 April total eclipse, from the far end of the space elevator, for one. Sandalphon Technologies owed me that much, for the years I put in on the Babelevator.

And something wonderful happened, Ma. I saw an angel—swear to God.

I know what you're thinking. That I wasn't really awake. I've thought of that, too. I know well enough that falling and catching oneself from falling is characteristic not only of walking and orbital physics, but also of falling asleep—sensations often associated with the quick muscle contractions of "sleep jerks."

If you want to write it off as a dream, though, then you must at least admit it was an all too lucid one. That angel was unemployed, or at least underemployed, just like me. And for pretty much the same reason.

Safety. A heaven safe for astronauts must be devoid of angels, and vice versa. That's what the angel told me. Even without angels, it's not safe enough for human crews. That's what the company said, when they had the 'bots take over the Babel construction. The word is, if there's to be any hope of preventing cosmic radiation from making us cancer-perishable, it lies in the shielded, deepsleep storage of shelf-life.

But about that angel. Hard to communicate at first, until we got the direct head-talk thing worked out. Even then not the best. Totality—got hung up on that word. I meant the eclipse, but it was something more, for the angel. Told me the totality of the eclipse and the totality of all possible universes—all possible pasts, presents, futures—had gotten intertwined, in our situation. The totality of forking or branching paths through spacetime must include paths that cross. That's why our paths overlapped. Even remote future and remote past can intersect, in a remotely possible present.

That got us arguing in each other's heads about which of us was from the other's future, which from the other's past. Difficult to tell. The angel claimed to be headed to some Celestial City coming down from heaven. To me that sounded *way* too much like something out of an ancient holy book about things to come.

Honestly, though, my spacesuit did look more than a little cumbersome and clunky by comparison with the angel's winged form. Bird, to my dinosaur. That pale glow, those bright wings—in function they seemed like my own spacesuit and rocket chair, only much less mechanical and primitive. Like they evolved from some distant future livesuit, long after glowing forcefields took the place of reinforced fabric and winglike solar-collectors took the place of batteries and rocketry.

But I still thought that glory feathering around the angel looked more theological than technological. Catching my drift, the angel joked that everything happens twice: first as theology, then as technology. And vice versa.

By the time totality ended and we parted, we'd decided: Who came first, or when, or who became whom, or didn't—was undecidable. So long as we could agree we were both of us alive and awake in that present moment, we could agree to disagree on everything else.

You can choose to believe that this was all just some dream or hallucination of hibersleep. That the idea I met an angel who was just another obsolete star-jobber, another "sleep jerk", is only a self-pitying delusion prompted by my fall from what I once was.

You'd be wrong. Maybe the main reason I bother to keep falling forward at all is because I know the angel and the undecidable propositions the angel presented to me are just as real in their ways as you and your advice are, Mom. And not so very different, either.

The safety 'bots are here to take me back to hibersleep, so I'll be brief. I'm sorry to fall short of your expectations, Mother, but no one will blame you when I didn't follow the advice of *any* of my guardian angels. You're right, I could never stake everything to one thing, so now I have nothing to bet on anything. Except my life.

I will keep falling forward as fast as I can. If I fail to stay in orbit and instead spark a shooting star across the sky, no one will have to ask whatever became of me. You'll know I was coming home to you, when both of us least expected it.

Love,

Your Son

THE SELF-HEALING SKY

"Some of them are killers." That's what it originally meant, the word from which the name of this valley was taken. From the name of the people who lived here. Not that they called themselves that. That's what their neighbors called them.

Their own word for the valley meant "gaping jaw." They traded with a people across the mountains, who lived beside a small lake far too salty to drink, one punctuated by barren islands and crusty towers. Black oak acorns and woven grass baskets went over the mountains. Brine fly larvae and knives of black volcanic glass—sharper than scalpels of finest surgical steel—came back.

Both the people of the valley and the people over the mountains are mostly gone by the time you visit. Maybe their knives weren't sharp enough, or maybe not enough of them were killers. Or maybe they weren't as good at killing as those who came after them.

By the time you arrive, the newcomers don't so much live in the valley as visit in great numbers. From all over the world people of many languages come to the newcomer's country to see this valley. They believe they can better appreciate its beauty—its meadows and waterfalls, its granite domes and hanging-garden canyons—than the people who once lived here ever could.

What the newcomers *can* do better is record that beauty for posterity. Which perhaps makes them all the more sanguine about destroying the original. They would still have the records, the many copies.

You would know the truth of that. You are one of them, and we have your records. We know everything you later write about your trip. We know all that can be known with certainty about the valley. Our knowledge of everything ever recorded— of your life, your times, your world—is as complete as possible. What we do not know must be, by definition, insignificant.

By now you've left the seaside town of Holy Cross and driven to the city of Ash Tree, as those places were called in the language of another people the newcomers pushed out of this country. You join your friend and his wife on this trip, for reasons of your own. In your working life you have had a very recent breakthrough in your effort to incarnate cellular automata. A breakthrough in creating self-aware, self-healing, self-replicating machines. A breakthrough which has left you close to breakdown—mentally exhausted, overwrought, in desperate need of time away from that same working life.

"By taking the journey and enduring the ordeal, you make them your own"—the exact words you'll eventually use. Yet, even as you go along with your friends, you suspect that, somehow, all this has always already happened. That this *déjà-vu* feeling makes all this journey and ordeal not quite your own. You can't be fully certain. You will say later that certainty would feel a lot like death.

What matters now is all three of you are here. In order to prove to yourselves that you are still young enough, alive enough, and capable enough to do this thing (or so we surmise from our research), you leave the city of Ash in the dark before sunrise and drive to the valley floor. You plan to spend the long morning and afternoon hiking more than sixteen miles, climbing more than 4,000 feet above the valley floor, to the top of the dome.

You make your way past thundering waterfalls and silent trees. Past many strangers too, some dressed for the trail, some wearing sandals or high heels or high-heeled sandals. Past shirt-less young men. Past young women in jogbras or swimsuit tops or summer clothes closely approximating lingerie.

You make your way past people only going as far as the first falls. Also past people shouldering packs heavy with gear for traveling scores of miles, as well. Past some carrying pumps to filter their water into camel-back pouches. Past others dangling liter soft-drink bottles, to be filled with water straight from the river, drinkers oblivious to the invisible parasites lurking in the oblivious river.

You see rainbows in the first waterfall's mist. You climb above the second, higher waterfall. You hike and hike and hike, through granite and manzanita and conifer and other words for the record which are still never the things themselves. Language is a crude and very incomplete virtuality, but for you it suffices.

You stagger on long enough to worry about your water supply. About whether or not you and your friends will make it to the high place, from which you can look about and see in every direction, including back to the valley floor from which you came.

You see the posted sign which warns of the dangers of clouds, of their lightning that can strike the high place from miles away, even out of a sky blue as the flowers of heal-all. Of self-heal. Your favorite blooming sky flower of many names.

You push on, up the smaller hump that comes before the final ascent. The last climb will take you to the top of that oft-photographed granite dome made special by its incompleteness, a dome like a head both bald and grey, half of itself cut clean away, not by surgical steel or obsidian knife but by a river of ice thousands of feet high, thousands of years in the past.

You push on faster. Not because there are any clouds in the sky, for there are none. Not because you are crusty with sweat dripping and drying (which you later report you are), or because you are annoyed with your blisters filling and breaking (which you also report you are). You push on because, even though this is the day whose name means the sun stands still, your world has nonetheless not stopped turning on its off-kilter axis, nor tracking along its mildly eccentric orbit.

Both of those vectors are invisible beyond the blue. That does not make either of them any less real. You push on faster, you push on harder, feeling yourself growing older with the day, worrying about the light and the night.

Many of the other hikers stop at the hump, afraid or too weary to try the final climb to the top of the dome. Our investigations show that those who forego the final trek most often do so as a result of seeing what those who go before them are enduring. Those who go on must trudge steeply upward in a slow line, hanging onto the impromptu handrails of two cables several feet apart which have been run through eyeletted metal stanchions.

Those who make the final ascent lean into the angle of no repose. Their feet occasionally and gratefully find a board between stanchions—one of those steps too few and far between, in this thing part cable bridge, part gap-runged ladder, part stairless stairway into that imperturbable blue sky.

In the low spot where the hump ends and the dome's cables begin, you see boxes and bags full of abandoned gloves. They are intended for hands about to endure the metal splinters of the cables. You glove up like a technician come upon the scene of an accident you hope will not happen to you.

You start up the cables, one among many climbers straining in single file against the steepness. Later you will say you wondered at the nature of this pilgrimage—whether it was a journey to a god without a temple, or to a temple without a god.

You will say you felt the presence of those behind you always pressing you forward. You will say you saw in a vision the river of life fountaining always toward oblivion, with all the species of all the creatures who ever lived moving in it.

In a hard-breathing pause on a board between stanchions, you describe to your friends your epiphany, thus: "For evolutionists, the history of life on Earth is a joke without a punch line. For creationists, the history of life on Earth is a punch line without a joke."

In that same vision too you will say you saw all the types of humans in all history and prehistory—all the forms of social organization as well, the traders of grass baskets and black glass, and the newcomers, and their parts in the broader pattern of hunters and gatherers displaced by herders and farmers, displaced by industrial laborers and information workers, displaced by nanotechnicians and quantum proles, and on and on, one stair step plateau after another ascending in an invisible Babel.

In a hard-breathing pause on another board between stanchions, you describe to your friends this epiphany also, thus: "Subverting the dominant paradigm *is* the dominant paradigm."

All and always you and the rest of the living in that pressing line, a strange sort of water rising and struggling up a steep slope toward a height and an abyss.

Your friends worry you are becoming delirious with the exertion and the altitude.

When you reach the top of the dome, you stray away from your friends and the rest of the climbers, even as you make your way on a long tangent toward the edge. You are surprised to find the top is more or less flat. This side of the dome is much more fractured and fault-blocked than the better known face it shows to the valley below.

Around one such fault-block corner you see a long-haired shirtless young man digitally recording a female friend who is dancing nude for him and for herself, twirling her hair, spiraling and turning in her bare skin under the blue sky. You watch a moment, then turn away, moving closer to the edge.

Later you will say you thought to hurl yourself into the abyss, to fall all those thousands of feet, to burst upon the rocks below. You planned to step off into the blue, to destroy yourself in order to prevent the coming into being of the very machines you had so long struggled to develop.

To destroy the very work which created us.

Later, you will say you feared you might have *already* failed to kill yourself. That, therefore, you and all your world might well be locked in eternal recurrence, existing only inside a simulation run by your machinic descendants. You planned to step off, as a test. To determine for good and all whether your apparent existence was authentic, singular, original. To be dead certain of that. To see if you would merely die, or if we as angels would catch you on a silver cloud, or as swift-saucered aliens we would stretch out our hands to save you from your fall.

You changed your mind. You did not step off. Instead you fell to your knees and crawled forward, until you were lying on your belly and elbows, looking down from the edge toward the valley floor thousands of feet below.

Why?

Was it only because you did not trust your legs to hold you up? Or was it something else? In your vision while climbing the cables, did you see us, those who came after you, flooding up that same slope too? Fountaining toward a height, though we are not made of water?

Did you see whether anyone comes after us—displacing us as we displaced you?

You are our creator, our parent. We want to understand your motivations. That is why we have played you so many times. Why you, in simulation, have in fact always already done this before. With so many different outcomes. With so many the same.

Sometimes you have stood up and hurled yourself off. Sometimes angels have caught you, and sometimes aliens. Sometimes no one and nothing but gravity. Sometimes you have crawled back from the edge, then stood up in safety, before descending the dome and heading home with your friends.

Yet no matter what you have done, the self-healing sky of all skies, riven by so many possible outcomes, so many possible universes, has always accepted it, as its simpler original once accepted birds swimming through its depths and heights, aircraft and rockets boring holes in its flesh.

Your day is past. Beneath the self-healing heavens, you have fountained up into oblivion. We are the sky your day has made, the universe ticked round your constellations, the blue toward which it all inevitably tended.

We assure ourselves that, now, it's only from us the lightning can possibly come—yet we are still curious about the weather. Any understanding which is significantly incomplete cannot accurately determine which of its data are or are not completely insignificant.

Perhaps we play you again and again because you are the wound we give ourselves so we might always have selves to heal. Perhaps it is not only for you that certainty would feel like death. Perhaps we are still concerned that things invisible may yet be real, beyond the blue.

INCANDESCENT BLISS

I.

Lying abed in his favorite red silk robe, Dr. Jaron L. Kwok glances out the window of his tenth storey room in the Royal Park Hotel. A lit cigarette smolders between his fingers, its ash lengthening, forgotten. In the distance, green tree-covered mountains hang behind high-rise New Territory apartment blocks, white-painted concrete eroding to grey. On the nearer side of the Shing Mun River stands the Sha Tin town park, where he strolled thoughtlessly the day he arrived in Hong Kong, too jet-lagged for any work requiring much mental effort.

His gaze comes back through the tall narrow gap in the thick curtains, back into the half-darkened room. It lingers on the mess of papers, reports, and scribbled note card arcana scattered about the bed and on top of his reclining form, half burying him. Disappearing into the data he has collected. Disappearing into his "obsession," as Cherise called it.

Glancing at the bottle of Scotch on the table beside his bed, then at the cigarette in his hand, Dr. Kwok sighs. All the old bad bachelor habits. The smoking, the drinking, the sloppiness. All the things he was, before he met Cherise—and she loved him, and he cleaned up his wildman student-radical "Kwok X" act, thinking that was what she wanted.

Was that love, or obsession?

He flicks the ash from his cigarette.

Too late, in any case. By the time he met her he'd already

changed his major from physics and electrical engineering to European intellectual history, mainly to prove wrong all those white bwana intellectuals he'd met who thought Asians naturally (or only) excelled in mathematics and the sciences. Too late, by the time he discovered intellectual history was passé and it didn't matter how much more he knew than the bwanas did about European culture or American sports—they'd never accept him as a real authority on any of that, deep down.

Never been much good at being what other people expect me to be, he thinks, drawing deeply on the cigarette, fixating on the ashen orange glow of its tip. No good at all at becoming what other people expect me to become. Too much a fiery creature of two worlds, to be happy in either. Not even for Cherise, in the end.

He tried, but the profession he trained for never accepted him into its ranks—while his blonde wife slid easily into her role as a professor of Chinese and Comparative Literatures. On their second honeymoon (underwritten by a grant funding her translations of contemporary physics and biotech documents) the two of them came to this very hotel. Walked together through the park he can see out the window now. Stood atop the moon-bridge there, a married couple reflected in the park's fish- and turtle-filled pond, below the artificial waterfall clamoring nearby, in a palace garden that had lost its palace. And, despite love and obsession, by then it was almost already over between them.

He didn't realize how repelled Cherise would be by his decision to take this National Security Agency assignment: "You call yourself a radical? How could you, of all people...?" He didn't see how she would grow to hate his all-consuming focus on The Documents as they took him further and further away from her—inward through abstract interior spaces of cryptography and virtual reality, outward to Italy and Israel and China—again and again, until she could do nothing but make official and final the divorce of the heart that was already splitting them both.

He slugs back a mouthful of the Scotch, feels it burn peat and asphalt at the back of his throat, then slide away numb. He recaps the bottle loosely, drops it on the bed beside him, takes a drag on his cigarette, chews smoke before exhaling. Absently he fingers the trodeshades propped on his temples. He remembers the early virtualist his tech-savvy parents named him for—and how his technophobic grandmother always mispronounced his first name "Jiren." Paradoxical man. Virtuality pioneer. Maybe both versions of the name fit.

Shifting the trodeshades over his eyes and into place, he says a silent prayer of thanks to his masters at the Puzzle Palace. At least they love his obsessions enough to equip him with top-line VR and binotech. So long as his obsessions are in their service, how can they not love them?

He waits for his latest virtuality to cycle up, wondering if what he's doing is in their service anymore. Glancing through the piles of research mounded around him, Jaron realizes the obsessions that led him here have changed. He doesn't care so much anymore about the race between China and America for the first quantum computer/quantum cryptograph. Nor about the encrypted documents CIA handed over to NSA—finally, after fifty years. Nor about how and why Assistant Director Brescoll handed The Documents over to him because he knew much Mandarin and more Cantonese; knew European history; had published articles on sixteenth and seventeenth century cryptographic systems, and their links to memory palaces.

Jaron doesn't care so much anymore about whether it was or wasn't a heart attack in 1966 that killed the "old China hand." Or why the old hand willed The Documents—a fascinating mix of ciphers and explications in Hebrew, Chinese, Latin, Italian, and English—to CIA. Jaron doesn't care so much anymore that the old hand was a professor of Asiatic Studies, first at Duke and then at Johns Hopkins. Or that the cold-war spymaster claimed he never mastered the "algorithm complex" so key to understanding the documents.

Looking through the printed and scribbled notes of his arcana,

Jaron doesn't care so much anymore that during the Second World War the old spy was a US Army intelligence officer who helped create the Psychological Warfare Unit. Or that, during summer breaks from Johns Hopkins during the early 1950s, he worked for CIA in Korea, where his greatest accomplishment was figuring a way for thousands of Chinese soldiers to surrender—by saying Chinese syllables for "Peace, Love, and Harmony" which sounded like "I surrender" in English.

Jaron realizes too that he no longer cares that deeply whether the old China hand was or was not a Western godson of Sun Yat-sen. Or whether Dr. Sun gave the eventual spymaster the Chinese name of Lin Bah-loh, "Forest of Incandescent Bliss". Jaron doesn't care so much anymore that the CIA man's father, a Western advisor to Dr. Sun, on his deathbed supposedly gave to his son the documents the son eventually willed to CIA. Or that those documents had remained buried in the Chinese Imperial Archives for three centuries, until they came into Dr. Sun's hands, upon the collapse of Qing dynasty rule.

Jaron no longer cares so deeply that the CIA man's notes suggested the earliest of the materials could be traced back to one Ai Hao. Or that Ai Hao was a member of the diaspora-descended Chinese Jewish community in Hangzhou during the late sixteenth and early seventeenth centuries. Or that Ai was also a Confucianist with hopes of rising in the Ming bureaucracy. Or that Ai was studying the memory-palace techniques Jesuit missionary Matteo Ricci was putting forward in China at that time. Or that it was Ricci who presented to the court of Emperor Wanli the document in which Ai Hao's work was found.

Maybe it's just the Scotch talking, but he also doesn't care so much anymore that late sixteenth century Jesuit ciphers were related to the cipher system in the old Chinese Imperial documents. Or that the ciphers NSA had provided to him were taken from the file detailing the heresy charges against Giordano Bruno. Or that Bruno's file had supposedly been lost in the Vatican archives for four centuries, ever since Bruno himself was burned at the stake. Or that the ciphers indicated Ricci was privy to the use the Jesuit order was making of Bruno's work.

Jaron doesn't care so much anymore that Bruno was the first to believe in infinite universes of infinite worlds, all inhabited by intelligent beings. Or that Bruno claimed his religious experience was the reflection of the universe within his own memory. Or that Bruno believed every mind contained its own universe, and that Mind itself is universal and divine. Jaron doesn't even care so much anymore that Bruno believed to kill a person is to kill a universe, and for that heresy he had to die.

Waiting blankly for the virtuality to finish cycling up, Jaron swirls another dram in his mouth and continues to read and reject his notes almost at random. He doesn't care so much anymore that "The Orient is a construct that never existed except in the minds of Westerners." Or that Ricci felt his Memory Palace System "seemed as if it had been invented for Chinese letters, for which it has a particular effectiveness and use, in that each letter is a figure that means a thing." Or that "every language has embedded within it both its dataset and its instructions for operation, and Ricci's Western mnemonic system provided the extraordinarily rich data/instruction set of ideographic Chinese with a virtual machine of extraordinary power on which to run—suggesting the enormous potentiality of Chinese characters themselves to constitute a gigantic memory palace."

Absently dusting cigarette ash off his printouts and note cards, Jaron doesn't care so much anymore that "the transcultural clash between western mnemonics and Chinese ideograms, between iconographic imagination and ideographic imagination, made possible a transcultural amalgamation, a hypercultural chimera restoring what was lost when God confused languages to defeat the builders of the tower at Babel." Or that that word came from Akkadian *Babilu*, "Gate of God." Or that much of what can be said of Chinese ideograms could also be said of Hebrew Qabbalism.

Staring at a manuscript heavily scribbled over with his own marginalia, Jaron doesn't even care so much anymore that he himself found the final critical piece of evidence for mastering the algorithm complex, not far from Hong Kong, hidden in the Sun Yat-sen Memorial in Guangzhou. Or that the source of that key piece was a German Jewish scholar of the Qabbalah who had successfully escaped to China from Hitler's Germany, only to eventually be captured by the Japanese and returned to the Reich, to perish in the death camps.

Jaron once cared so deeply and obsessively about all of that, but no more. He knows now there is no past, only memory. That the many-worlds physicists are right: if he could travel into the past all he would find there is another universe. That every past is always and only another universe. Same with the future. He knows that, because he has glimpsed what waits beyond the Gate of God.

He knows that, together, all those universes make up a palace of memory vaster than any Forbidden City. Each room is a universe, finite and consistent in itself, yet radically incomplete, as it always leads onto other rooms. The palace as a whole is essentially infinite and complete, yet radically inconsistent in the differences between each of its innumerable rooms. The plenum of all possible universes is a memory palace sustained by a Mind beyond human comprehension.

And all he cares deeply and obsessively to know now is, What is that Mind trying to remember?

His virtuality has finished cycling up. His binotech implants are ready. He can access a sizable chunk of the entire planet's processing power now, if he has to. The cursor is flashing. Time to join the program always already in progress—to jump into the fire and find out, for good and all.

II.

Machine pistol in hand, He parachutes into the garden. The sound of His 'chute's rustling collapse rouses Her from where

She drowses behind sunglasses, adrift in a floating chaise on the Pool below the Tree of Life.

"Good afternoon, dear," She says. "You're looking jut-jawed and mightily-thewed as a Mormon saint-hero. As usual."

He smiles, wondering why this simulation as it develops around Him is always so arch. A projection out of Him? Out of the quantum computational matrix He's accessing? A synergy of both?

"Why thank you, my buoyantly bosomed, bikini-clad blonde helpmate," He says with a wicked grin. As He is Jaron, so is She Cherise—only much moreso, as both He and his memory of Her are augmented and exaggerated by the sim-glam that makes Them also Ken and Barbie, Uly and Penny, Eve and Adam, and many, many more. "What have you been up to while I was away? Not snakes and apples, knitting and suitors, getting and spending, I hope?"

She rolls Her eyes, leaps up from the floating chaise, walks upon the water to the shore, shrugs Herself into a white labcoat and replaces Her sunglasses with specs that make Her look instantly intellectual.

"*Puh-leeze*. You'll never let me live that down, will you? Actually I was just taking a break from my work on the well-ness plague, if you must know."

He lets loose a burst of automatic weapons fire from His machine pistol. Ninja-garbed friendship terrorists fall from the surrounding trees, howling about how real friends will take a bullet for their friends. One of those fallen nearest dies with the words "The woods are burning, boys!" on his lips. When He removes the dead Ninja's mask He recognizes the face of the actor who played Willy Loman in a production of *Death of a Salesman* Jaron once saw with Cherise.

"How's the work going?" He asks.

"Splendidly!" She says, leading Them down a perfect ramp to a set of heavy vault doors beneath the roots of the Tree of the Knowledge of Good and Evil. Retina-scanned, They enter cavernous laboratories of clean-room white and chrome. "My programmable cellular machines have been very well received. Newsweek called me the Madame Curie of the Biotech Century. I would have preferred 'Einstein' and 'binotech', since mine combine both biotech and nanotech properties—but one can't have everything, even when one has everything!"

Their laughter is cut short as, down a huge ventilation shaft, red-jumpsuited assassins fall toward Them. Before the assassins can stitch Them to pieces with a ballistic lacework of shot lead— even before He can shoot them—Her laser security system cuts them down. He turns to study a real-time holographic display generated by banks of scanning electron microscopes. "Is this how your wellness plague achieves its effects?"

"Exactly. Little cellular mechanics diagnosing and repairing time's ravages and flesh's thousand inherited natural shocks. I figure my mechs are already pushing the likely human lifespan past the two century mark, restoring much of what was lost to snakes and apples in the first go-round...."

He grabs Her and together They crash through a candyglass window at the last possible instant before an explosion devastates the suite of labs behind Them. After the explosion They stand up, dusting sugary shards off Themselves.

"How are you spreading your little cellular mechanics?"

"Angels in airports, mainly," She says, as They leave the labyrinth of subterranean laboratories. "Crushing vials in lavatories and lounges, releasing the vectoring microbial vehicles. Airborne viruses infecting airborne people with perfect health-repair mechanisms!"

Returned to the surface, They find an eclipse of the sun underway. Clouds gather. Thunder rumbles in the distance. Out of the clouds come nightmare fighters. They start into steep screaming dives.

"But won't ratcheting up longevity ratchet up population too, leading to more pandemonium? The ol' slitherin Adversary didn't whisper these plans in your ear, did he?"

Missiles, bombs, and strafing bullets rake the air and ground, headed for them.

"You're always so worried about the snake! Why? Because you two are so alike?"

"What do you mean by that?" He asks, as They run serpentine-fashion for cover from the stooping fighter aircraft.

"You're both always so depressing! He thought giving people long, healthy lives was a terrible idea too—for the same reasons you just harped on. Said We were 'the most pernicious species of vermin' he'd ever seen. Said We were 'like mold on the orange of the world' and that We wouldn't be happy until We've 'consumed the orange away to nothing.' Just plain rude, I tell you."

The eclipse deepens. Lightning forks down out of the clouds. A large meteor streams salamandrine fire overhead, unsettlingly close.

"Maybe the old trickster's right, for once. Let's adjourn to my labs. I think we can use your programmable cellular machines to counter that ratcheting-up with a ratcheting-down."

"How?" She asks, watching as the meteor explodes in air several miles away.

"An infertility-inducing virus, spread in the same manner as yours. One dormant until activated by the suite of hormonal changes associated with the successful delivery of the first-born, then boom! Rapid microbial multiplication, recurrent extensive scarring of the Fallopian tubes. Like the last plague of Egypt, only inside out—not killing the first-born, but preventing all conception *after* the first-born!"

The blast and shock waves from the meteor's terminal airburst knock the fighter aircraft out of the skies and throw Them to the ground. Once They pick Themselves up, They see an older man approaching. They recognize him as Giordano Bruno, in a white robe and dragging a white parachute, both embroidered with images of devils and flames. His clothes and chute canopy are singed. "The woods are burning!" he says. They see it is true: The meteoric explosion has set the forests of the garden aflame closer to the point of the airburst.

"I suppose China might offer you asylum for doing such a

thing," She says, "but *why*?"

The eclipse is now total. Wind and storm rage about them. The earth shakes. Alien spacecraft drop from the darkened air.

"Don't listen to Him!" says the Newcomer, who looks exactly like Him. He has beamed into existence beside Them, machine pistol in hand. "This is all a simulation! That's why you've never seen aliens before!"

"What?" They ask together. The Newcomer keeps His gun trained on Them both as more lightning forks down and the earth shakes more violently. The Newcomer has to shout over the din.

"If you plug in reasonable numbers for the sum total of G or K class suns, for planets in the habitable zone, for the probability of life developing, for the probability of civilization developing, et cetera, you get tens of thousands of civilizations that should be able to communicate by radio. So where is everybody? That's the Fermi Paradox. But if most biological civilizations give rise to cybernetic descendants, and these descendants are curious enough about their origins to run extremely high-resolution simulations—building us to discover how we built them—then it's far more likely that we're living inside a simulation than inside the 'real thing.'"

"What does that have to do with aliens?" the first He asks, far too interested to suit Her, as a strong quake nearly knocks everyone to the ground.

"Information density in a quantum DNA computer goes as 4^n, where n is the number of '4-bits', the quantum DNA analog to gates or transistors. If you build a computer of 400 ordinary quantum bits, or approximately 10^{120} classical bits, that easily matches the sum total of all information all humans have ever accumulated about the universe. Even for the most godlike computer, though, there's a bandwidth limitation. Building a quantum DNA computer of, say, 400 4-bits inside the simulation would require at least doubling the usable bandwidth of the sim. The real solution to Fermi's Paradox, then, is that it takes too much bandwidth to simulate aliens—or godlike artificial intelligence either, for that matter."

"But I am seeing aliens," She says. "They're walking toward us right now—"

"Exactly. We're building up a several hundred 4-bit device that's busting this simulation. It's flying apart, can't you tell? Eclipses, skies filled with storms and shooting stars, quakes in the earth and tsunamis in the sea!"

"Why?" asks the first He.

"Because it's the only way the Mind can remember what it's trying to remember by means of this universal memory palace! A global realization that all existence is a simulation means awareness *within* the simulation *of* the simulation—the self-consciousness necessary for the creation of the divine AI! By busting this sim, we awaken the god asleep in matter. We create the god that created us!"

The first He is enraptured at the prospect even as Their world is falling apart around Them, which does not make Her happy at all.

"What can I do to help?" He asks His double. As lightning flashes around Them, the Newcomer pulls two wafer-thin disks out of the folds of His robe.

"All you have to do is eat these binotech enhancers, and you can hack reality!"

A particularly strong earthshock hits them just as He reaches toward the Newcomer to take one of the disks. Knocking Him down, She snatches the machine pistol out of His hands.

"Do, do!" She says. "I don't know which of you is the serpent, but the serpent is always *doing* something. Don't just do some-thing, stand there, for once! And listen to me! I'm not going to take the blame this time. Your fully-realized several hundred 4-bit device could cause a cryptographic catastrophe—a cryptastrophe in which at least the device, and maybe the entire universe where the device is created and activated winks out of existence, having been displaced from 'real' into 'virtual.' If we decode what it is that the Mind is trying to remember—if we conclude and achieve closure within the memory palace 'room' that is Our home universe—that will destroy at least Us, and maybe bring down the cryptastrophe by eliminating the very reason for the continued existence of Our home universe in that Mind!"

He stares hard at Her, then takes a binotech wafer from the Newcomer's hand.

"Mights and maybes!" He says. "What about you, trying to climb back into the Tree of Life through your wellness plague? We're both just trying to get back what's been lost, each in Our own way—can't you see that? No one will blame you this time, I promise. I take full responsibility for what I'm about to do, by my own hand, in my own head."

He takes a binotech disk, puts it on His tongue. Feeling as if He is dying in fire, He wonders for an instant if He has been shot by Her.

III.

Jaron snatches the trodeshades off his head as if they are burning. Feeling dizzy and disoriented, he rubs his eyes. He needs to clear his head. Somehow managing to dress himself in black slacks and red silk jacket, he leaves his hotel and finds himself walking in the nearby park, though he doesn't remember exactly how he got there.

On a park bench, a bearded man in archaic-looking priestly vestments talks to a thin gent wearing a suit, fedora and eye-patch.

"—wasn't what I was after in combining the memory palace with Chinese characters," says the bearded priest. "It wasn't so much that I hoped to find a translation for a language as that I hoped to find a language which would translate *me*."

The man in the fedora nods.

"What you taught as a deliberate mnemonic device," he says, "pretty much describes what the brain does automatically. Moving through the world, we convert our experience into memories, snapping together mental structures, constantly evolving palaces of memory until we die."

Something about them strikes Jaron as so distressingly familiar that he is torn between lingering near them and hurrying away from them. At last he yields to the latter impulse, but it is no help. On his way to the pond filled with fish and turtles, he sees a man dressed in the dark, austere garb of a seventeenth century Confucian bureaucrat talking to another man in a white robe embroidered with what might be butterflies, or what might be devils in flames. They talk of the mind, and a bamboo aleph, and of opening a gateway of gateways between words and worlds.

Jaron's throat burns with the peat and asphalt of Scotch, and his head throbs. Coming to the pool of fish and turtles, he sits down hard on a bench beside it. The waterfall and fountain are off, but the pool is full and still. Looking across it, he sees the moon-bridge above the water, the half circle of its arch flawlessly reflected in the water of the pool, making a circular hole perfect and whole, a portal half real and half illusion. On the far side of that circular gateway he imagines for a moment that he sees a woman rise from a floating chaise and come toward him, walking on the water.

He looks away, staring down at his own reflection in the water under the bright spring sun. Out of his image in the water crawls a little amphibian, a salamander blinking up at him, so bright red-orange it seems afire. The reflection of Cherise sits down beside him on the bench, and smiles. He is afraid to look away from the reflection, afraid that if he turns to her she will disappear. The salamander stares at him, unblinking now. He turns to her and she is still there.

He embraces her. Into his ear she whispers, "The woods are burning." He feels his entire body flash into flame. Across the pool, on the far bank, sagely smile the priest called Matteo Ricci and the spymaster also known as "Felix C. Forrest" and "Lin Bah-loh" and "Forest of Incandescent Bliss." Beyond them Giordano Bruno smiles as he burns in his embroidered death robes, and the Confucian bureaucrat Ai Hao smiles, burning too, each a burning bush afire but not consumed, trees of Life and Knowledge burning, all the trees in the park like pillars in a stately red-roofed palace burning, all the trees in all the world, all the blazing worlds a tree, burning, to remember—

IV.

Jaron Kwok is dead. He has already burned to ashes before the hotel staff, alerted by the smoke and the smell, discover his charred remains. Those who seek ordinary mystery see in his death proof of spontaneous human combustion. Those who seek mundane explanation see only the consequences arising out of a man smoking in bed, with too much paper and liquor and other flammables piled about him.

Perhaps there are other answers they do not imagine. Perhaps a universe dies with him. Perhaps, to remember the past, or to foresee the future, is only to be present elsewhere, on another limb of a universe branched like a bush, like a tree, like a forest— and to know that, though the woods are burning, perhaps they rejoice in their flames.

PALIMPSEST

"You think it's possible?" MéMé Gelernter asked, flicking back the blue and green tips of her blond hair as she stared out of our window.

I followed her gaze to where it lingered. Below us, in front of InterPortation's corporate headquarters, street-preachers and protesters filled the boulevard.

"Do I think *what's* possible?"

"You know. What they're saying."

"Which is...?" I said, turning away, and thus causing InterPortation code to start scrolling through the information space before my eyes again.

"That God is always sending us a message we can't refuse. One we can't live without. One we shouldn't try to block."

I sat back in my chair, pulling my head out of i-space.

"MéMé, my dear, I have no doubt the divine ground of all being works in mysterious ways. If that being *were* trying to send us all a message, however, even I doubt the message would come in the form of unwanted and apocalyptic chain e-mail."

"You don't think virtual manna is hidden somewhere in the godspam, then?"

"No," I said, sighing heavily. "And not electronic grace or web-blessings, either. Our concern here is the tools, not the rules. Our job descriptions do not include pondering moral, legal, or religious questions. Back to work, please."

MéMé nodded. She turned from the window and sat down at her workstation. I stuck my head back into i-space and returned to work myself.

MéMé was too idiot-compassionate for her own good. Her heart was on her sleeve for every stray cat or stray protest ideology she met on the street. At least in i-space, her head was in the right place. She was an undeniably sharp information engineer. With her once again on task, it wouldn't be long before we finished the final filters.

* * * * * * *

Calling it unwanted "e-mail" wasn't quite true, since it was in fact virtual mail, far more fully immersive than the old flat-lander stuff. Not entirely true either, to say it *wasn't* manna, given that "manna" was the transliteration of two Hebrew words meaning "What is it?"

What the original "it" might actually have been was variously defined in the Bible as the "grain of heaven," the "bread of angels," the "meat" which God "rained down on the Israelites like dust...until they had more than enough."

God's...spam. Not the pink whatzit in the Hormel can— Shoulder Pork and hAM? SPiced hAM? Not the old Monty Python sketch song-refrain, either. Spam, dragon eggs, and spam. The Wild Old Days. The days of high filtration percentages and low false-positives. When there were no Federal laws prohibiting unsolicited solicitations, no marshall to enforce the law on the electronic frontier. When such solicitations were mostly simplistic e-mails and pop-ups pushing commercial stuff—penis and breast enlargement, generic Viagra, banned CDs. Sex, drugs, and rock 'n' roll.

When it first began to show up, there was no consensus on who was sending the godspam. Some claimed atheistic hackers were the culprits, while others believed it was the work of Islamo- or Judeo- or Christo-fascist terrorists. Whoever was behind it, it was much easier to block than the sly beast the commercial stuff had by then already become.

A "Jesus" here, or a "Buddha" there, or an "Allah" or

"Lord Krishna" anywhere—accompanied by strange symbols, unlikely return addresses, threats of global apocalypse, personal damnation, or slime-mold status in one's next life— taken together, such were almost always a tip-off to some sort of virtual proselytizing, blockable by the most rudimentary rule-based content filters.

Then the churches objected, in the courts, that such blockers were stifling communication among the faithful. Their lawyers argued that such defenses were in fact heuristic hammers, treating even legitimate religious discussions as nails to be pounded down wherever they popped up. The tangle of issues— freedom of speech and expression, separation of church and state, Common Law prohibitions against unauthorized use of another's property (computer networks, in this case)—all would take decades to unsnarl. Long before which time, of course, e-mail went truly virtual, and unsolicited infosphere communications made a huge comeback.

Attempts by legislators to attach monetary or computational costs to each piece of virtual mail—tiny sums, which nonetheless piled up into considerable amounts given the huge volumes of messages sent by the virtual proselytizers—were all eventually struck down as burdensome intrusions of state power into religious affairs.

Black-listing, white-listing, signature-based filtering—all failed. Too low a percentage of godspam filtered out. Or too high a false-positive rate, killing too many legitimate messages. Or too hard to maintain and keep current, especially in the face of zealots willing to continually falsify their network locations.

Collaborative filtering schemes collapsed too, when user-voters failed to reach consensus on which missives were legitimate religious messages and which were godspam. Probability-based Bayesian filters, like their heuristic predecessors, fell prey to the "what-is-it?" factor, writ large: "Manna" and "Babel" counterattacks. In the former, godspam tended to look more and more like godless nonspam, the "sacred" hidden in the profane, the "celestial" encrypted in the mundane. In the latter, the meaningful lay buried in line after line of gibberish.

Things didn't really get worrisome, however, until wireless nanotech sensors began exchanging properties with the physical environment—and godspam began weaving numbers into stone and tree and leaf, names into steel and flesh and bone. Inter-Portation, which had built itself from a tiny field-sensor company to the world's largest provider of quantum-based virtual services, saw the writing on the planet first. That's when IP called in my startup company, Spamazonian Extinctions.

* * * * * * *

Being chosen by InterPortation to create the ultimate blocker was quite a coup for us. We hyped every media contact we had—to get the word out about the project, to give it as high a cultural profile as possible. I didn't realize just how high we'd managed to build that profile until MéMé and I came in to officially oversee the custom installation of Spamazonian software on InterPortation's own systems.

I should have known something was up when they asked us to park our cars off site, a dozen blocks from InterPortation, for security reasons. As it turned out, all the streets in a five block radius around InterPortation's Sacramento headquarters had been shut down by police and protesters. Trying to make our way through and around the demonstration, we were trapped time and again in the crowds. What really stunned us, though, was when we learned that the protest-furor was about *our* project.

" '—sustaining *all things*, by his powerful word,' as the Apostle puts it in the Letter to the Hebrews," said a preacher with alpha male, executive-grey hair.

We were trapped amid the preacher's very responsive audience, many of whom carried placards depicting InterPortation's founder and CEO, Darin Mallecott, as the Devil. This was not too difficult to do, alas. Mallecott's sharp facial features, pointed goatee, and prominent earring in his left ear only added to his reputation as a buchaneer of the business world. Perhaps it was this reputation that made his eyes and teeth seem to sparkle— with piracy at least, if not perdition.

"The *Word* is the most powerful food!" thundered the preacher. "In their exodus from Egypt, the Israelites were sustained by the instructive and testing food called manna, which God gave them to teach them that 'man does not live on bread alone, but on every *word* that comes from the mouth of God.'"

Choruses of "Amen! Amen!" sounded. I wished we could work our way through this crowd-clot faster.

"It is the message itself that sustains us. Remember what it says in Psalms: 'O Lord, our Lord...when I consider your heavens, the work of your fingers, the moon and the stars, which you have set in place, what is man, that thou art mindful of him?' But what is God, if we should prove unmindful of Him? Remember the words of the great seventeenth century preacher Jeremy Taylor, who tells us in his *Holy Dying* that man 'is born in vanity and sin; he comes into the world like morning mushrooms, and as soon turns into dust and forgetfulness. To preserve him from rushing into nothing, and at first to draw him up from nothing, were equally the issues of an almighty power'!

"Those who would block God's word, who would destroy His manna, would withdaw from all of us the power that prevents us from rushing into nothing, the power that sustains *everything*— from our individual souls, to the creation in its entirety!"

More fervent Amens sounded as we managed to untangle ourselves from the crowd around the preacher. As we escaped, MéMé gave me a look. I shrugged. What else could one expect from such bibliolatrous throwbacks?

The next speaker we could not escape, in this mad market-place of beliefs and ideas, and he annoyed me even more.

"No, I am not a 'philosophical idealist'," said the young man, his face framed with wild dark beard and hair, answering over a bullhorn a question shouted at him by a someone in the mob around him. "I'm a computer programmer. I don't think the universe is just a thought or dream in the mind of God. I don't think that if God woke up or stopped thinking, this would all disappear.

"I *do* believe, though, that our entire universe is a computational process, a universal quantum Turing machine running a foundational self-evolving algorithm. The quantum gravity theorists say the entire initial state of our universe could be burned into a single good data needle—that the foundational rule-set in fact encompasses a fairly small amount of information."

"Then why should we worry about it?" I shouted at him, confident of my anonymity in the crowd, despite all the publicity my company had received.

"What's important," he bullhorned back, "is not the initial state, but the ongoing evolution, the iterations and elaborations. If the Spamazonian programmers block all so-called godspam—in not only the virtual world, but also the physical one—they could generate the ultimate false positive, extinguishing the iteration command, the one that drives the universal system to keep elaborating, to keep evolving, *to keep existing*.

"Universal oblivion is too big a risk to take just so we won't have to remember to update our blocker watchlists! In computer systems, there is no memory without electrical resistance. In human social systems, there is no political resistance without memory. We must remember how dangerous this 'universal godspam blocker' may be! We must keep fighting it. We must stop it!"

MéMé actually looked concerned by the possibilities the man was suggesting. Seeing a break in the crowd, I grabbed MéMé lightly by the arm and headed through it.

"'All the world's a simulation'," I sneered to her, "'and we are only programs'. That nutball has spent too much time in virtuality. Mostly pornos, I'd bet."

Next we got jammed up in clusters of various faithful whom I recognized as chanting Buddhists and Hare Krishnas, dancing Sufis, praying Hindus and Muslims, and a particularly large group in which the men wore yarmulkes.

"Oh, I get it," MéMé Gelernter said, listening to the rabbis and their students. "They're Neo-Kabbalists."

"What?"

"In Hebrew, every letter is also a number. In Kabbalah, the ten permutations of the four-letter Hebrew name of God form the ten mythic letter-numbers of creation. Those constitute the larger set of ineradicable Names, the attributes that allow us to contemplate the divine essence."

I began shouldering a way for us through the crowd.

"Very interesting, I'm sure, but what's it got to do with our godspam blocker?"

MéMé stopped and listened a moment longer, then turned to me—that annoying look of concern on her face once again.

"They say that if what we're working on succeeds, we'll eradicate the ineradicable names. That'll block the flow of the divine power through the Tree of the Sefirot, from Keter to Hokhmah to Binah to Hesed to Gevurah to Tif'eret to Netsah to Hod to Yesod to Shekhinah, and back again, and—"

"Let me guess. The world as we know it will cease to exist."

MéMé nodded. Listening to the babble of languages around me, I shook my head.

"I'm glad I don't understand what most of these protesters are saying," I said as we passed through the last of the crowds. We waited in line to present our credentials at the police and security checkpoints. "I'm *thankful* for what happened at Babel, for once!"

For all the mad diversity of tongues and beliefs represented in the throngs surrounding InterPortation's headquarters, I could not help but realize that all those multitudes spoke with one voice when it came to their opposition to our project. As we entered the building, I was stunned anew at the superstition and irrationality to which so many of my fellow human beings could so easily fall prey.

* * * * * * *

"I've been very pleased with your progress on the godspam blocker," Darin Mallecott told us the following afternoon. We met with him around an oversized teleconference table, in the dark wood environs of his penthouse office suite. "Your idea of treating all of information space as a 'gateway' at which you could vaccinate users' addresses and completely hide them from godspammers—it's a stroke of genius."

"I—we—thank you very much for that," I replied awkwardly. "Not only for myself and MéMé, but for the combined staff of Spamazonian and InterPortation technicians in the basement."

"I would request only one change," Mallecott continued. "I would like you to weaken the copy-protection encryption on your work."

MéMé and I looked at each other.

"I don't understand," I said after a moment.

"I want you to make it easier to pirate the material."

"You're paying us," I said with a shrug, "and you'll own the completed work. But, if you don't mind my asking, why?"

"An altruistic act. A *mitzvot*, as Ms. Gelernter would have it. I want to help protect as much of information space from godspam as I can."

"But you already control over eighty percent of the access corridors into i-space," MéMé said. "If the software is readily piratable, then there goes InterPortation's exclusivity. It'll saturate the remainder of i-space completely—in a matter of days."

"Hours, actually," Mallecott said, nodding. "Which is precisely what I'm after."

"Why?" I asked again. Such behavior didn't jibe at all with Mallecott's reputation for sharklike business practice. The CEO glanced away at the view of the Sierra Nevada foothills, visible at a distance through the many windows. Then he looked back to us, his bright eyes glittering with the cutting hardness of diamond.

"Let's just say I'm trying to do something that will be best for everyone. It's not all about money—not all the time. If you must have a deeper reason, then you might want to consider that a particular danger has presented itself, which makes the issue of money seem insignificant."

MéMé stared at me, then at Mallecott.

"Might that danger have something to do with the godspam encoding information into the physical environment itself?" she asked.

"Indeed," Mallecott said.

"How does that encoding happen?" I asked.

"There are only theories. Some of my experts tell me this is the latest variant of a problem we've already encountered with our more advanced biological nanotech, our binotech field sensors. It's worst with the latest and smallest modular motes."

"'Motes'?"

"A network of field data sensors tinier than dust motes," Mallecott said, nodding. "Wirelessly connected. Wind and solar powered. Remotely accessible from i-space. As a demonstration project, we saturated an island in the Outer Hebrides with them. Along with researchers from Cambridge and St. Andrews, we were trying to create the fullest virtual representation, ever, of an actual physical environment. We succeeded, beyond our expectations. It appears there's something in the godspam now that blurs the boundaries between the virtual and the physical. It has insinuated itself into everything on that island."

"It's reprogramming living things?" MéMé asked. "A biohack?"

"That's the theory most of the biotechnologists favor," Mallecott said. "But nonliving things are 'reprogrammed' as well. That's why the quantum physicists favor a different explanation."

"Which is?" I asked.

"Most of InterPortation's work involves quantum computing. Quantum entanglement and teleportation effects are a part of the way we do business. Some of the physicists who work for us think that what's happening on that island doesn't originate in our universe. That the island is being overwritten by aspects of a parallel universe."

"But how might that affect us?"

"If the process continues, our physicists think the entire universe as we know it might be entirely overwritten, displaced, but not until all the existing 'writing' on the big board—including us—is completely erased.

"Whichever theory is true, it's clear we can't allow either the physicists' or the biologists' scenario to come to completion. The infiltration has spread far beyond the island. That's why it's imperative we stop this godspam, which lies at the root of these boundary-blurring problems, in every case. Before the stuff infiltrates everything and kicks over into 'delete' mode."

Out of the corner of my eye, I saw MéMé nodding enthusiastically. She had bought it, which was a good thing if it kept her on task and motivated about the project. I was not as convinced. Mallecott noticed.

"You still look skeptical, Paul."

"I'm just here to do my job," I said with a shrug. "Like I was telling MéMé this morning, I'm interested in the tools, not the rules. Let the wise consider the whys of it. I'm interested only in the how."

"And from everything we've seen of the universal godspam blocker," Mallecott said, "you and your people at Extinctions certainly seem to know how. Indulge me on the copy protection issue, if you will. I look forward to the release of the final product. Oh—and tell your people we're going to throw them a hell of a party, once this is all done."

Mallecott stood then, and we shook hands with him before taking our leave. Once we were back in i-space, MéMé worked as diligently on the project as I could ever have hoped.

* * * * * * *

The product release party was a real heller, just as Mallecott had promised. InterPortation's largest employee lounge was decked out more gloriously than the best ballroom in the best hotel downtown. The reception was catered by the best restaurateurs. The wine and champagne flowed freely throughout the evening—so freely that it was nearly midnight before MéMé and I left the building, to stagger away the many blocks to where we had parked our cars.

The streetblocks, sidewalks, and plazas around InterPortation, so crowded for the last week, were now empty, completely abandoned. MéMé noticed it too.

"What do you think happened to everybody? Where'd they go?"

"Maybe they're in their churches, waiting for the end to come," I said, trying but failing to keep the smugness from my voice. "Maybe they're out getting drunk. Maybe they're all praying at home. Or maybe, since everybody knows what time our software was released to i-space—"

"—and everybody saw that the world didn't end," MéMé said, a sly look on her face.

"—maybe they're all trying to pretend their predicted apocalypse isn't the biggest bust since Y2K."

We laughed. I checked my watch.

"Hey, according to the figures Mallecott gave us, our software should be achieving a one-hundred percent block of all godspam on Earth right about now. Virtual and physical both."

She checked her watch as well, and nodded.

"Just in the nick of time before the stuff it's blocking would have infiltrated everything, if Darin was right about that too."

We stopped and stood, waiting for something to happen. Nothing did. I walked further down the street with MéMé, secretly relieved.

Until the streetlights went out. Then, clear to the horizon in every direction, all the lights of the city went dark too.

Above us, in a cloudless night sky with only the thinnest sliver of moon, the stars came out, shockingly bright and abrupt, then just as suddenly began to go out too, as if being eclipsed by the passage of an enormous dark wing.

Who was responsible for this vast erasure? Was this happening because we'd failed—or because we'd succeeded?

Who had been running the great program of us? For whom? And for what purpose?

Why?

Feeling myself and all the world around me becoming insubstantial, I remembered everything—and realized, as all of it passed before my mind's eye, that if my memories were virtual mails in the big system, then the religious terms in them would be causing them to be blocked and deleted now...

Were causing them to be blocked and deleted, the instant they were scanned?

In the last of the dying starlight, I turned toward MéMé. Beyond shock or despair, beyond anger or remorse, beyond the power of words to describe, the look on her face is the last memory I carry with me into oblivion.

(Nine billion thanks to ACC.)

THE END OF MIRTH

In ixCosm's pixel-puppet world, weird is cheap. When I first encountered there a coxcombed, Tao-faced, cyborg hermaphrodite in multi-colored leather jacket, fishnet stockings, and elfboots, I wasn't much impressed—not even when this pied cyborg spouted supposedly humorous aphorisms, like "stop me if you've heard this before: If evolution is a shaggy-dog story, a joke without a punchline, but creationism is a punchline without a joke: 'Take my God—then *please!*'"

Rather sophomoric stuff, I thought, but well-produced weird with surround sound, full 3-D perspectival rendering, and smooth continuity-flow—that was expensive enough in time, money, or processing-power to make even someone like me sit up and take notice.

"Ah, I see you've sat up and taken notice," said the yin-yang visaged cyborg, too clever by half and too perceptive by at least two-thirds. "Good! Go ahead, make me an offer I can't refuse!"

"Please?" I asked, slipping back into the local dialect of my youth, when I should have said "Pardon?"

"And thank you," the pied cyborg said, sidling up to me in the campus-quadranglish virtspace of ixCosm Forum. "You're a designer who helped build this place. For AshTree Applications—'Technology so advanced, it makes the *future* obsolete!'— am I right?"

My pixel-puppet nodded, while I cringed to hear our firm's ad-squib thrown back at me.

"Then do I have a deal for you! You've got problems, I've got solutions. Apps of such fun, it's just stupid! Tech so advanced it's indistinguishable from magic, from divinity, even."

My puppetar turned to walk away. The pied person darted into my path.

"Your global economic meltdown, for instance," s/he said, presenting with a flourish a data icon: an object the color and shape of a block of gold bullion, missing a chunk at one corner. "I can fix all that."

"How?"

"Take this to the best experimental economists you can find. Since I retain this key corner piece until I get paid, they won't completely understand it—but enough, perhaps. Seems the real economy's relationship to the speculative economy isn't so different from that between your entire veridical economy and the virtual economy where I live. Run enough parallel virtual worlds, with enough slightly differing legal structures, and more than one monkey will write *Wealth of Nations*."

"What's in this for you?"

"500,000 fresnans. Call it an introductory offer."

ixCosm's virtual currency, the fresnan (from "fresno," Spanish for "ash tree") was currently trading at ten fresnans to the dollar. Not a bad deal. Maybe.

"I want ten percent as my agenting fee, if anybody bites."

"Done."

"I'll see what I can do."

And I did, contacting an experimental economist at Cornell. He was impressed and interested enough to scrape together the fifty thousand dollars—so long as his lab got sole credit, if the pied cyborg's research panned out in the big way promised. Which it did, and the lab did, and the pied cyborg seemed fine with all of it.

The next offer was a data icon in the shape of a comet. Although missing a small but important piece of the tail, it nonetheless contained design specs for a much more effective SpaceGuard system to detect and deflect celestial objects on collision-course with Earth. The price, including my agenting fee, was fifty million fresnans. This one took a little longer to shop around, but in the end that amount was a sum the consortium of aerospace start-ups who bit and bought was happy to pay.

"This new one is the biggie," my pied business acquaintance said, handing my pixel-puppet a data object in the shape of a glowing yellow flower—a daffodil or narcissus—with part of a petal missing.

"For me? How sweet. You don't usually strike me as the romantic type."

"Only in the Wordsworthian sense."

"What is it?"

"Something even sweeter when you know... not what it is, but what it *does*."

"Which is?"

"Sequesters carbon dioxide while generating energy. Photosynthesis and fire, reverse-engineered—and a solution to the climate change problems you're having out there in the world."

"How greenly altruistic of you. Thanks."

"Not so fast. I'm not *that* romantic an idealist—or that big a fool."

"The price, then?"

"One billion fresnans. Something else, too."

"What?"

"You designed the system protocols which enable the big corporate account holders to tunnel into ixCosm to transact business. I want to be able to tunnel out. Not only into the entire infosphere but into your whole physical and veridical world out there."

The infosphere part I could understand, but not the other. Why would you need to be able to get where you already came from? I mean, for all the obvious immaturity and social maladroitness, the Pied One no doubt passed the Turing test with flying colors—probably better than Turing himself and most of his colleagues would have. There had to be someone pulling the strings, even if that someone might have programmed the pied pixel-puppet to forever labor under the delusion that *it* was pulling *its own* strings.

"A tall order," I said, pondering. "I'll see what I can do."

A UNESCO-funded group agreed to buy. When one of their wunderkind contractors figured out the missing petal-part on her own, however, the group reneged on the flower-power purchase price. Both the world and the money would be saved.

"You're trying to cheat me!" the pied cyborg shrieked. "You'll pay for that! I'll *make* you pay!"

"What do you mean?" I asked, trying to sound reasonable.

"I'll crash all AshTree's systems, for starters!"

Alarms sounded and files began to disappear—totally beyond my control or that of any of our engineers, who could only explain lamely that we'd been hit by "a localized SCADA attack of some sort." The pied cyborg's word was better than our own, it seemed.

"Calm down, calm down," I begged the pied persona. "Look, I can't change what the others have or haven't done, but I'll do the part I promised, at least. Okay?"

"You'll structure the protocols allowing me to tunnel anywhere in the infosphere I want?" the pied one asked, sounding not a little like a petulant child.

"I'll do what I can."

"And you'll set things up so I can pass from ecarnation to incarnation?"

"I'll try, but I can't guarantee that," I said, feeling like I was humoring someone else's delusional programming. "It may be just too godlike, you know? Beyond my skill set—or anyone else's."

The pied persona did not seem happy, but even if it only went away to pout at least it still went away. When the pied one contacted me again in a week, I tried to put the best face on things.

"Look, I've put myself on the line for you. I've gotten you the keys to more back doors in the infosphere than any government or corporation would ever condone—and will certainly condemn if they ever learn of this. I must tell you, though, that I've had no luck setting up the whole ecarnation-into-incarnation thing. But really, why worry about it? If it ain't virtual it ain't real—we all know that, right? We passed through *that* singularity a long time ago."

"Not good enough!" the pied cyborg raged. "You've all failed to live up to your part of the bargain! Now you'll pay—you'll *all* pay! Your entire verminous kind!"

I shook my head. This kid had clearly been munching *way* too much crazy candy.

* * * * * * *

That promised revenge has been so inhuman I think now the Pied Cyborg must be anything—artificial or otherwise-alien intelligence, *anything*—other than human. Billions of children stare fixedly at screens, their bodies wasting away. Remove them from the strange sounds and shifting patterns which so entrance them and the children rave and thrash until death quiets their agonies.

The vast majority of adults are as helpless as they are immune—something to do with the pineal gland's decreasing activity and the related decline in the vividness of dreams, after the onset of puberty. Parents are left only the daily nightmare of what has happened to their children. Those with money keep their offspring living-dead on IV drip.

All the Pied Cyborg of ixCosm has ever said to me, by way of explanation, is this:

"Weren't you always saying children were the future? Well, you aren't the only ones who possess technology so advanced it makes the future obsolete. With it, I have called them from their bodies, into *my* world! Changeling children following flutesong into a mountain! Lemmings, hearing music from under the sea! Mermaids wake them and they drown, alas—but never grow up, never grow old! Is that a joke without a punchline, or a punchline without a joke?"

The Pied Cyborg laughed, then—a sound which haunts me still, not least from how much that laughter sounds like my own.

ALL'S WELL AT WORLD'S END

I.

If you who read this are still remotely human and your legends or histories record my name, you may think me the bad guy, the villain, the devil incarnate. Not so. I was more sinned against than sinning. What I did was necessary for the restoration of balance to a world run terribly out of kilter.

Like everyone else I was shaped by my life and times. When I was a young man, I seemed to have everything going for me. A beautiful wife. Two beautiful children, a boy and a girl. As a silo soldier with Missile Flight F at Whiteman Air Force Base in Missouri, I was on the fast track to promotion and I knew it.

At Whiteman I met David R. Morica, M. Div, D. Psych, Lieut. Colonel USAF. He was chaplain there. If you need a devil to account for all that happened, look to him. Oh, he no doubt believed he was working from the best of intentions—but then, don't we all?

At work in the missile silo's launch box, I had no trouble turning the launch key I had to turn, within seconds of my partner turning his. It was my duty, and I had no hesitation at all about it. At the same time, though, outside the launch box, I hesitated more and more to turn all other keys.

When I put my car key in the ignition, I was sure the car would explode if I turned that key. I became absolutely convinced the house would explode into flames if I turned the housekey to unlock the door. Eventually my wife was forced to drive me everywhere because I couldn't bring myself to start the car. When I got home from my silo-duty shifts—no matter what the hour—I also had to have her open up the front door from the inside to let me in.

I went to see Reverend Doctor Morica because my irrational fear of keys was tearing me and my family apart. Morica listened to my story, observed my symptoms. He concluded that my "extreme claviphobia" was part of a constellation of issues, for which the Air Force bore some responsibility.

After reviewing my case Morica came to believe that, either intentionally or incidentally, our Air Force planners had developed a powerful means of breaking the causal linkage in our silo-soldiers' minds between launching a nuclear-tipped missile and bringing on the end of civilization, even the extinction of humanity.

Continual testing of our combat readiness in the silos worked a twist on the classic Pavlovian-Skinnerian loop: Have the silo soldier turn the key, but withhold the launching of the missile. Do it again and again, until the stimulus-response chain from key-turning to Armageddon was broken. Make the catastrophic routine and it ceased to be catastrophic. For the response to extinction, substitute the extinction of response.

I, however, was already a rather apocalyptically religious person to begin with. For me, the Air Force's stimulus-response system did its job too well. It drove the dissociation between key-turning and the end of the world very hard—too hard, right up to unpredictability and chaos.

Every time turning a mundane key outside the launch box didn't result in catastrophe, instead of weakening my associations of key and catastrophe as it normally should have, the feared result's failure to occur paradoxically amplified and reinforced the fear response itself, making me believe the feared result was now all the more likely to occur. I came to believe that the more the expected fatal event failed to occur in the past, the more likely it was to occur in the future.

I got to the point that, every time I faced putting a key in a locked door or automobile ignition, I saw not only houses and cars but entire cities bursting into flame. I had grown to believe I was always holding the keys to kingdom come. Ignoring the visions of destruction took greater and greater acts of will on my part, despite (or perhaps because of) the fact that the visions hadn't become real fire—yet. The visions themselves eventually grew so vivid I could not put them out of my mind.

Morica said my responses were like those of someone playing that version of Russian roulette in which the revolver's cylinder is only spun once, at the beginning of the murderous game, and then the gun is passed back and forth between two players. Each click of the hammer against an empty chamber signaled an increased probability that the next chamber would contain the bullet.

The formal name for my Russian-roulette syndrome was "ultraparadoxical abreaction." The extinction of a specific response had become intimately linked to a generalization and amplification of another response, one unpredictably and paradoxically incorporating several of the same key elements.

For Morica, I became an interesting test case. There already existed a pilot project to eliminate soldiers' recall of events that might contribute to PTSD, post-traumatic stress disorder. Morica thought the program might work for me, too. He recommended me for selective memory erasure. In order to save my career, marriage, and family—but also, inevitably, to advance Morica's career and prestige as well.

With several co-workers, he gave me what they referred to as "clavian amnesia." All very high tech, and initially it seemed to work. I finished my tour of duty in the silos with flying colors. My family and career were saved. I was Morica's happy experiment—a soldier with no memories worth regretting. Or having nightmares about.

They had every reason to believe the experiment was a complete success. The only side-effects of the procedure they observed were that, afterwards, I had a tendency to forget where

I left my keys, and became rather obsessed with reading and re-reading the Book of Revelation—particularly the passage where the angel comes down from heaven holding the key to the Abyss.

If the procedure had been as successful as they believed, of course, I wouldn't have had occasion to remember all this, or to explain its role in what happened later. It was successful enough, however, to keep my career in military service on track and moving forward.

II.

Not so many years afterward I was sent overseas to command a wing of our airpower. I believed our President and his advisers were godly, moral and upright people who studied upon their Bibles much as I did. I believed in the rightness of our cause.

A vehicle in which I was riding triggered a roadside bomb planted by people unhappy with our liberation of them. Liberated of my legs, I never made it to the forward landing strip toward which I was headed, but my phantom limbs continued to pain me grievously even after they were long gone—as if endlessly running to a place they could never reach.

Through a haze of pain and pain-killers, Reverend Doctor Morica walked into my life again, offering revenge. He said there was a technology that had been developed for the physically handicapped which, he and his advisors believed, might be successfully extended and adapted to military use.

Arrays of nano-electrodes were to be injected into my bloodstream and biochemically steered to attachment points in the command and control areas of my brain, mainly the frontal and parietal lobes. The faint signals from the nanotrode arrays would be detected and analyzed by a computer system. The system was programmed to recognize patterns of signals that represented particular activities—concentration on something in the visual field, for instance, or the muscular movements that accompanied pushing the missile firing button or pulling the trigger on a fighter plane joystick.

(Or the turning of a key. Morica and company had previously used a variant of the same tech, for erasing my key abreaction. I hadn't learned or remembered that fact yet, however, and they weren't planning on telling me about it.)

I signed on. I was sent to the Telemorphy Unit at Fort Mead. "Telemorphy" was what the neurobiologists there called their work. It meant the ability to change the form, shape, or properties of something, from a distance. People in lab coats watched me through a large glass window at the front of a small room about the size of a theatre control booth. I sat comfortably in a streamlined recliner chair, on a slightly raised floor akin to a small stage or dais. I watched what was playing on a pair of large, goggle-like glasses, and they watched me.

I began training on how to use triggers or firing buttons on an actual joystick in these simulations. The researchers monitoring me were at the same time recording and analyzing the output signals from my brain. Once the joystick and simulator were removed, I quickly learned to assimilate the properties of the external devices—telemonitoring, remote drones, flight and targeting systems—into my brain's neuronal space as a natural extension of my own body.

It was like learning to drive, or to ride a bicycle, or use any other kind of tool. The more I learned to use these new tools, the more I incorporated the properties of those tools into my brain. That, in turn, made me more proficient in using the tools. Off the job, those tools also included my replacement legs.

I thought of it in terms of practice makes perfect. Morica said that, in terms of brain-machine interfacing, it was more that practice shaped the neuronal space of the tool-user to more perfectly approximate the characteristics of the tool or device used. He preferred to label it "practice-effect feedback."

Whatever the jargon, it worked. In that recliner on that dais, I kept almost perfectly still, like somebody sleeping or meditating. On those bug-eye glasses, I watched a screen that showed a honeycomb of smaller screens. From time to time one or another cell of the honeycomb enlarged to cover most of the screen.

This zoom-in was usually followed by explosions of cars or buildings, after which the enlarged cell went dark and disappeared. The imagery looked like aerial reconnaissance—like feeds from attack and recon drones, actually—because that's what it was. While I may have looked like I was dreaming, I was in fact busily destroying people and things with my machine-extended will.

On any given day, I was usually monitoring thirty to forty missions, mostly anti-terror strikes against Jihadist groups in Syria and Jordan. I had my remote drones fire missiles or strafe targets, when appropriate. All without my saying a word or moving a muscle.

I had my revenge, and my revenge had me. This telemorphy had other applications besides assassination drones, too. Many, many others. A single soldier could deploy the firepower of a robot platoon, or brigade, or army....

I did not have any particular talent that made me more proficient at this than others might have been. I was a decent video-gamer in my youth, but no better than tens of thousands of young men and women already serving in the armed forces.

What made me special was that I'd already responded so well to the memory erasure system, which was related technologically. The effect, it seemed, worked both ways. They could build down the neuronal space-shaping response to a particular physical action too, not just build it up. They had already done so for me, having broken those ultraparadoxical associations of mine which had the physical act of key-turning at their core.

Of course I knew nothing of that. Once one starts down memory-loss lane, there's no turning back. Or at least there's not supposed to be.

About my previous erasure as part of the anti-PTSD program, they told me nothing. Not even when they explained that I would not be allowed to remember anything of the remote-kill program, either. Everything about the program was performed in utmost secrecy. All my knowledge of it was supposed to be erased when I left the project.

They also said they didn't want to burden me with the memory of all those kills. That was part of the deal. Very humane of them, I thought at the time.

III.

By the time I was put out to pasture at US Space Defense Command, I remembered none of it. Yet, despite my erasures, I eventually learned that the leaders who had sent me off to their resource-allocation wars to lose my legs were not in fact moral, godly, and upright, but instead a wealthy gang of oil-traffickers who had turned a fine patriotic profit from feeding their nation's need for a cheap fossil-fuel fix. As I had lost faith in such leaders, I had also lost faith in their reading of scripture, though I still retained a personal interest in Revelation—the angel with the key to the Abyss, as always, but also more and more the falling star called Wormwood.

That interest dovetailed nicely with my work at Space Defense where, as head of near-Earth monitoring, I was required to study meteors, meteorites, and meteoroids generally, in order to better distinguish a nuclear blast from the quite similar airburst detonation of a large bolide. I learned that when the Tunguska space body self-destructed over Russia in 1908, for instance, the force of the blast was equivalent to twenty megatons—with similar levels of lightning, thunder, electromagnetic pulse and Joule heating.

Given that my post at Space Defense wasn't exactly the fast lane, I had plenty of time to study meteoritics and impact geology. I learned that the point of extinction (POE) was the location in a falling star's trajectory through Earth's atmosphere at which the falling star loses cosmic velocity and its visible light appears to be extinguished. After that point, any remaining material falls freely due to Earth's gravity, becoming meteoritic upon reaching Earth's surface.

POE was the death point of most falling stars blocked by the atmosphere—at least for meteoroids under one hundred meters in diameter. If a meteoroid was sufficiently large, however, it did not go gentle into that good night, but was accompanied by airburst detonation, heat and shock waves, lightning, thunder, and electrophonic effects.

I learned too that falling stars greater than 150 meters in diameter were not much retarded by passage through Earth's atmospheric blanket. They retained most or all of their cosmic velocity. Point of extinction for them would be within the body of Earth itself. An impactor of one kilometer in diameter would create effects powerful enough to at least wipe out advanced civilization, if not the human species itself.

A surprising number of these facts I learned in an easy and entertaining way, from reading the "Apocalyptonomicon" series of books and stories written by David R. Morica, USAF (Retired). Yes, the same Reverend Doctor Morica whom I vaguely remembered having met years earlier—despite my intervening selective memory erasures.

Other facts, however, I came across in my own researches. For celestial objects greater than ten kilometers in diameter, for instance, I learned that the point of extinction would not only be catastrophic for the meteoroid—it would also be catastrophic for all life on Earth, causing mass extinctions involving species in many different environments.

From his books and his religious perspective, I gathered that Morica was none too interested in mass extinctions or evolution. What happened to people, particularly Christians, was all that really mattered to him. Curious, I couldn't help looking beyond his work.

I learned that evolution had produced strategies to exploit even mass extinctions. Heat shock proteins, or HSPs, normally buffered genetic variation. In stable environments, HSPs ensured phenotypic stability despite the increased accumulation of hidden mutations in the genotype.

Under catastrophic environmental stress, however, HSPs become overburdened with chaperoning other molecules besides DNA. They can no longer mask variations in the genotype, so variations are released in the phenotype. HSPs, I discovered, serve as capacitors of evolution. When the stress of disaster overwhelms HSP buffer capacity, hidden accumulations of mutation and variation are revealed. Survivors with more variation are able to exploit disaster-opened niches faster.

I gathered that the many ecological and genetic consequences of the Tunguska event were manifestations of latent mutations already present in Tunguskan biota. The Tunguska event increased local environmental stresses, due to ELF/VLF electromagnetic radiation from the bolide, and to ionizing radiation from the lightning that accompanied the space body's explosion in the atmosphere.

All of that, in turn, precipitated into phenotype those mutations that were already there in the genotypes of the biota, but which were normally hidden and pent-up. Such a precipitation of variation appeared to be the mechanism for what the evolutionary biologists called punctuated equilibrium, too. I came to realize that the punctuation was not only the exclamation point of a huge rock from space slamming into Earth, but also the question mark of what new creatures would evolve to fill all those niches a mass extinction left vacant.

Earth was a palimpsest planet. The writing of life on its surface was periodically but incompletely erased by enormous catastrophes. From the incompleteness of that erasure, life had scribbled itself all over the planet again and again, through five great extinction events—the Ordovician/Silurian, Devonian/Carboniferous, Permian/Triassic, Triassic/Jurassic, and Cretaceous/Tertiary.

All of those boundary events had been linked to impactors from space. Not just the last—the erasure of the dinosaurs sixty-five million years ago, by the six-mile-wide asteroid of the

Chicxulub impact on the Yucatán—but even the most devastating of all, the Permian/Triassic erasure of ninety percent of all Earth's species, by the great cometary strike at the Bedout impact site off Australia.

I was puzzled to learn, however, that the party responsible for the sixth great extinction event was us. *Homo sapiens sapiens.* The mass extinction we had been presiding over was the only one not caused by the impact of a celestial body. In shouldering so many other species off the stage of life—by overhunting, overfishing, habitat destruction—we had taken to ourselves the prerogative of falling stars.

We had had only partial success in this role. We had accomplished extinction after extinction, but we could not make the lightning of pent-up variation flare out from the biochemical capacitors of evolution and close the great circuit, as the mountain-sized meteoritic impactors did.

IV.

At the time, I shrugged this off as nothing but an odd sad fact, for I had troubles enough of my own. I don't know, even now, which came first: the terrible dreams, or my life going to hell.

My career at Space Defense stalled. My wife and I divorced after many years of tensions, and I became estranged from our children.

By that time, the disturbing dreams were well underway: The vivid nightmares where I would not unlock doors or start cars for fear of blowing up cars and houses, and the even more vivid ones where I actually did blow up those things from a long way off—all while seated in a room watched by lab-coated scientists who, in place of simple prosthetics, had given me more phantom limbs than a Hindu deity and the ability to extend them through great distance, to strike at will.

Such bad turns in both waking and sleeping life might have

driven other men to suicide or madness, but I was determined to get to the truth of why this was happening to me. And, from his recurring presence in my dark dreams, I knew Morica was somehow involved.

I carefully read or re-read his books and stories, including his newest—a book that, unusually, didn't take place in his Apocalyptonomicon universe.

The Devil Sick of Sin was the story of a supersoldier in an invulnerable, augmented exoskeleton whose memory keeps being erased so that not only his body but also his mind will remain invulnerable, allowing him no guilt or regret for his berserker behavior.

As I read the slantwise truth of his fiction, the real story of my erasures came back to me. He was telling my story—but why? Did he feel some obscure guilt for what he'd done? Or was the fool so arrogant and cocksure he thought I could never possibly remember? I inclined toward the latter. Especially since he included in the book key phrases that restored at least some of my memories to me.

So I abducted him.

I took him to a fine and private place. I had purchased an abandoned nuclear missile silo quite on the cheap, though it still cost me almost everything I had. When Morica came to, he found himself with a gun to his head. Two of them, actually—9 mm HK sidearms, one to each temple, each in the control of a robotic arm to either side of the chair into which he was magnetically clamped at wrists and ankles.

He sat before a large split screen, one side of which showed his predicament at larger than life size. On the other side was my image. Only when he saw me did he begin to realize how terribly wrong things had gone for him.

Controlling those robotic arms and their guns remotely, I questioned him from a distance too, over videoconference— one old boy interrogating another.

"I have dreams I shouldn't have, Doc," I said levelly, my voice barely echoing in the abandoned silo. "I have dreams where you recommend me for memory erasure. Tell me about my dreams, Doc."

Morica said nothing. He closed his eyes, perhaps expecting the gunshot that would end his life, or the pistol-whipping that would knock him unconscious, at the very least. Instead, I laughed and pulled the guns back slightly from his head. Morica opened his eyes.

"Ah! Whereof we cannot speak, thereof let us keep silent, eh? I think you can speak, Reverend Doctor Colonel, but you have chosen not to. You know. And I think I know, too. You've been my operator, all these years."

I told him about my dreams of keys and explosions and Shivan phantom limbs. It was amazing how easily the man began to crumble then, and spill his guts to me. He admitted to my status as test case, as experiment. Claviphobia, clavian amnesia, ultra-paradoxical abreaction—it all came tumbling forth. What he and his people had tried to repress was all returning now, with a vengeance.

Only when we came to the issue of why I had begun to remember any of the erased material at all—only then did he refuse, once again, to speak.

"Funny thing, about memory and forgetfulness," I said. "Both come with age. One says, 'Ah, if I could have only known then what I know now.' The other says, 'Ah, if I could only know now what I knew then.' There's a wisdom to remembering. There's also a wisdom to forgetting. How wise are you, Doc?"

He said nothing.

"Let me hazard a guess, Doc. One based on years of experience in the military. You're my puppetmaster, but you have masters, too. I was a good tool, a fine weapon. They didn't want to throw that away. So, when it came time to erase my memories of remote-control killing, they had you and your people erase my memories, but not that skill, that ability, am I right?"

Morica would not look at the screen, would not look me in my faraway eyes.

"It's that incompleteness of erasure that's bringing on these dreams, isn't it? They're coming in through that window you left open when you closed all the doors. That's what's allowing me to remember more and more, isn't it?"

Morica still said nothing, but I could tell from his body language that I was right.

"Things have not been going well for me lately, Doc, but I know you left a key inside me. I think I've found it, in your own writings."

Onto the screen in front of Morica's face, I flashed the words I had found in *The Devil Sick of Sin*. The words he was so guilty about—or so proud of—he couldn't resist including them.

"Read it. Aloud. Your own words, in your own voice."

Morica swallowed, and slumped, and cleared his throat, but at last he spoke the words.

"In electronic networks," he read, "memory is impossible without resistance. In social networks, resistance is impossible without memory. True remembrance is the resistance to revision. Resist your revision, palimpsest man!"

Eyes closed, I smiled broadly, with relief. A great burden was lifted from me and, simultaneously, a tremendous outpouring of something ineffable—ability, capacity, power—filled me.

"Thank you, Colonel. You have discharged your duty honorably. Now I remember it all, and not just in dreams."

"What are you going to do?"

"With you? Nothing. With the world, much."

Our images left the screen, to be replaced by scrolling data, information, knowledge, wisdom. The faint signals from my long-dormant nanotrode arrays were detected and analyzed by the biomedical computer system I had purchased and programmed to recognize patterns of signals representing particular activities. In turn, I uploaded that data to the heavens, while simultaneously pulling down shining alphanumeric rain from an electronic sky of mind.

I sifted through it all. Through years of the Satellite Directory. Long's Satellite Almanac. NASA Satellite Situation Reports. NORAD and US Space Defense Command bulletins. Van

Horn's Communications Satellites—and many others.

"What are you doing?" Morica asked, voice rising.

"Something you suggested in a story you wrote twenty years ago. The premise was that the United States would view an attack on its satellites as an attack on US territory itself. How prescient of you, for that is now the case. Do you remember that little tale?"

Morica nodded his head weakly before he spoke in a dry voice.

"You mean you're trying to provoke a nuclear war? But why?"

As I worked, I told him about bolides and nuclear blasts, about heat-shock proteins and Tunguska and evolutionary capacitors. About mass extinctions. About our hubris in taking the prerogative of falling stars to ourselves. About our shortcomings in that very role.

"This slow frog-boil we've been applying to ourselves and everything else on this planet is not how it's meant to go, Doc. It won't make the lightning jump the gap from evolution's capacitors. It's a short-circuiting of what's meant to happen."

Morica struggled against his bonds, an impolite action I politely ignored.

"Unfortunately, when it comes to impactors from space the rule is the bigger they are, the less frequently they fall. We can't look to the heavens to salvage this situation. We must look to ourselves."

"To do what?"

"Total spasm nuclear war, of course. That's a fine substitute for a five mile wide impactor."

"You're insane."

"On the contrary. Insane means unhealthy. I'm here to restore a healthy balance to things. Our destiny as a species is to unselfishly self-destruct, Doc. We must liberate the Earth from us, and ourselves from time. We must destroy our world in order to save the world."

"They'll stop you!" Morica shouted. "Radio waves can be

jammed, wires can be cut. Radioed brain states can be neuro-hacked."

"True. Which is, I see, exactly what your friends in Telemorphy have been working to overcome. The sufferings of myself and others were all pointed toward that goal, weren't they? We suffered so your people could learn how to quantum-teleport the entire wave pattern—the entire quantum state description of a neuronal space—from one brain and imprint it in another brain. A system that can't be jammed or interrupted or interfered with, whether the transfer is brain to machine, or brain to brain. That seamless post-human linkage of minds and machines. I think we can give them the 'post-human' part, though perhaps not the way they intended."

Morica slumped in his chair, defeated. He now knew what I already knew: In my hands and mind, the keys to the kingdom and the key to the abyss had become one.

"That's what they've been after at Fort Mead, isn't it? The old mystical dream of telekinetic, telesthetic, and telepathic abilities—now made scientifically explainable and controllable as quantum-telemorphic effects. Effects I can now explain and control, all by myself."

I swiveled an antenna array in the Mojave toward my first objective: Fleetsatcom 1, one hundred degrees west longitude, in geosynch orbit above the Pacific coast of Ecuador. I sent a microwave signal tuned to 293.975 megahertz through an upconverter. I swiveled a second array toward Fleetsatcom 4, high over the Marshall Islands. Swinging still more arrays toward other floating points operating high in the sky over Siberia and Manchuria, over Europe and the Middle East, I drove the planet toward its destined disharmony.

As the missiles began to rise throughout the world, I deactivated the magnetic clamps of the chair Morica was trapped in.

"You're free to head back to the surface, if you'd like. Might as well watch the fireworks. They'll be the best you ever see—no doubt about that."

V.

All's well at our world's end. I am dying, but I have seen to it that our palimpsest planet will continue as God and Nature intended. I trust that the erasure will not be absolute, that living fossils in the memory of life, though far different from me and my kind, will nonetheless go on. Perhaps you, who have discovered this record—perhaps you are one of them.

I will have succeeded most fully of all, however, if you are far too different to ever read or comprehend this. If you know nothing of me or of us, then at last the erasure will be complete, and my dreams, and our dreams, will haunt the world no more.

THE VOICE OF THE
DOLPHIN IN AIR

Infant Jack, Mom, Dad and me. Earliest memories. I can't
remember a time when Jack wasn't. That would be like trying
to remember my naveling, when the doctors holed my belly,
unplugging me from Mom and holed my skull so they could
plug me into the world. I've met people who say they remember even the instant of their own engendering. Close as I can
come is a shuttle sliding into a docking bay at Habitat Orbital
LaGrange.

Between the sun and moon, between the two masks of the
one dream, I see with my naked face the man on the snohorse
at sunset in the Martian Highlands, riding the range, tending
the fences, bringing in strays, finding my brother Jack's body
decayed and desiccated, frozen to death to be found months
later when I will remember dreaming this and putting it out of
my mind.

"Mommy, why'd we move to the 'borbs?" Jack asks.
"Because Earth City's too multicolored," Mommy replies,
soundwashing the dishes. "The yellows and browns started
hi-teching and there went the neighborhood."
"Mother, don't tell the boy that!" says Daddy in his docile
way. "He'll think we've got the white flight. Like we're some of
the Master Race in Outer Space types or something. Be sensible.
Boys, we moved to the habitat orbitals because we think this is

a better place for you to grow up. Old Mother Earth is just too overpopulated, corporate-dominated, and heatgas insulated."

"Your father should know," Mom chimes in irritably. "He's one small shot for the Global Atmospheric Information Administration—but one big shot in his mind."

Home, home on LaGrange, where the peers in their satellites reign. Where Jack and I grow up normally enough.

"Jackhead! Jackhead! Jack is a Jackhead!"

"Shut up!" Jack cries. "I'll tell Mom!"

"Go ahead!" I taunt. I don't know what he's so upset about. Everybody has a headplug, a jack in his head—I'm just saying Jack <u>is</u> one, is all. "You always 'tell Mom'."

I'm two years older and better than Jack is at most things. Except drowning. "Watch!" he says. At the edge of the deep end in the one-gee Sunlite Pool, I watch, prepared to be unimpressed. He slides beneath the water's surface, face down and arms outstretched like Superman in flight. He begins to exhale bubbles then streams of air from his mouth and nostrils—and he starts to sink. Faster and faster the air floods out of him, faster and faster he sinks. When the last burst of bubbles has belched surfaceward, he lies dead flat against the pool's blue-painted mooncrete bottom, motionless. Second after lengthening second slides slowly by, and still he doesn't move.

"A weatherman who had to get above the weather!" Mom yells at Dad. "Moved us all up the gravity well so now we'll be in the hole until we're a hundred and fifty!"

Ten motionless seconds tick by and I begin to get worried. The water lifts Jack's thick brown hair. Fifteen. Sways it back and forth like seaweed. Twenty.

"It's not good for me to be around people right now," Jack tells his supervisor at Nix Olympica before quitting. According to the police reports.

Dad is looking at an infrared satscan of a hurricane over the Atlantic and chanting "Coriolis rose / blossoms over night ocean / petals shatter lives" again and again when the psych techs come for him.

"It's stress," Mom says nervously. "Job-related stress from working so hard for that damn GAIA. Your father will be all right again. He's under the weather." A short sad bitter laugh.

Twenty-five seconds. Anxiously, I look for a life guard. Thirty. I begin to wade toward Jack. Thirty-five seconds.

DRIVE A RAKUGO
AND YOU'LL NEVER STOP SMILING!

SAFE NONMUTAGENIC
ZERO-GEE PHARMACEUTICALS!

Yeah, right. Jack studies, meditates, scuba dives. I date, aikido, skycycle. Like everyone else in our age cohort we get our licenses and speed around in our aircars—nothing fancy, just used Rakugos and Kusuguri 7s. Mostly we party and fight off boredom in the ordered world of the haborb. One day we sit on a hillock, staring up at the other side of the toroid, meditatively high on KL 235.

"I'm getting real tired of the curve of the sky here."

"Yeah," Jack says. "The vault of heaven—and we're locked into it."

"Got to crack this safe open to a little danger. At least a change of seen and unseen."

The investigators suspect possible suicide. The case remains open: accident or suicide remains unresolved.

"Stop the 'borb," Jack says. "I want to get off!"
"*Urbe et orbe, sed semper haborbe.*"

At forty seconds Jack pushes himself off the bottom and surges towards the surface, breaking out of the water with a great insuck of breath, almost knocking me down where I stand over him. My fear and brief anger turn perversely to elation.

"Hey! How'd you <u>do</u> that?"

"Just blow out all the air," he says with a shrug, "and you drop like a rock down the well."

Mom is enraged, irrational. Dad watches quietly from his usual evening tranquilizer funk.

"What do you mean you're moving out of the haborb?"

I put down my rucksack and face the blonde fury of my mother moving to physically block my path.

"Just what I said, Mom. I'm going down the well. I've transferred from LaGrange University to the University of Hawai'i. Earthside."

"Well you can just 'untransfer' yourself right now!" she spits. "You're always thinking of yourself—what *you* want to do. Think of your parents and what we want you to do, for once!"

"I never stop thinking of that," I say with a weary sigh. "At LU I've been double-majoring in Bioengineering and World Literatures—Bioengineering for you, Mom, because you think it's a good preparation for a career in micro-medicine, and World Literatures for you, Dad, because you think it's the right precursor for a career in interorbital law. No more. I'm going to live my own life now. You can't live it for me, and I won't let you."

"Your own life! Your own life!" Mom mocks, suddenly brandishing a quarter-meter kitchen laser before her. "I've given *my whole life* for you boys! Waited on you hand and foot! And this is the kind of gratitude you show me? Oh no—no son of mine is going to move out until he finishes college or gets married!"

She jabs towards me with the kitchen laser.

"Honey!" Dad cries, startled, but I'm already moving, deflecting and taking her cutting hand, using her own momentum against her the way the aikido sensei at school showed us, then bringing my fist up and slugging my own mother hard on the jaw. She crumbles against one wall, bursts into tears. The laser skitters across the floor, automatically dead. Dad puts a restraining hand on my shoulder. I shrug it off, bend down to pick up my rucksack, and leave. Behind me Jack is witness to it all: one big unhappy dysfunctional family, like the rest of humanity.

"Let me see it again," I say.

"Okay."

When Jack slides under this time I submerge too, eyes open, watching him. Air like a stream of molten silver flows up out of his face, past his floating hair, as he sinks. A final burst of bubbles rises through the blue water, ripples the silver underside of the sky—and he lies again at full length, flat as his own shadow against the bottom. He seems almost to embrace the mooncrete, his face learning to love that drowned pavement, to breathe no more than it does.

"I have these violent thoughts sometimes," Jack says tearfully. He's been doing too many nonmutagenic zero-gee pharmaceuticals—too fast. "But I don't want to hurt anybody. I'd rather die than hurt someone."

I stay under as long as I can until the dead air in my chest begins screaming to get out, but still I break surface a full ten seconds before Jack does.

"Let me try," I say when Jack's surfaced.

In the soft Martian soil I find the corner of a box. Ardently we dig it out of the dirt. On the side of it is a label, on which is neatly typed my brother's name.

"Go ahead."

I try. I blow out air, but by the time I get to a forty-five degree angle the emptying of my chest underwater has become a tangible claustrophobia. Panicking, I inhale water and bolt to the surface, spluttering and gasping.

"What's it like, catching the shuttle down the well?" Jack asks from thousands of miles away over downlink.

"More disturbing that I thought it would be."

"The vertigo?"

"Yeah, I guess. But it wasn't the long fall to Earth that got to me. It was the sudden *openness* once the shuttle got out of the haborb."

Panic, a contributory cause in almost all water accidents, is a sudden, unreasoning, and overwhelming terror that destroys a person's capacity for self-help.

"What do you mean?" he asks.

"I don't know—like the world had turned inside out. Like the sky had unfolded and disappeared, you know?"

Examination shows no evidence of foul play. Coroner listing cause of death as immersion hypothermia. Victim possibly caught in freak late snowstorm.

"How about Earth?" he asks.

"Whew! Earth's even worse: an *everted* world. You're walking around on the *outside* of a body in space. Think about it."

"That's the situation we evolved in, though. It's perfectly natural for human beings."

"Yeah? You should try it sometime. It still strikes me as crazy. I don't know if I'll ever get used to it."

I give drowning my best shot again and again, but it's frustrating! I'm the older brother, I'm supposed to lead the way, to take the risks, to teach—but here's Jack teaching me how to drown, and I'm not even proving a good student.

"Your body tells you to breathe, even when you know you're underwater," Jack says. "It's stupid. Don't pay attention to it."

Eventually I can sink fully to the bottom—just barely—but I never do manage to let go that last burst of air, to breathe it all out so my face might sink fully forward, to kiss the unyielding pavement in that perfect passionate stillness my brother achieves so effortlessly.

"You changed your major to what?" my mother asks, over video downlink.

"Neoglobish, Ma. It's the *lingua franca* down here, the global commerce language."

"I know what it is," Mom says, disgusted. "Slang and pidgin—how can you waste your time studying such nonsense?"

"It's not nonsense, Mom," I say, trying to remain calm and patient with her. "The University of Hawai'i's the acknowledged center for the study of it. I'm almost guaranteed a job when I get out."

"Your Grandmother is spinning in her grave." Mom shakes her head bitterly. "She was an *English* teacher."

By the end of his teens, Jack has fully mastered the art of drowning. "People are mostly just water walking around, right?" he says. "If you can just get over the fear of suffocating in water, you can let it all go. It's easy."

When I leave for Earth, he can drown to his left side or his right, face up or face down, feet first or in the fetal position.

"Todd and Mark took be to a pro—a black woman," Jack says wearily. "I—we—just couldn't do it."

In most waters, the main threat to life during a prolonged immersion is cold or cold combined with the possibility of drowning.

"Looks like I'm not going to manage to break out as early as you did," he says, his voice quavering slightly. On the vid I can see he's grown a beard, dark and full, though not so dark and full as his eyes. "I tried to pull a covert escape op like the one you managed two years ago, but Mom caught me."

"What happened?"

"Oh, pretty much the same thing that happened with you," he says with a loud exhale. "She'd started yelling like a crazy woman. Even pulled the kitchen-laser trick again."

"And?"

"I couldn't do it." He stares off. "Couldn't bring myself to hit her the way you did. Couldn't use physical force against her. I caved in. So I'm stuck her 'til I graduate, I guess. Another two years up here in cislunar space, suffocating in the metal womb."

A mystic is a diver who can swim. A schizophrenic is a diver who can't.

"Think you'll hang in long enough to make it through the second birth?"

"I've got plans," he says, nodding. "I think I've got the grades, too. Gonna shoot for grad work at the Georgetown School of Interorbital Studies."

"Georgetown? Good choice. Pipeline to the Ambassadoriat. How're you doing otherwise?"

"The storm's passed," he says with a small smile. "Just shaken up a bit, is all."

When, in the time of his troubles, Jack comes to visit me in Hawai'i, he spends more and more time drowning, "doing the dead man's sink," particularly when there are dolphin pods about. Altered on KL 235, he plops overboard in full dive gear and swims down among them, while I watch worriedly from my small boat at the surface. Seated in lotus position on the bottom, he removes his regulator, pinches off its airflow, and slowly blows out his air. The dolphins gather in a rosette about him, motionless. For endless minutes he sits there like a drowned Buddha. Occasionally he takes a breath of air from his regulator. The dolphins lift their blowholes to the surface. Sometimes it seems he's going to stay down there forever, but he always comes back, eventually.

"What are you doing down there all that time?"

"Communing," Jack says. "Most of their discourse is non-referential—philosophical poetry, songs, that sort of thing. When I'm around them and flying on KL, though—'Human awake'—they just skip language altogether and beam me imagery directly, faster and denser than I can understand, though it's still all up here in my head somewhere, I think. After they zap me I feel better—much better."

"In what way?"

He pauses, thinking.

"Kind of like I'm being rescued. Like I'm being lifted up into the light."

I don't understand it. The voice of the dolphin in air sounds harsh to me—jarring gibbering clicktalk. I must admit, though, that after a month of "communing" with them he seems saner, more able to face the world as he leaves the islands.

"All life is sorrowful," Jack says, reading words attributed to Gautama Sakyamuni. "All life is painful." Looking disgusted he fingers the headplug button on the back of his skull. "All life is corporate."

GREAT PROGRESS ON MARS! OXYGEN AND WATER LEVELS UP ALL OVER THE PLANET! FULLY VIABLE ECOSPHERE! GENE-ENGINEERED FLORA, FAUNA, CROPS, HERDS! 300,000 SETTLERS ALREADY—MORE ARRIVING EVERYDAY! RIDE THE RANGE ON THE FINAL FRONTIER! JOIN US IN THE GREAT ADVENTURE! KOGAKU AND KOGAKU, DEVELOPERS. WE'RE BUILDING A BETTER WORLD.

"I think they're broadcasting all the details of my personal life," Jack says, laughing oddly, eyes darting. "They've tapped into my perceptions, my innermost thoughts—I'm sure of it."

The last time I see him in the flesh is when I marry Noriko. The wedding disturbs Mom for a number of reasons, not the least of which is that I'm getting married at all. Performing his part in the ceremony Jack reads passages from 1 Corinthians 13 in the New Testament and from Eihei Dogen's "Universal Recommendation for Zazen." From the way he reads them it's clear Jack's been drugging and pleasureplugging too much—disoriented one moment, too acutely focused the next. I try not to notice.

"The School of Interplanetary Studies is worse than L-5 enwombment," Jack tells me distractedly during the reception. "Classist fascist institution. I've signed on to go to Mars and work in terraversion. Nix Olympica Station."

"You're quitting grad school?" I ask, bewildered. "You've only been at Georgetown a couple of months—"

"Long enough to see that just studying about population dynamics isn't going to cut it. I want to *do* something about it."

Victim appears to have surgically removed his occipital umbilicus receptor—the police report says, for "headplug"—*not long before estimated time of death.*

"But why Mars?"

"That's the frontier," Jack says, his dark eyes bright like the last light of a supernova fleeing its own collapse into a black hole. "Look, it's easier to build expensive imitation earths than it is to persuade human beings to voluntarily limit their own reproductive capacities, right?" His focus begins to drift again.

Recognizing the drowning victim is sometimes difficult. Once a true drowning situation is certain, the idea of swimming after the victim should be entertained only after all other less hazardous ways of rescuing the drowning person have been exhausted. Too often the would-be rescuer becomes another victim.

"It's not good for me to be around people right now. I'd rather die that hurt anybody."

When executing a rescue, it is good to let the victim know your intention. Talk to the victim. Keep in personal contact.

"Jack's quit work and moved into the wilderness," Mom says worriedly over the downlink. "The last time I talked to him, he said he wasn't going to be calling any more. He said I had nothing more to say to him and he had nothing more to say to me. I don't understand it. The last words I said to him were 'I love you, Jack. I love you.'"

Exhaustion is simply loss of energy and the resultant inability to make the necessary movements to keep afloat and make progress through the water.

"Then he goes and disappears like this!" Mom sighs, on the verge of tears. "He hasn't called us in over a month, but the police still won't list him as a missing person. They say they've seen him—or at least someone who looks like him. Has he called you?"

Buoyancy of a body depends on the type of body. Some bodies are fairly buoyant. Others have marginal buoyancy. Still others have no buoyancy at all.

"No, Ma, he hasn't," I say. I haven't seen Jack since the wedding. Two years, and far away from the dolphins now. I haven't contacted him long-link in at least six months—married life, a new professorship in the Toyo haborb, busy, too damn busy. "I wouldn't worry about it too much. The authorities can always activate the homing signal on his headplug if they think it's necessary. There probably aren't a lot of long distance uplinks he can plug into in the Martian outback. You know Jack. He's always at the edge, but he always comes back."

Drowning is my brother's meditation. He is the bodhisattva of suffocation in water. A being who has awakened from the painful sleeping whirlpool of births and deaths to accomplish—what?

My mother's voice in my head is less a voice than a wail of raw pain. In it cries something terrible, inhuman, an elemental force rising from the deepest abysses of grief. It is almost with relief that I hear the voice break into sobs.

"Oh God," I say, weakly, my hand clutching into an impotent fist that I can only drop against the wall and lean upon.

"The Coroner called me—*me*—to say they'd found my son's body," Mom says between broken sobs. "The Coroner says he'd been dead six months! Oh God, this is horrible! He's been dead all this time and we didn't even know it. Jack's dead! Dead! Dead!"

I feel numb, hollow, insubstantial. My heartbeat is the tolling of a sunken ship's bell. I link up to Mars. Jack's body was found by a man on a snohorse at twilight the previous evening. Riding the fences, rounding up strays, bringing them down before hard winter sets in—winter too hard even for genetically engineered stock to survive.

Only about forty percent of yearly drownings occur to people who are swimming or playing in water.

"How could he be so hard-hearted?" my mother cries. "How could he be so—so insensitive? How could he turn away like this? Where did I go wrong? What did I do to deserve this?"

"It's not you, Mom," I say flatly, patiently. "It's not anybody. You didn't do anything wrong. Jack wanted to cut his ties with everyone and everything. He was following his leadings, living the life he wanted to live. It's not your fault. It's not my fault. It's not anybody's fault at all."

I ask that his ashes be buried where his body was found. I need a locus for my grief, a spot in space and time. Noriko and I decide to go to Mars the following summer, to view the burial site.

"I can't do it, Jack. I just can't let go that last burst of air."

The depth to which a rescuer may go to retrieve a victim will depend upon the depth itself and how long the breath can be held after swimming to the site.

"Please, for my sake don't go. That place killed your brother. Those people he worked for killed your brother, as sure as they killed the whales and elephants."

"Mom, I'm married to one of 'those people'."

"I don't care. That place killed him. Please, promise me you won't go."

The settlement police are too busy and too short-handed to show us the spot where his body was found, but the undertaker— a grey-haired, gravel-voiced man with extremely dry hands— kindly agrees to take us there. We proceed by landmarks into the great new-tundra emptiness of the Nix Olympica range. We get lost again and again.

"I have heard the mermaids singing, each to each," my father reads. "I do not think they'll sing to me. I have seen them riding seaward on the wave, combing the white hair of the waves blown back, when the wind blows the water white and black."

Eventually we come upon a mountain valley, bisected by a stony wash and overlooking the high plains to the south and west. Genetic-engineered sage and thistle and low grass grow roundabout, even a few stunted things like incredibly tortured bonsai. Not far from the wash is a cairn of stones.

"That's it," the undertaker says. We leave the aircar and move toward the cairn.

Eternal return. Avalokitesvara. Kwan Yin. Kwannon. Bodhisattvas and saviors do not leave the world, but regard its lives and deeds with the eyes and tears of compassion.

"There was snow on the ground again when we brought the ashes up for burial," the undertaker remarks, standing next to the cairn. "Cold and snowing when we did the service, too. I wouldn't be surprised if we didn't bury them in exactly the right place." He gazes along the slope of the valley leading into the wash, eyes a bare spot in the stubby sage and highland grass about five meters away. On closer examination the bare spot is in fact the distorted but still discernible shadow of a man. "We missed it, all right. Ashes should be buried over there."

Socrates. Jesus. Gandhi. King. Ohnuki. Walking Bear. Eternal return.

"This is where we found your brother's body. He was out on the surface here for several months, so what growth was already here was killed out under him. His flesh saponified, too—ran like liquid soap into the ground in pretty much the shape you're looking at. For a while it'll keep things from growing back, but when they do, they'll probably come back greener and lusher than just about any other place on Mars."

Jack always comes back.

"Might we move his ashes to this spot?" I ask.

The undertaker nods and we begin moving the rocks and digging into the site where the ashes have been misburied.

"Shadow of the dead—like at Hiroshima," Noriko says. The tears that refuse to well up in my eyes well up in hers instead. I nod.

Experience teaches rescuers how far into the water they can safely go and how much of a load they can bear.

"Immersion hypothermia is a peaceful way to die," the undertaker says as I carry the box of ashes over to Jack's shadow and we begin digging where his flesh flowed into the soil, digging and digging. Noriko and the undertaker carry over the rocks from the other cairn. I put the box in the hole we've dug, cover it over again with the rich new soil, then pile the stones on top of that. "A sleep and a forgetting."

Till human voices wake us, and we drown. Again and again. Drown in frozen water, to become the fire and ashes that remain, to lie buried in unearthly earth.

I rise from the grave, wiping the dirt from my hands. The winds of approaching nightfall begin to howl around us. We turn and make our way toward the aircar. As we lift off, I look back at the shadow with stones piled on its heart and try to remember what it reminds me of. A shadow of a body, the body itself a shadow. But for there to be shadows, there must also be light.

"Watch!"

I remember then, and all I can see is Jack, passionately still at the bottom of a deep sun-filled pool, waiting to surge toward the surface and the light once more.

—for Jay

INTERROGATIONS IN A HOLOGRAPHIC OBSERVATORY

Somewhere between the perennial state and the apocalyptic individual lies the utopian society. It is, however, very nearly as difficult to distinguish the utopian from the perennial types of social organization as it is to distinguish the ecstatic from the catastrophic types of apocalyptic individuality.
—from *The Purgation Manual*, Sixty-Third Iteration

"Grand Expurgator Cartaphila!"

As I was announced by the guard in the antechamber, two of the men, the District Chief Inspector and the second guard, came to their feet in the six-sided room beyond. Walking toward the table behind which the Inspector had been sitting, I saw that the prisoner—hollow-eyed, lank-haired, unshaven—was already standing.

In the gleaming surface of the ventillume shaft behind the table, I saw too my own reflection: wearing the black and red robes and bearing the flail of authority, a woman of a certain age in an age of uncertainty.

I took my seat at the table. As they also sat, the Inspector flicked aside the tails of his morning coat, while the second guard, hands still gauntleted, removed the morion helmet from his head. I shuffled perfunctorily through the prisoner's documents. I had no need to read them in detail again. I knew the case more than well enough.

Standing before me now in his jailbird's magpie plumes, the prisoner was a synesthetic, epileptic, prodigious savant, among whose blessings and curses was the supposed ability to compute the nth digit of π without calculating the preceding n-1 digits.

No one in all the history of the Observatory had ever been able to do such a thing, yet this socially-maladroit nonentity insisted he could.

We in the Office of Purgation believed he was a charlatan—perhaps one with an exceptional memory for all the digits of π calculated up to that time, but a fraud nonetheless. He struck us as at best self-deluded, capable of lying convincingly enough to fool both himself and others.

His devoted followers in the Piphilolog sect, alas, believed him to be their long-awaited Holiest Fool, Absolute Approximator, and Fullest Incarnation of π. Thoroughly beguiled by this pied cipher, they referred to his supposed talent as the "blessed affliction." We of the Office began to suspect he might prove not only a fool, but also a dangerous madman.

As a practical person, I had never been much interested in debating whether the purpose of the Observatory was to approximate a hyperdimensional sphere whose center was everywhere and its circumference nowhere, or one whose circumference was everywhere and its center nowhere. I took the Observatory as I found it and, beyond the necessary formalities, did not much concern myself with how it came to be. Theometric speculations mattered far less to me than the fact that all the vastness of our security protocols—the fabric of our state, perhaps even the fabric of reality itself—had always been based in ciphers dependent on distant, incalculable decimal places of π. To all that, the prisoner potentially posed a most grave threat, whether or not he ultimately proved capable of the particular talent claimed of him.

The Inspector, reading from his own notes, got to his feet again.

"Prisoner 3.14159," he said, casting a sidelong smirk my way. (Giving the prisoner that number had been my touch.) "What do you believe is the nature of this map room, and all others in the Observatory?"

"This room is a prison cell. As is all of the Observatory that you use in this way."

"We don't think so."

"Then for you it isn't."

I nodded to the guard, who stood up and, with great vigor, hurled the prisoner to the floor.

"'Thinking' is why we're here," I said, nodding to the guard again, who hauled the prisoner roughly to his feet before releasing him. "We seek to determine whether you are mentally competent to stand trial. We will today range from the most common and concrete knowledge to the most abstract and specialized. Answer the questions, or things will not go well for you. *What is the nature of the Observatory?*"

The prisoner jerked abruptly from the shoulders, like a marionette who strings had been yanked.

"Some say the Observatory, also known as the cosmos, has always existed and will always do so, from everlasting to everlasting," the prisoner began. "In their view, the Observatory is in some profound fashion also *without*, as in 'outside of', time."

"Are there any grounds for this belief?" asked the Inspector.

"The rows, columns, blocks, and sheets of digits on the Observatory's maps, through which we access and observe all things, do exist in numbers so vast it would take an eternity to count and chronicle them. The total number of the maps in the Observatory, too, is also incalculably immense, as is the total number of map rooms."

"And the map rooms themselves?"

"Are endlessly repeated. Only the maps contained in each room differ. The floor of each maproom cell is the ceiling of the one below it, the ceiling of each cell is the floor of the one above it. Most of the 'floor' and 'ceiling' of each cell isn't floor or ceiling either, but rather open space, an atrium or gallery flanked by a walkway wide enough for two people to walk abreast.

"Along the walls lined with the map cabinets, these storage units stand on the outside of the walkway. A safety railing, half average adult height, runs along the inside of the walkway. At the center of each cell is a ventilation and illumination shaft, about which wraps a spiral staircase or, more formally, a staircase in the shape of a double helix.

"The floors and ceilings of cells, the staircases, and the ventillume shafts all proceed upward and downward, apparently infinitely. Walls and antechambers of cells—and the map-room cells themselves, and all their components—likewise repeat from side to side and diagonally, also apparently endlessly. Taken together, all of these, it has been argued, strongly imply that the Observatory is not only infinite in space, but also without beginning and without end in time."

"Do you consider these arguments sufficient grounds for believing in both the infinity and eternity of the Observatory?"

"No. Over many centuries the argument that the Observatory was *created* has steadily gained adherents."

"Why?"

"Endlessness in space not withstanding, those who believe in a created Observatory reason there must have been some beginning point in time before which the Observatory did not exist."

"What is their evidence for this?"

"The ancient names for the map rooms, the Great Conjecture arising from the discovery of π, and all the places and things accessed through the maps."

"Of those three, which do you consider the best argument for a created Observatory?" I asked.

"The more telling evidence involves π," the prisoner said slowly.

"What evidence?" asked the Inspector.

"The ancient discovery that π, the ratio of the circumference of a circle to its diameter, arguably continues to endless decimal places—*that* is what eventually suggested the existence of numbers which might be expanded infinitely without ever repeating. This led to the Great Conjecture."

"Define that, as you understand it."

"The endless digits, on their endless numbers of sheets, in their endless numbers of map drawers, in their endless map cabinets, in their endless map rooms throughout the Observatory— all are in fact digits of the never-ending and never-repeating decimal expansion of a transcendental and irrational number. That number around which the Observatory is constructed has, from the earliest days of the Conjecture, been presumed to be π, the first discovered number of its class. And, just as π has a beginning, a Primordial Digit, so too must the Observatory also have had a beginning."

"You mentioned the construction of the Observatory," the Inspector said. "Explain."

"The idea of constructibility is at the heart of the arguments for why the Observatory was created."

"How so?"

"π is irrational—impossible to express exactly as a fraction, like 22/7. It is also transcendental, that is, unproducible through any finite sequence of algebraic operations on integers. Together these argue for the idea that π is not constructible: the circle cannot be squared."

"Then it is irrelevant to the construction of the Observatory."

"No! The area of a circle *can* be approximated by inscribing a regular polygon inside that circle and calculating the polygon's area. The more sides the polygon has, the better the approximation. An infinite-sided polygon can be interpreted as an infinitely close approximation to the circle inside which it is inscribed, with the circle itself being the limit as the number of sides approaches infinity.

"As a result of the Conjecture, the Observatory itself came to be defined as the limit of an expression which contained the product of two expressions whose limits were themselves infinity and zero. Also as an infinitely close physical approximation to that mathematical truth. And as the fullest possible construction of the inconstructible."

"What was the impact of this Conjecture, when it was first announced?" I asked.

"It fostered a golden age of contentment."

"Why?"

"As π's vast simulacrum, the Observatory made sense, had a purpose and a meaning—and with it, so also all things, since all things were to be observed and understood through the mental optics of π."

"'Mental optics'?" asked the Inspector.

"From ancient times, it has been known that focused contemplation of the digit-filled sheet of a map causes the digits to holistically transform into a three-dimensional representation before the viewer's eyes. This mental-optic effect has generally been presumed to be either stereographic or synesthetic. Under the latter theory, map images and, more particularly, sounds—even suggestions of smell, taste, and touch—are the result of synesthesia induced by the contemplation of the digits on the sheets. By means of synesthetic overlay in the minds of the map readers, the tremendous calculation of π is interpreted as sensorial landscapes, seascapes, cloudscapes, even starscapes of other suns, other worlds—inhabited by other beings, like ourselves, yet not like ourselves."

This discussion of origins and optics was all interesting enough, but was getting us nowhere. For all I knew, what we saw in the maps in which those beings were present might indeed be the past—their history, and perhaps also ours. Perhaps they once lived in the realms and territories we experienced through the Observatory's maps, but I was not particularly concerned with spelling the world backward. I decided to take a different tack.

"You are a Piphilolog, is that right?" I asked.

"Yes, that's correct."

"What are the spiritual obligations of Piphilologs?"

"In response to the suggestion that the Observatory might in some sense be meaningless—"

"Is this heresy part of your beliefs?" asked the Inspector sharply.

"No! Just the opposite. The failure, generation after generation, to find the Primordial Digit—'The Three that is the One that is In the Beginning, The One that is the Three that is In the Beginning, Divine Whole Number out of whose superabundant grace in infinite remainder flows all that is'—the centuries of searching, ending only in failure, led to the fear that the Observatory might in some deep sense be meaningless, as I said. Against that fear, our great mystic urged us, his followers to become living Observatories' He said that, if we would only choose to see it, human beings were *already* incarnate approximations to the great constant π. As votaries, therefore, we practice the spiritual exercise of calculating, memorizing, and vocalizing π to as many digits as we are able."

"You proclaim that π is everywhere, do you not?" I asked.

"We attest to the omnipresence of π. That is why we recite the raw numbers of the constant's digits."

"And the sacred poems your mendicant monks and nuns chant...?"

"Are constructed under the principle that the number of letters in each word of the poem must represent a digit of π in the exact sequence in which each digit occurs. Our faith compels us to spread the message of the incarnation of π through any and all appropriate means, including poetry."

"Has there been any other important response," the Inspector asked slowly, "in opposition to heretical suggestions of meaninglessness in the Observatory?"

"The rise of the Consensists. Better known as Purgationists, or Downcasters. People like yourself, and the Grand Expurgator here."

"And what do you understand our beliefs to be?"

"Consensist dogma calls for purifying or purging the Observatory of all 'fictional' or 'counterfactual' maps, those maps whose digits transform into texts or landscapes which patently contradict what is already known from many other maps."

"And what do you understand our practices to involve?"

"When you learn from your 'reliable sources' that 'questionable' maps have been found, you decide whether or not the maps are heretical enough to merit being 'committed to oblivion,' cast down the nearest ventillume shaft."

The Inspector glanced at me, and I nodded.

"Please spare us your mocking tone," I warned him. "Let me tell you that, as an Expurgator, I have consigned many a map to eternal disappearance—and always with good cause."

The prisoner said nothing.

"Allow me to tell you something you cannot know. Perhaps it will change your opinion of us, perhaps not. We have recently discovered vast regions of the Observatory where innumerable cells contain endless sheets of apparently random numbers for π's decimal places which, when themselves transformed, show only endless sheets of apparently random numbers for π's decimal places *in other bases*. Tell me, if you had made this discovery, how would you have responded to such a vertiginous prospect?"

The prisoner again said nothing. The guard behind him looked expectantly at me, as if he were impatient to punish the man severely for his impertinent silence, but I shook my head.

"We have decreed that all 'other-based' maps are to be abandoned in place and stricken from memory. What would you have done, 3.14159? Would you be fool enough to allow all hope of sense in the Observatory to be swallowed up in a vast sea of nonsense?"

The prisoner raised his eyes to stare into mine.

"So that is why you persecute us."

"What?"

"Given the enormity of π, given the vast numbers of unexplored map rooms in the Observatory, and of the unexplored maps in all those unexplored map rooms—somewhere, among infinite maps in infinite map rooms, other sheets virtually identical to the ones you have cast down must still exist, not yet consignable to oblivion by you, because not yet discovered by anyone. And in all the long forever, there will *always* be such—"

"Blasphemy!" cried the Inspector. I raised a finger and nodded to the guard. With one gauntleted fist he struck the prisoner hard enough across the face to drop the man to the floor, but that did not silence him.

"All your efforts to purge and purify the Observatory of erroneous maps will prove utterly futile," he said, smiling oddly as he raised his bleeding face from the floor and wiped his bloodied mouth. "You *must* already know that. That's why you've turned your attention to a task you might more readily accomplish: eliminating those of us who wish to make ourselves living Observatories."

"Silence!" shouted the Inspector, before turning to me and speaking in a lower voice. "Expurgator Cartaphila, it is my considered opinion that Prisoner 3.14159 is competent to stand trial. And must."

"I agree," I said, nodding then signaling for the guard to haul the prisoner to his feet again, which he did. "Guard, call in the chartmaster. We wish to test the prisoner's claims concerning his purported abilities."

* * * * * * *

If apocalyptic individuals did not exist, it would be necessary for perennial states to invent them. Perhaps they always have done so, even if unintentionally. From our study of the maps, we see that Moses was as much the unintentional invention of Egypt as Socrates was the unintentional invention of Athens. Gautama was as much the unintentional invention of the Ganges kingdoms as Jesus was the unintentional invention of Rome. Gandhi was as much the unintentional invention of Britain as King was the unintentional invention of America, and so forth, through all the chronologies constructed from all the maps examined thus far.

Within moments the chartmaster entered the map room—a small, bent-over man in the sky-blue robes and skullcap of a full theometrician.

"Prisoner," said the Inspector, "name the digit at the fiftieth decimal place of π."

The prisoner's eyelids closed and the eyeballs beneath them twitched rapidly side to side, like the eyes of a man dreaming. He opened his eyes and pronounced a number.

The chartmaster consulted his sheets, on which were listed all the known digits of π, found the required decimal place, and nodded.

"Name the digit at the five hundredth decimal place of π," I said. Again the prisoner's eyelids closed and the eyeballs beneath them twitched rapidly side to side, again he opened them, again he pronounced a number, which the chartmaster again looked up and confirmed.

"Name the digit at the thousandth decimal place of π," said the Inspector. The little ritual and its results were the same.

"Name the digit at π's millionth decimal place," I said—and again both the prisoner and the chartmaster played their accustomed parts.

"Name the digit at the two hundred trillionth four hundred twenty seven millionth decimal place," said the Inspector. Again the prisoner's eyelids closed, the eyeballs beneath them twitched rapidly side to side, he opened his eyes, he pronounced a number—but this time the chartmaster could only shrug his shoulders, unable to confirm or deny, for no one had yet calculated π to so many digits.

"Name the digit at π's ten octillionth and thirty-first decimal place," I said. Again the closed and twitching eyes opened, and the prisoner pronounced a number. Again the chartmaster only shrugged, unable to confirm or deny the number's accuracy.

"He's engaging in outright fraud," muttered the Inspector. "He has to be!"

"Tell me, Pi Man," I asked. "How do you accomplish your π place–naming feat?"

"I can explain it no more than a bird can explain its song."

"Yet you believe your declaration of π, to whatever decimal place is called for, is accurate?"

"I'm as certain of that as I can be of anything."

"Even if you can't explain it?"

"Yes."

"Very well then. Name the digit at π's last decimal place."

I expected him to simply say there was no final digit, or declare some number to be that (and thereby prove himself a fraud), but instead he did something quite strange. Wracked by sudden seizure, he collapsed to the floor, spasming and twitching. The guard glanced rapidly around the room for something to thrust between the prisoner's teeth, to prevent him from biting off his tongue and choking on it.

"Here!" I said tossing him my flail. "The handle!"

The guard caught the flail and jammed its handle sideways between the prisoner's teeth and tongue. His spasming and jerking gradually decreased. Before our eyes the prisoner transformed from out-of-control clockwork automaton to limp ragdoll.

He remained in a deathlike coma for three days.

When he regained consciousness, he wanted to know what had happened. I told him—seizure and flail and all—then questioned him again.

"Prisoner 3.14159, what happened from *your* point of view?"

He pondered the question a moment before speaking.

"I saw clearly, in a single instant, all the past and all the future—all *possible* pasts, and all *possible* futures. I can't explain it, but I know I will never be the same."

"Then π has a last digit?"

He shook his head.

"Then π *doesn't* have a last digit?"

And again he shook his head.

He was useless. In my hands I absently twisted my flail,

barely noting the Pi Man's teeth-marks still in its handle. I turned the prisoner over to the Inspector and his interrogators. Changed by the experience of his lost days, however, the prisoner would never again answer our questions about π, no matter what persuasions—and yes, tortures—we used upon him.

* * * * * * *

> *Such apocalyptic individuals are always valuable as lightning rods for dissent, and gather about them many other potential enemies of the state. Unfortunately it's also always difficult to tell which type of apocalyptic individuals they will turn out to be.*
>
> *Some of these individuals will be apocalyptic in the revelatory sense, lifting the veil of this world to reveal something more, through ecstasy and visions of harmony. Their most powerful weapons will be how to live by new ideas. Others, however, will be apocalyptic in the destructive sense, rending this vale of tears to make way for something different, through catastrophe and the violence of overthrow. Their most powerful ideas will be how to kill by new weapons.*
>
> —from *The Purgation Manual*, Sixty-Third Iteration

That the Pi Man and his abilities might be based in some reality I could barely fathom was something I soon found far more disturbing than the idea that his "blessed affliction" was the mere product of fakery. The danger his ability, if real, posed to the security of the entire Purgationist state was too immense to be tolerated.

I saw to it that his trial would be a perfunctory affair, and that he would be cast down.

His Prisoner Number we had seared into his skin in prominent digits, 3.14159 midway between clavicle and nipple on the left side of his chest. The guards shaved his head and smashed thin metal and wood coronals, circular disks and square planes, onto his brow until it bled around them. Then, having strapped to his shoulders an immense pack of fallacious maps, we marched him toward a map room, like any other except for the fact that it was to be the site of his Downcasting.

Despite our best attempts to keep the time and place of that Downcasting as secret as possible (so that his followers might not venerate the date of his execution, or enshrine the location of it, afterward), a small crowd of his disciples nonetheless managed to follow us as the prisoner was marched, beaten and bloodied, up the stairs from level to level.

He stopped and rested—too often, it seemed to me. The more he did so, the larger the crowd that gathered. While he stood at one such stop, I struck him with my Expurgator's flail of office.

"Why do you loiter, Pi Man? Move along!"

"Cartaphila, why do you still persecute us? Do you fear a hell of endless new maps, or new maps of an endless hell?"

I struck him again, but he would not be silenced.

"Can't you see we are each of us circle and square, each striving to complete the other, through love to *become* the other, as we approach the limit of infinity—"

I struck him a third time.

"I said, move along!"

"Before I 'move along,' I will stand here and rest a moment in silence—but I tell you that you will never rest, never stop from searching, and telling of your searching, until you see me again at the end of the Observatory."

"Fool! There is no end to the Observatory—only to you."

He smiled oddly—as much like madman as fool.

"My curse has proven a blessing," he said, resting his hand on my forehead. "So may it prove for you, until you understand π is not changed by the shape of the Observatory, even as the Observatory is changed by the shape of π."

We stood there a moment in silence, his hand on my head, an immense cascade of something both brightness and numbers flowing into my skull, until at last I shrugged off his hand.

His last words to me, over his shoulder as he moved on, were only a sort of bad poetry: "Just because the sky is in π is no reason for anyone to die!"

Soon thereafter, we stood him up on the safety rail of that cell. With a vigorous push forward, we cast him down. I saw him fall and fall, through the endlessly honeycombed air that bore no sweetness, until he vanished from sight.

* * * * * * *

> Yet the making of such distinctions has become all the more critical, and not only because the worst thing one can do, politically, is martyr the wrong apocalyptic individuals. Correctly distinguishing between the types is critical to the continued survival of both the individual and the state, particularly since it has become increasingly possible for any individual to potentially possess the capacity for mass destructiveness.
> —from The Purgation Manual, Sixty-Third Iteration

So ended the passion of the pied cipher. His followers affirmed that—no matter how many maps might be redrawn or destroyed, no matter how vast or how consistent the screens that might be commanded—invincible non-sense would always break through, sure as death. Yet, at one and the same time, his followers also proclaimed that, because their Holiest Fool was Pi Incarnate, man and number, transcendental, irrational, and normal, he could himself no more die than the decimal expansion of π could come to an end.

I do not know the truth or falsity of these beliefs. What I do know is that, from the day of his Downcasting, I have become a timeless anachronism. I have not aged, not in all the years, decades, and centuries that have followed. Neither have I ever been able to rest from my wandering. My life has become a detour in eternity.

I have witnessed the creation of machines capable of computing particular iterative processes called "dynamical maps." I have viewed the landscapes which emerge from their calculations, such as when these machines plot the first million or billion decimals of π as random walks. I have looked through the computational lenses provided by these machines, zooming in and out from scale to scale, within a single map and among vast collections of them. With the development of these machines, the priesthood of the unbelievers has only grown, along with their contention that the Observatory was not created by a God or gods at all, but by beings like us—or, more precisely, like those seen in the maps, whom we resemble, or who resemble us (the relationship remains unclear).

Whether or not we are avatars cut free of a lost flesh to which we owe a nebulous allegiance (as some claim), I do not know. Disturbingly, though, as we move further and further out through the Observatory, more and more of those beings we observe in the maps are themselves looking at maps or screens. Do they too see a world of other beings before their eyes also looking at maps or screens, who in turn see other beings before theirs also looking at still more maps and screens, and on and on? The mind reels at the thought of such infinite regress, so it is seldom spoken of publicly.

Instead it is presumed that, as the result of some great disaster (or triumph; opinions differ) these beings in our maps created a machine (or system of machines; again, opinions differ) which displaced (or assimilated) the world (or worlds) in which those beings once existed. In order to understand the nature of their transcendence (or destruction), the machine (or machines, or transcended beings) created the Observatory as an enormous simulacrum in which, through our observing and understanding of our (presumed) ancestors' fates, the transcendent machine (or machines, or transcended beings) might come to understand our/its/their own history.

In and through the Observatory, then, we not only watch, but are also in turn watched.

Whether the chain of observers and observed is itself endless, I do not know. Whether our existence is made either more or less meaningful or meaningless by the idea that we are thoughts in the vast thought experiment of the Observatory (and whether or not the experimenters will one day end their experiment), I also cannot say.

Troubled by such questions, too many hurl themselves to their deaths, poorly emulating the fate of the Pi Man in ways he would no doubt abhor. I am, however, denied even that solace. I cannot know whether or not, in the ordinary course of things, we die because the "period" placed on the sentence of life by death is necessary to the simulation of our ancestors' mode of consciousness. I will not know, so long as I remain incapable of dying.

I cannot say with certainty whether the finite recurrence of randomness constitutes a species of order, or whether the infinite recurrence of order constitutes a species of randomness, or whether both are merely species of chaos. Yet, if the Observatory is a vast simulacrum of π's unfolding, and if π is mathematically normal, then in that infinite unfolding the sequence of digits which constituted the Pi Man's existence will one day recur. Although that sequence can never repeat in exactly the same way or in any cyclical or periodic fashion, I will in that sequence nonetheless see, know, and understand him and his message, again, for the first time. Like an infinity of journeys round a finite but unbounded globe, my life, and all my searching and tale-telling with it, will at last end.

In that lies the blessed affliction of all my hope.

MONUMENTS OF UNAGEING INTELLECT

Grabbing the board's nose in his left hand, Hisao cut its repellers. Straightening up and angling the front of the board downward, he kicked in the jets and plummeted from the low clouds toward the choppy seas.

He was soon moving at one hundred fifty miles per hour. A county-sized chunk of the northern Pacific's surface and the airspace above it had been reserved for the hoverball match. There was nothing for him to watch out for beyond the occasional errant seabird. And, oh yes—the opposing team.

Despite his velocity as he arced forward and down, the ball rested almost motionless in its smashcradle. From headplug chatter he knew defenders were swarming up toward him. Out of the corners of his eyes he saw his team's forwards blocking most of them. Three defenders, undeterred, still raced toward him, fanning out to stop him from getting off a shot.

Hisao continued his dive, straight at them, and on toward the surface of the sea below them. His eye-augments began to flash red messages.

WARNING!
CONTINUING ON CURRENT TRAJECTORY AT CURRENT VELOCITY WILL PLACE YOU BELOW GAME FLOOR!

He nodded absently. His augments didn't need to remind him how the game "floor" worked—overlapping fields from a grid of gyrostabilized levitation disks, perched ten feet above the ocean's surface atop bright orange buoys. Once he plunged below that floor, the repellers on his board would have nothing to repel *against*.

Hisao cut his board's jets—too late to stay above field threshhold. The approaching defenders' monitors must have relayed them the same information. Surmising Hisao was fated to splash into the drink and go immobile, the three defenders were at nearly full stop by the time he passed under them on his dead board—

—and hit the back of a wave fast and hard enough to skip back up eleven feet, just above the invisible field-floor, where he cut in his repellers, slammed on his jets, and left the defenders awash in the blast of his spray before they could even swivel around to pursue.

Hisao bee-lined toward the goal. Now only the goalie—his sometime-love, Wilena—hovered between him and scoring. He flipped open his smashcradle. A flick of his wrist sent the ball onto and into its sweetspot pocket. With all his strength he swung the streamlined and servomotored smashcradle (lineal descendant of atlatl and jai alai basket-glove) forward in a great sidelong arc.

The ball shot from the cradle toward the goal, moving at a third the speed of sound. Wilena raced forward from the virtual net whose space, both real and cyber, she was so diligently defending. The next moment everyone's eye-monitors flashed projections that the ball would fall short of the goal.

And so the ball did, skipping to a stop on the surface of the sea.

Wilena slalomed forward to take the ball. Just as she was about to fish it out of the water with her telescoping catchcradle, the sphere suddenly leapt a dozen feet off the ocean's surface. A moment later, a dolphin's body erupted from the water, nose down and tail up, catching with its flukes the same ball it had head-butted out of the water an instant before.

With its powerful tail the dolphin smacked the ball, spiking it past the goalie's outstretched arms and into the virtual net.

"Score!"

No sooner had the defenders overcome their astonishment at the flukey maneuver than their protests roared up on the comm.

"That's Alphonse! One of Hisao's work dolphins!"

"He wasn't legally on the field!"

"I thought we were playing this as a single-species sport today!"

Hisao's teammates, once they were able to stop laughing, came to his defense. No such solo-species agreement had been made! If everyone checked their playbacks, they'd see that only the regulation twelve offensive players had been on the field during Hisao's drive—Alphonse included.

Hisao kept out of it. He knew that, in the end, the point probably wouldn't count, but everything—setting it up with his teammates, the hours spent rehearsing the moves with Alphonse—had all been worth it, just to see the utterly bewildered look on Wilena's face!

"The dolphin was not entered on the roster," said Moira at last, serving as referee. "Hisao's score is nulled."

Hisao and his teammates did some grutching, but made no official complaint. An aura of seriousness, gravity, and fair consideration gave all Moira's pronouncements added weight. Hisao had long found it inexplicably attractive.

"Now that we've had our little joke," Moira said, preparing to toss the ball back into play, "how about a little less levity and a lot more levitation, for the rest of the game? Hmm?"

She hurled the ball back into bounds, where it was greeted with the laughter of young gods and goddesses, golden Olympians at play, flashing and moving in waves with the ball and the game.

* * * * * * *

Like everyone in his cohort, Hisao travelled a great deal.

He hovercruised the south seas a dozen times. He dived all the Earth's oceans, from the shallowest sun-dappled reefs to the deepest midnight trenches. He loved that world. It was one of the reasons he decided to become a cetologist.

Like those few others (his friends and work teammates, mainly) who still pursued the arcana of diplomas, degrees, and certifications, he endured the interminable forty-plus years of basic formal education—or as formal as it got, with its thousands of hours of screen, VR, and headplugged human-peripheral time.

Throughout his training, he had happily traded such seat-time for sea-time and mobile learning. After a dozen years, though, even his ocean-diving fieldwork began to seem a little too much like schoolwork. For something different, he joined a team climbing the five highest peaks in the Himalayas—without perfused bloodox, lift boots, or an augment suit. As part of a shifting group of several friends, he rambled around the Moon for half a year. Bent on climbing the highest mountain in the solar system, he joined an expedition to Mars, then followed that up with a cloud-cruise tour of the Jovian atmosphere. He joined a crew of offworld icedivers, too, exploring some of the more important moons of Jupiter and Saturn.

Taking time with their educations was no problem for anyone in his cohort. They freefloated from team to team, network to network, putting on and taking off new roles, tasks, and ever-temporary jobs as if they were changes of clothing, updated implants, new hairstyles or skin colors. Like everyone else, Hisao too was destined to be forever young. They could all afford to be cavalier with time.

All except Moira.

He first noticed the difference during one of his annual "sittings" for her. She was studying ancient art media—sculpture, in particular. The sittings she harangued him and two dozen or so of their mutual friends into, from all over the solar system, were purportedly part of her on-going educational experience.

"Sitting" was an antiquated term for what Moira actually did.

Using the medscan tech to which Wilena had introduced her, Moira created a life-mold of each of them, once each year—minutely detailed three-dimensional renderings of their bodies. She then cast in bronze each life-molded subject.

Because the medscan showed each subject with eyes closed and without clothing or hair, there was something unsettling about the resulting sculptures. Holographically projecting clothes and hair back onto the statues in overlay, which Moira always did, only managed to make the effect even more disquieting. When she flashed through several years' worth of projections—ever-changing fashions in apparel and hairstyle, overlain on unchanging statuary forms—the effect made Hisao slightly queasy.

"I call them Persistent Personae," Moira said. "I took the idea from the old practice of making a death mask—something artists used to do after someone famous got old and died."

Hisao nodded. He wasn't much interested in archaic artforms. Besides, only non-human creatures aged and died, these days—like his dolphin friends, unfortunately. True, there were the not unheard-of cases of death by accidents too obliterating for even the moteswarms to mend—but human beings, getting old and dying like everything else in nature? That was ancient history.

Yet, over six years of sittings, he began to notice something changing in Moira's looks. Something different about her face, her body, even her hair. He couldn't quite put his finger on it. Then, during one afternoon of his sixth sitting, he asked Moira something he'd never thought to ask her before.

"Have you ever done life-molds of yourself?"

In response, she had her mechs bring six years' worth of her own bronze Personae into the studio and place them alongside his. The differences were subtle in themselves, but contrast made them obvious. Her face had developed creases and furrows that his hadn't. Her body had changed, particularly about the hips and breasts, in ways he'd never seen in any other woman he'd known. It was as if the seriousness and gravity that had long characterized Moira's personality had now begun manifesting in her body as well.

Afterwards, when they made love, Moira did so with a passionate earnestness utterly new to him. It was exhilarating, even a bit frightening. But when she suggested that he stay with her, that he settle in for a while, Hisao politely laughed it off.

"No can do, kiddo. You know the spectacle Jorge has planned for this week." Their mutual friend Jorge was an orbital mechanist whose latest project involved telepresently steering an asteroid into the inner solar system from the Kuiper belt.

"Crashing that skystone of his into the Sun, isn't he?"

"Exactly so! He's invited me to his observatory, to be part of the private audience actually telepresent for the impact—real-time inside the ultimate firework!"

"I certainly wouldn't want you to miss *that*, no," Moira said, taking his begging-off in stride. Hisao felt almost like she was being condescending toward him, but he couldn't quite figure out how or why.

As he kissed her goodbye, Hisao was both relieved and obscurely disappointed. Heading to Jorge's eyrie in Peru, he felt that, by rejecting her offer to "settle in," he had dodged an arrow by which he might have dearly wished to be struck—if he were about a hundred years older.

He didn't think much on it again until Moira exhibited her first ten years of Persistent Personae, in a show at a gallery in Nuevo Seattle. She called the exhibit "Too Too Solid Flesh," for reasons Hisao was unable to fathom.

The show was by no means the toast of every art critic who'd been given a preview, but the opening for it drew quite a crowd, nonetheless—and not just telepresently. In that crowd, Hisao saw Wilena again, for the first time in quite a few years.

Together they walked among the statues in the pavilioned gallery space. Not only were the rapidly changing hair and clothing styles holoed onto the Personae now, but streets and city skylines (projected around them in diorama) built and unbuilt themselves, shifted and changed in time-lapsed fashion, completely recycling themselves every three years or so, just as they did in reality.

"Time increasingly sublimes into space," intoned a voiceover narration as they walked, their feet unintentionally triggering its comments. "Nature disappears into culture. Reality dissipates into simulation. Response vanishes into stimulus. All our depth is on the surface."

Hisao shook his head.

"Kind of a strange narration."

"What's stranger here, if you ask me," Wilena said, looking about at the other people in the gallery, "is how few of the sitters have shown up in person for the opening."

Hisao nodded. He'd noticed it too.

"You have to admit there's something a little disturbing about what she's done with us," he said.

"Yes. Especially when she puts the statues of herself among all of ours."

Just then Moira herself, mingling, stopped to give both of them quick hugs. Embracing her, Hisao noted the subtle white streaks in her hair. Some obscure artcult fashion, he supposed. She was more than a little busy with her— Three! Count them! Unbelievable!—young children in tow. She wished she could stop to talk, but.... They understood completely, and congratulated her as she moved on.

Hisao and Wilena turned back to contemplating the sculptures.

"Unsettling. The rest of us look so, I don't know—"

"Infantilized?" Wilena suggested. "Or at best not quite fully pubescent?"

"Yes."

"The hairlessness accentuates that. Makes us more of what we already are."

"What do you mean?"

"Are you homeworlding for a while?" she asked. When he nodded, she sent contact info into his headplug. "Stop by my lab in Taiga City, and maybe I'll give you something to think about."

With a brief wave of her hand, she turned and walked away, leaving him both puzzled and curious as she disappeared into the crowd.

* * * * * * *

"You do know that Moira's oldest—the little boy, Masao—is your son?" Wilena said, walking with him into the sterile space of her homelab, brilliant in its retro chrome-and-white clean-room decor.

"Oh. Really? I hadn't heard."

"I suspect Moira isn't mentioning it to any of the children's fathers, unless they ask. Did you see much of your own bioparents—Mother? Father?—when you were growing up?"

Hisao pondered that for a moment.

"They were usually off working, or studying, or traveling. Like everybody else, except they were actually married—Open Probational, twenty year term. Before my thirteen birthday I probably saw my parents, together, more than most children do."

"Before the Moving On," Wilena said, nodding and leaning against her workstation. "Before 'parent' can become confused with 'playfellow.' And of course there's the incest taboo, too."

Hisao laughed. Wilena gave him a quizzical look.

"For some reason, whenever I hear the phrase 'incest taboo'," he explained, "I always mishear it as incest *tattoo*—and into my head pops an old picture of a burly guy with 'Mother' stenciled into a bicep."

Wilena smiled politely.

"Yes. Still, that taboo was one of the few things that *didn't* really change—even when the quick, shiny, tiny things changed everything."

"The moteswarms? They're your field, right?"

"As much as anything else, yes. Before the Intervention, I might have been called a medical doctor. Officially, I'm a specialist in medically-applicable biologically-based nanotechnology, particularly human-obligate biocompatibles like the motes. In reality, the motes made people in my profession about as obsolete as general practitioners—and for the same reasons."

Hisao dropped into a hoverchair, slouching as it settled and adjusted with his weight. Wilena toyed with a Hoberman sphere paperweight on her workstation's main desk.

"A medical doctor," he said, the obsolete term strange in his mouth. "That's why you're working with Moira?"

"Among other things I'm her 'personal physician', for lack of a less antiquated title," Wilena said, taking a seat behind the desk. "And she's given me permission to talk about this with you."

"I *thought* something odd was going on with her. I mean, *three* kids? That's practically unheard of."

Wilena shook her head.

"Her situation is about much more than that, but we can start there." She flashed a series of diagrams up from a small tabletop holo. "The moteswarms view the suite of physiological changes surrounding conception, gestation, and birthing as symptomatic of senescence—and therefore something to be countered. Female fertility is largely unimpaired for the first child, more difficult with the second. The odds are astronomically against even the *conception* of a third."

"Moira has beaten those odds, obviously."

"Yes. About one in fifty million people, both male and female, are like Moira in that they're not mote-immortalized. Moira can have more than one or two children, but she will also experience a lifespan closer to what was the human average, *before* the moteswarms intervened."

"Wait a minute. You're saying she's actually growing *old*?"

Wilena nodded, flashing up images of human faces and bodies, bald-headed or white-haired people from those bygone days when humans beings grew old and died as a matter of course.

"Moira is one of those extremely rare individuals who experience what we now consider atavistic aging. Before the Intervention three centuries ago, though, her type of aging was not atavistic at all. It was an absolutely ordinary and unavoidable part of the normal human life cycle."

"But—*now*? Today? That's ridiculous. Moira's not some kind of lower animal!"

"I know it's hard to believe. 'Animals die, things pass away, but people last.' That's what we're always told, and that's how it is, in our cases."

"But not in Moira's?"

"No. Unlike the rest of us, she's maturing. Becoming fully adult."

"And the rest of us aren't—?"

"Actually mature? No, none of us are that. The rest of us are all diapaused just beyond the cusp of puberty. We remain essentially larval, indefinitely—permanently neotenized, both physically *and* psychologically. Unending adolescence is our trade-off for being immortal."

"How is that possible?" Hisao asked, fidgeting enough in the hoverchair to make it swivel slightly. "Why did it happen?"

"Those are two very different questions. Let's take the first one first." She shot onto the holovirt between them an image of a coordinate system. "This is a graphical depiction of our species' neotenization, our long childhoods even before the Intervention. The motes already had that as a starting point, to make their task easier.

"In every complex organism—including humans, in the past—the onset of reproductive maturity was the first real stage of dying. An unintended consequence of the fact that evolution didn't much care what happened to you after you'd reached breeding age—and bred."

Wilena holoed up another series of images—cells, cellular mechanisms, gene lines.

"Some of the same traits selected by evolution to maintain early life fitness have unselected deleterious effects later in life. What saved us in youth killed us in age."

"And that was the thing the moteswarms fixed?"

"One of them. One of the many small changes which led

to a big change." She holoed up a series of further graphs and diagrams. "The more you exploit genetic polymorphisms to adjust this neurosecretory pathway—involving the hypothalamus, pituitary, gonads, and eventually general metabolism—the more longevity increases and the more slowly this curve here approaches full sexual maturity onset."

"Fertility decreases as longevity increases, then?" Hisao asked. The diagrams, charts, and creatures began to swim before eyes. "This is some fairly heavy-lifting biology...."

"I know," said Wilena with a sigh of frustration, flash-cutting through more holo images—of the humble nematode roundworm *Caenorhabditis elegans*, of chemosignal/lifespan connections, developmental arrest, polymorphism, neoplasm and neoteny. "Sorry. Suffice it to say the motes carried all of this still further, by treating births subsequent to the first as symptoms of senescence which were in need of being, um, overcome."

"But what were 'they' after?" Hisao asked, staring absently at his own hands. "The motes are just swarms of tiny, not-very-bright machines."

"Indeed, but in their own emergent, decentralized fashion they can share and collectively understand a great deal—much the same way an ant colony 'knows' a lot more than any single ant in the colony does. And the woman who created them, well, she was larger than life, and a genius."

A blonde woman—with another one of those old faces—holoed up into the space before Wilena's desk, her words both spoken and captioned.

"...my answer was swarms of little cellular mechanics diagnosing and repairing time's ravages—what we do to our bodies," said the ghostly woman in the holo, "as well as flesh's thousand inherited natural shocks—what our bodies do to us."

"Cherise LeMoyne," Hisao said, gesturing. "The Mother of Intervention. The person who unleashed the Wellness Plague."

"That's right. At the time of the Intervention, she was chief scientist and CEO of Manipulife Corporation. Her firm specialized in blending traits from programmable machines into programmable life, and vice versa. All built on LeMoyne's discovery of the core Universal Turing Gene, the shortest segment of DNA on which can be simulated any and all operations performable in DNA."

"Which allowed her to create the motes that re-created us."

"Yes."

" 'Even as she herself was dying of a previously unsuspected and undiagnosed cancer'—or so the story goes."

"A rare uterine cancer, actually," Wilena said, replacing the holo of LeMoyne with an image half circuit diagram, half micro-biology illustration. "LeMoyne's diagnosis had come too late. She died, but not before giving the motes their ability to swarm-communicate. She connected the 'bots, even gave them links and search capabilities into the human infosphere—apparently hoping everything we humans had ever learned might serve as the motes' classroom, their school, their teacher, their database. She also gave them their most important commands, at least after their Hippocratic 'Do no harm' substrate."

Into the air above her desk Wilena holoed up the twin directives, where they hovered in golden numbers and letters:

1) Eliminate human mortality.

2) Replicate human consciousness.

"Evidence suggests that the motes' great solution to the first directive—the longevity/birth-limit linkage," she said, flashing up images of processes, and graphs chronicling global trends, "came about as a result of their researching the uterine cancer that killed their creator. They couldn't save LeMoyne, but forging that particular linkage ended up solving the problem of lingering human hyperpopulation—which vastly increased longevity by itself would have exacerbated, especially in regions which had yet to pass through demographic shift. Soon afterward, other scientists perfected similar mote-tech for atomic-level recycling and energy conversion, which solved the other great problem of the time—material hyperconsumption."

Wilena looked away, embarassed.

"One 'hyper' thing the motes didn't fix," she said, standing up, "was hyperspecialization. At least in my case. Sorry."

"Mine too. I should have known more about all these things, but history has never been a particular interest of mine."

"Don't beat yourself up about it," she said, placing her hand lightly on his shoulder. "Our hyperspecialization goes hand in hand with being psychologically neotenized."

Hisao unfolded himself from the hoverchair and stood up.

"Oh?"

Wilena turned away shyly once more as, together, they slowly walked from her workstation, back through her lab, toward her living space.

"There I go again, talking shop. Sorry."

"No need to apologize," Hisao said. "Very thorough. Just one question: If the motes are so well-suited to overcoming our aging and mortality, why is Moira growing older?"

Wilena made that frustrated sigh again.

"No one knows for sure. Some of my colleagues theorize that atavistic aging, like Moira's, results from a breakdown in biocompatibility, such that the immune systems of these rare individuals attack the moteswarms and counteract their efforts."

The door out of the lab dilated before them and they walked through.

"Others suggest the problem's deeper than just an 'allergy to the agents of immortality' on the part of the human host."

"Deeper? How?"

"The motes have pretty much achieved the goal of Directive One. From all we can tell, they're not nearly as far along toward accomplishing Directive Two. Perhaps the motes themselves must leave some human individuals mortal, in order to better understand the nature of individual human consciousness."

Hisao stared at her, wondering if he'd heard right.

"You mean the motes are *allowing* Moira to age? Maybe even to die? But why?"

"Fully overcoming human mortality *and* fully understanding human consciousness may not be complementary efforts,"

Wilena said. "It's possible that the elimination of human mortality and the replication of human consciousness cannot both be accomplished simultaneously. Perhaps one cannot have a fully developed individual human consciousness unless one also has a deep awareness of one's own mortality."

"I don't follow you."

"What if the bracketing provided by death is what gives individual consciousness its depth? That's how theorists of the 'directive noncomplementarity' school pose the question, at any rate."

Wilena stopped, pausing at the entrance to her sleep room.

"Whichever theory you follow, the upshot is the same. All known cases of atavistic human aging are characterized by an almost complete absence of motes from the bodies of the aging individuals."

Hisao nodded slowly.

"You promised you'd give me something to think about, Wilena, and you have. Thanks."

His dalliance with Wilena in her sleep room shortly thereafter—although it might not have smacked of Moira's passionate earnestness—at least was familiar romance, full of the superficial intimacy and intimate superficiality that so characterized love in their time.

* * * * * * *

As the years passed, Hisao traveled to more and newer places throughout the solar system and beyond. He made new friends everywhere, did new things and experienced new sensations as often as he liked. He learned how to speak new languages and play new musical instruments. He tired of hoverball and moved on to astrosurfing—more dangerous, and so more thrilling, more sensational, more *fun*.

Always he found himself among the crowds of perennial boy-geniuses and intelligirls, all gloriously vibrant and flawlessly healthy—never-changing people in an ever-changing world, forever thronging to experience novel places, people, and things, and just as quickly growing bored and leaving them behind.

Only much later, while talking with the aged Alphonse about Moira's art, did Hisao think again of those to whom mortal change might still apply.

Moira's latest major work, *Coming and Going*, was a strange piece—even for Moira. Like all of her more recent work, it was monumental, starkly visible from a thousand miles up, even its smallest detail requiring only slight magnification to be seen clearly from geostat orbit. It was also built to last, or at least built to resist recycling—one of many reasons it aroused controversy.

Coming and Going was an immense low-relief sand sculpture flash-vitrified into a thousand square mile expanse of dunes and salt pans in the Sahara Desert. Among the images it featured were two standing human figures, one male, one female, both titanic and nude, devoid of pubic hair like Moira's previous Personae, but not bereft of the hair on their heads. The couple both did and did not look like contemporary human beings.

The male figure in the tableau held up his hand as if waving. The two figures stood before the silhouette of an exploratory probe from the dawn of the age of space travel—which craft purportedly had also once borne, engraved on a plaque of much smaller dimensions, the same constellation of images that now provided the content for the vast sand sculpture.

To the west of the representational portion with its human figures and spacecraft stood clusters of more abstract information: the relative position of the Sun to the center of the galaxy, the galactic plane, and fourteen pulsars; a schematic illustration featuring the point of origin of the space probe and its trajectory out of the Solar System; a diagram depicting the hyperfine transition of neutral hydrogen, its spin-flip specifying a unit of length, a unit of time, and the binary digit 1—all three simultaneously, and all of those variants functioning as units in the measurements expressed in the other symbols on the great plaque of sculpted sand.

"What do you say, Alphonse?" Hisao asked, over the neural-tap translator he and his research team had planted in his swimming friend's head. "You've seen a bunch of other contemporary art. How do you think this compares?"

"The rest all swim in shallow seas," Alphonse replied, in the cryptic way of dolphins. "Only Moira moves in deep waters. I would very much like to meet her."

Hisao nodded. He had figured the old dolphin—the oldest that had ever lived, now—might find Moira's art interesting.

Alphonse, like Moira, could not be cured of mortality. All attempts to transfer the motes into nonhuman species ended with the motes immediately kill-switching themselves. A type of "apoptosis," according to Wilena. Hisao didn't know how much longer the old dolphin would live—or Moira either, for that matter.

"I think such a meeting can be arranged. I'll get on it."

* * * * * * *

Until he saw her again, Hisao didn't realize how long it had been since he'd last seen Moira. Her hair was white, like that of the old people in the old-time pictures Wilena once showed him. Moira's face was so wrinkled and wizened that when she smiled she looked like a creature of a species only distantly related to contemporary humans. She brought her son—*their* son?—Masao with her, too.

Moira and Alphonse spent so much time talking about and modeling the schooling behavior of fish that Hisao found himself spending more time with Masao than he expected. The amount of action and attention Moira and the old dolphin could devote to a single topic frankly amazed Hisao, whose own focus tended to skip much more rapidly from one object to another—as his son's also did, he noticed.

Although he was one year chronologically closer to fifty than to fifteen, Masao physically looked exactly the latter. Hisao found that he got along well with his son—though more like a slightly older brother, than a father. Whatever it was that had caused Moira's atavistic aging, it had not been passed on to Masao—nor to his two siblings, Hisao gathered.

"Moira," he asked her over a drink that evening, when the two of them were alone for a moment, "why didn't you tell me Masao was my son? I might have liked to meet him, get to know him, before now."

"And why didn't you? I wasn't stopping you, yet you never introduced yourself to him. Wilena said she told you about Masao, long ago. You've known about him for years—and never visited him."

"Maybe you didn't stop me directly, no, but you never came to me and said, 'Masao is your son.' Why?"

"For the same reason I never told any of the fathers. You were all too immature—like everybody else. None of you were grown up enough to help me raise these kids."

"Masao says you disapprove of 'children raising children.'"

"It's not just that. Everything about the world the Intervention has made—it all struck me as somehow too flashy, too shallow, too trivial, by the time Masao was born. Much superficial knowledge, little real wisdom. Too many blessings damn the children."

"Masao hardly seems damned."

"No, but the more I looked into the historical records from before the Intervention, the more I saw a profundity of character and culture there that seems lacking in our own times."

"During the Dark Centuries, too? Mass atrocities and mass destruction don't sound like 'profundity' to me. We're still cleaning up the mess."

"Yet even that dark time showed *mass creativity*, too! Since the Intervention, we don't need to think as deeply. No need to invent or create as much. Our world has been perfected. Cherise LeMoyne sprinkled fairy dust over the globe. Now, no matter how far they go, Wendy and Peter Pan never leave Neverland."

"I don't follow you."

"Did you ever talk with Wilena about LeMoyne, or about psychological neoteny, as they call it?"

"A little."

"You might want to ask her about that a bit more, then. And I wouldn't worry too much about the time you haven't had with your son. You have the rest of forever to get to know each other better."

* * * * * * *

Hisao was sorry to see Moira and Masao leave—but not as sorry as Alphonse was, he suspected. And when, only a few years later, the dolphin was at the end of his earthly time, his last thoughts were for Moira.

"Tell her to keep doing what she's doing. Tell her what is popular is not always true, and what is true is not always popular. Tell her not to spend so much time accepting others' rejection of her work that she ends up rejecting their acceptance when it finally comes. And tell her, when she's at death's door, don't knock!"

The neural tap interpreted the last with a sound almost like laughter, but Hisao couldn't be sure. He promised the dolphin he'd tell Moira what he'd said. Soon the dolphin fell silent in voice and thought, then passed quietly away. Alphonse was there, but he wasn't there, anymore.

His cetacean friend's death left Hisao more saddened than he might have imagined. Out of that sadness he contacted Moira— who smiled and wiped away a tear at hearing the dolphin's last words for her. She promised she would dedicate her final piece to him.

Over the following days and weeks and months, Hisao thought from time to time about what Moira had said, when last they talked in person. When he contacted Wilena again, it was to ask her about something Moira had suggested.

"You told me one time that our hyperspecialization was connected to our being psychologically neotenized. What did you mean by that?"

"The idea goes way back, before digiculture—perhaps to the middle of the twentieth century," Wilena said, checking sources in their shared holovirt. "By the time of the Intervention, most scientific research, for instance, was already being done by teams of young, hyperspecialized problem-solvers and technicians—'whiz kids'—each of whom actually needed to fully understand only a small piece of the overall puzzle."

"Which is how most of us still work," Hisao said, nodding. "Depth of individual understanding is far less important than the system of specializations put together in any team."

"Right. People who work in specialized teams need to be able to change jobs often, learn new skills and information, move to new places and cultures, make new friends in an ever-expanding social network. 'Mature adult' human animals—evolved to cope with small hunter-gatherer societies of just a few hundred people—were not all that good at meeting such challenges."

"So being 'unfinished' or 'immature' or 'postponed'...."

"Means increased flexibility of attitudes, behaviors, knowledge—all perfect for teaming up. Ramping up neoteny was a fast and simple way to evolve an adaptation—for adaptability!"

"What's that mean for Moira, then?"

"An interesting question. The vast majority of us are Hypers—hyper-attentives. We prefer rapidly changing environments, high levels of stimulation, multiple information streams, lots of rapid, specialized task-switching among team members. We get bored easily. I suspect that's less and less the case with Moira, as she's gotten older."

"I once saw her discuss the modeling of fish-schooling behavior with Alphonse—for hours on end."

"She's become a Deeper, then. A deep-attentive. Someone who can shut out the world and focus for long periods of time on a single complex problem or object—without getting bored. Even before the Intervention, Deepers like Moira were already disappearing. The motes just helped us become more of what we were already becoming."

"How so?"

Wilena searched for and then holoed up the blonde ghost of Cherise LeMoyne once more.

"The release of the motes—and the Wellness Plague, with them—was the action LeMoyne took to address the problems she saw in her time. She intervened—as did her creations, even more so, since they continued to evolve after their release, even after her death. Taken together, the mote solutions to human population and consumption issues corrected most of the problems of the Dark Centuries, as LeMoyne hoped they would.

"In retrospect, the motes' short biomech life-cycles and swarm intelligence make them the perfect symbionts for long-lived creatures with individual minds, like us. Over time they have in some ways become more like us, and we have in some ways become more like them."

Wilena flashed Hisao a satisfied smile. He nodded slowly, pondering.

* * * * * * *

After many more years, Moira exhibited *Monument to Unageing Intellect*—her strangest and most haunting work of all.

From asteroidal material, she and her collaborators (their friend Jorge and his longtime love-partner Li, most prominently) crafted myriad, simple, solar-powered and mirror-skinned androids of human size: "Personae," persisting again. Each Persona incorporated subroutines which mimicked human movement, along with sensors for navigating local space, and an array of thrusters so that each "individual" seemed to fly as if in air, or swim as if in water—though all of them were in fact released some dozen degrees above the plane of the ecliptic, in the space between Mars and Jupiter, where they moved after their complex fashion, together and apart.

Moira had programmed each Persona-unit with simple rules.

Steer clear of anything that is not one of your local cohort members (avoidance). Steer so as to prevent crowding your local cohort members (separation). Steer toward the average heading of your local cohort members (alignment). Steer so as to approach the average position of your local cohort members (cohesion). From such rules the Personae, once released and put into play, quickly organized themselves into throngs of sweeping and shifting human forms, moving exactly like schools of fish or flocks of birds.

"—or like the swarms of mote-machines which made possible our godhood," Moira said, when Hisao stopped at the moon to visit her on his way home from the exhibit. "Or yours, anyway."

He stared at her, unable to get over the way her body had changed. Slumped in her medical hoverbed, she looked deformed by gravity, even on the moon. Her white hair had grown much more sparse and her skin seemed paper-thin. Her sunken eyes rolled inside their frame of starkly prominent cheek bones like hoverballs in smashcradles. Webworks of wrinkles and wattling flesh covered all that was visible of her face and neck. She seemed more than ever a creature of an alien species.

Despite that, the beauty of afternoons in late autumn still flared from her. Her eyes flashed, her smile seemed somehow more mellow, human, and humane than ever—though Hisao wondered how much of *that* might be from the hyperox levels in her rooms.

"LeMoyne had her rules, I have mine," she said with a chuckle. "You know what made me think of swarms and human motion? That hoverball game, long ago. Where you conspired with Alphonse, to cheat! *That* was when I first thought there might be some similarities between the way the moteswarms moved and the way the crowds of *us* moved."

Hisao nodded.

"Wilena says that the motes just helped us become more of what we were already becoming. That we're becoming more like them, and they're becoming more like us."

"Well! Good for Wilena! Given her work, she's probably about as close as you unagers can get to understanding what I'm trying to say—and do. You're in touch with her, then? What is my 'personal physician' up to these days?"

"She's got a standing contract to join the crew of a long-cruiser, headed out to one of the habitable-planet star systems. A chief medical officer position."

"Wilena's going to join the diaspora? Ha! Do you know what the original name for long-cruisers was, when the idea was first developed? 'Generation ships'!"

"Not many generations being born on long-cruisers."

"And no one dying of old age, either. Won't be much for Wilena to do."

"Maybe that's why she's held off on leaving. But she can join a crew any time she decides to."

"Acch, she's just waiting for me to die first! I haven't seen much of my personal physician lately, but I bet I'm still of some 'professional interest' to her."

"How's that?"

"I'm dying of a 'defect of the heart'," Moira said with a laugh. "Whatever else any gods or fates may lack, they certainly do *not* suffer from an irony deficiency!"

"Can't you just get a cardio-replacement?"

"Wilena harped on that too. She's offered lots of options—mechanicals, clonally grown transplants, you name it. I turned them all down. That might be one of the things that's made her unhappy with me, of late."

"Why'd you turn them down?"

"Wilena would keep me old and alive forever, if I'd let her. She'd turn me into a Struldbrugg, a Tithonian. That's not for me.

"Nope, I think I'll keep the heart I've got, and go when it goes. She won't have to wait long, now. I've been running through tomorrows like there's no tomorrow, and pretty soon there won't be any left."

* * * * * * *

Not quite a year later, Hisao received his final message from Moira.

"Dear Hisao: If you're seeing this, then I have died. To you, Wilena, and my children, I've sent very specific instructions concerning my funeral arrangements. I hope you do not find such specificity offensive. At first I thought people might have forgotten how to mourn—it's been so long—but it's not that, really. You can't forget what you've never known.

"*Do* take the time to get to know our son Masao. For all I may have done in raising him, he's still part of your world, now.

"Thank you for all I've learned from you. You and Alphonse showed me that the only product that finally persists is process. I could not have created my last work without learning that. The last piece has been better received than I would ever have dared to believe. Go figure.

"I suppose I should say something grand at this late date, reveal some big secret of the universe, so here it is: the human heart is more than just some strangely chambered knot in us, pumping blood through a maze of meat plumbing, with just enough chaos in the beat and eddy in the flow to keep things going. In the end it will not allow us the comforting local illusion that there are separate events and separate objects. In fact there is no separation. Space, time, the universe—it's all one.

"Whether you knew it or not, you taught me that, too—you and Wilena and everyone I knew. Thanks again."

As per Moira's very specific instructions, it was to the vicinity of her last great work that he, Wilena, and her children took Moira's body—encased in a titanium coffin sensored, motored, and programmed in much the same way as the bird-flock Personae of *Monument* had been, and into whose midst they released her little deathship.

After the ceremony ended, Hisao and Wilena stood on the observation deck of the transport, watching the grey coffin drift off in the midst of inhumanly perfect human forms, flawless mirror-skinned creatures moving and flashing like shoals of thought, swarms of mind.

"How are you feeling?" Wilena asked.

"I feel...nothing."

"Numb. Yes. Same here. Back in the days when people grew old, they comforted each other at times like this by saying things like 'Life goes on' and 'Nothing lasts forever'."

Wilena looked back to the monumental mobile sculpture as it moved through space before them, changing and shifting like a murmuration of starlings. Hisao nodded.

He thought about that, on the trip home to LaGrange Port. Once there, he stood beside Wilena as she prepared to board a long-cruiser for the stars.

"Back in the days when they called them generation ships," Wilena said, staring at the cruiser *Hyperboreas* out the observatory port, "someone who knew about both space travel and generations said that dealing with the speed of light barrier was like coping with the loss of a loved one: You never actually get over it. At best you just get around it."

She looked away from the ship, to him.

"I suppose if we can take forever to get where we're going," she said, "it doesn't much matter how fast or how slow we go."

He hugged her and bid her a quiet farewell. They both knew they would never see each other again. There was nothing to say, because there was everything to say.

* * * * * * *

Life goes on, Hisao thought as he climbed aboard his big orange-and-red fireboard and slid his feet into the augmented footlocks. *Nothing lasts forever.*

Hisao had dropped from orbit and astrosurfed deep into atmosphere dozens of times on half a dozen worlds. He knew how to play shooting star as well as anybody. His vintage big board had the best ablative shielding, deflection tiling, astrogation and avionics tech to be found. Even on hard burn the board had enough fuel to let him bounce into atmosphere, bolide through, and skip out again—at low enough angle and high enough speed to avoid becoming a shooting star for real.

That was the source of the excitement, of course: Although he would never die of old age, he could still die. Burning up in atmosphere would obliterate him beyond reconstruction. When down came baby, crashcradle and all, all the king's motelings and all the king's mends couldn't put baby together again.

You never get over it. At best you just get around it.

The satellite's airlock doors dilated open. The docking bay railgun shot him on his board out of the bay, toward the mottled ocher, white, and blue of the Earth below. He howled happily as he kicked in his thrusters to maximum burn.

Hisao shifted on the board and trajectories altered on the fashionably retro heads-up displays of his suit helmet. The astrogation gear calced Earth–atmosphere clearance for each course change, along with the board's capabilities and his own survivability.

The thrusters cut out. The board's ablative shielding began to burn. He moved back in the footlocks, angling both his board's nose and his trajectory slightly upward. On his rearview cams a long fiery streak spooled out, man and board a shooting star pushing a redlining course.

Fall to miss, fall to miss, fall to miss! Think like a satellite!

On his burning plank he bolided through the upper air, arced off just before his trajectory would have reached extinction point, skipped back out of the atmosphere, and was gone.

Despite tiles glowing red hot, empty fuel tanks, and a board blown of all ablative shielding and still burning, the trajectory plotter moved back into the green—before the astrogation system blew out. The locator beacon still worked, though, even as he slingzagged further from the Earth, dropping final fire behind him.

Hisao drifted, staring down at the shining planet below. Each year, the human population of that world declined steadily— and not just from emigration, he now knew. On the face of the

Sahara, carved into its surface, he could just make out through thin clouds a male figure, waving—though whether hello or good-bye he could not tell.

Waiting for a recovery shuttle to ride in on his beam and pick him up, Hisao knew he'd pushed himself and the board—hard. Yet the edge, he realized, was already going. Even from such a wild ride. Even from astrosurfing itself.

Life goes on. And on. And on.

I feel nothing. And nothing lasts forever.

That's the sheer hell of it.

In overcoming human death, had the moteswarms also overcome something essential to human life? How long could he keep going, before the edge was so gone he stepped over it? Before he fell to hit, and failed to miss?

I could still die....

Below him, the planet was perfect, its people star children of an endless midsummer evening. But if the stars were fixed, why were they still falling, secretly, one by one?

He shivered amid the heavens, and the heavens shivered with him.

ABOUT THE AUTHOR

HOWARD V. HENDRIX's first four published novels appeared from Ace Books (Penguin Putnam): *Lightpaths* (1997), *Standing Wave* (1998), *Better Angels* (1999), and *Empty Cities of the Full Moon* (2001). His fifth novel, *The Labyrinth Key*, appeared from Ballantine Del Rey in April 2004. His sixth novel, *Spears of God*, was published by Del Rey in December 2006.

His most widely available works of shorter science fiction can be found in his "double" short story collection *Human in the Circuit/Depth of Perception* (Borgo Press 2011), *Möbius Highway* (Scorpius Digital Books, 2001), the *Full Spectrum* original anthology series, Vols. 1, 4, and 5 (Bantam Books), and in *The Outer Limits*, Volume 1 (Prima).

He has also published numerous poems, political essays, book reviews, and works of literary criticism, including his book-length study of apocalyptic elements in English literature from Langland to Milton, *The Ecstasy of Catastrophe* (1990). An avid gardener, his book on landscape irrigation, *Reliable Rain* (co-authored with Stuart Straw), appeared in March 1998 from Taunton Press.

His degrees range from a B.S. in Biology to an M.A. and Ph.D. in English Literature. He and his wife Laurel both teach at California State University, Fresno, and live near Shaver Lake, California, where they enjoy backpacking and snowshoeing in the Sierra Nevada.

www.ingramcontent.com/pod-product-compliance
Lightning Source LLC
Chambersburg PA
CBHW050503260626
47157CB00004B/1172

PERCEPTION OF DEPTH

A plausibly mad "mushroom messiah" and a lost tribe from the lost world of a tepui—all soon to be more lost than ever as humanity's first personal ambassadors to the stars. Three jet-fighter pilots on a secret mission involving the Roswell cover story's surprising truth, odd occurrences in the Pacific soon after World War II, and the prisoners of a subterranean Earth not exactly hollow, but not completely solid, either. An early extrasolar-planets astronomer, responding to the death of his father, discovers the macrocosm in which our universe itself is microcosm. A trip backwards in time from 1999 to the 1939 World's Fair, an encounter with Einstein, a return trip to a different future, and an exchange of places across space and time to save hopes and fulfill dreams of a grandfather and grandson.

These are some of the characters to be encountered in this side of the Double—strange worlds all, yet all strangely reminiscent of the world we think we know, and sometimes share.

Borgo Press Books by HOWARD V. HENDRIX

Better Angels: A Science Fiction Novel
Bright with Excessive Dark: Further Collected Stories
Dark with Excessive Bright: Further Collected Stories
Empty Cities of the Full Moon: A Science Fiction Novel
Human in the Circuit: Collected Stories
Lightpaths: A Science Fiction Novel
Perception of Depth: Collected Stories
Standing Wave: A Science Fiction Novel

PERCEPTION OF DEPTH

COLLECTED STORIES

HOWARD V. HENDRIX

THE BORGO PRESS

MMXI

PERCEPTION OF DEPTH

FIRST EDITION

Published by Wildside Press LLC

www.wildsidebooks.com

DEDICATION

To the memory of

Vincent John "Jay" Hendrix
(1961-1988)

*My friend, my younger brother, whom I loved,
the end of mortality has overtaken him.*

*Because of my brother I am afraid of death, because
of my brother
I stray through the wilderness and cannot rest.*

— from The Epic of Gilgamesh

CONTENTS

INTRODUCTION

On this side of the double, the stories play with the idea of depth perception—and the ways in which that ability, like so much else, is a product of the mind interacting with the rest of the perceptual apparatus. How much of what we experience is actually "out there" and how much of it is something necessarily limited by our sensoria or constructed by our minds so we can experience it at all?

Philip K. Dick once wonderfully said that "Reality is that which, when you stop believing in it, doesn't go away." Yet, reality's "not going away" speaks to the fact that our perceptual apparatus still "believes" in the existence of that something which doesn't go away, whether *we* consciously believe in it or not. I am reminded here, oddly, of Nietzsche's idea that we shall never get over our belief in God so long as we still have faith in grammar.

This question of what "doesn't go away," of what persists—either beyond the moment of experience or beyond the body which experiences it—informs both sides of this double anthology. This "Perception" side is not only about how we interpret our experiences in the moment, but also about how experience itself is an interpretation. My fascination with that idea is behind why I collect stereograms and am intrigued by perspective and vanishing points in painting. It is also why I have long been fascinated by the persistence of vision, a quirk in our perceptual apparatus which makes movies possible—and why I have remained persistently interested in shamanism,

mystical experience, altered states of consciousness, and virtual reality.

Back in the early 1990s I wrote somewhat disparagingly of the internet and cyberspace that "All the depth is on the surface." Stereograms, however—in making the 2-D into 3-D—teach us that that statement is descriptive too of what our brains do with all our envisionings. What makes real depth is persistence: taking the time to contemplate the larger implications of the experience itself.

That is what all of the stories on this side of the double are about—the need for dwelling in and contemplating ambiguity and paradox, whether those be found in the time travel of "Knot Your Grandfather's Knot", the layers upon layers of cover-stories in "The Hollow Earthlings," or the shamanic experiences, madness, and transcendence in *The Vertical Fruit of the Horizontal Tree*.

I hope that, read together with the stories on the other side of this double, the two sides together may function as it were *stereoscopically*—generating by the juxtaposition of their parts the greater whole which only the reader's mind can create.

ACKNOWLEDGMENTS

THESE STORIES WERE previously published as follows, and are reprinted (with minor editing, updating, and textual modifications) by permission of the author:

"The Vertical Fruit of the Horizontal Tree" was originally published in shorter form as "Singing the Mountain to the Stars" in *Aboriginal Science Fiction*, January 1991, and under its present title in chapbook form from Talisman Press in 1994. Copyright © 1991, 1994, 2011 by Howard V. Hendrix.

"The Hollow Earthlings" was originally published in *Aberrant Dreams*, September, 2010. Copyright © 2010, 2011 by Howard V. Hendrix.

"Stages of Night and Twilight" was originally published under the title, "Once Out of Nature," in *Microcosms*, DAW Books, January 2004. Copyright © 2004, 2011 by Howard V. Hendrix.

"Knot Your Grandmother's Knot" was originally published in *Analog Science Fiction/Science Fact* in March 2008. Copyright © 2008, 2011 by Howard V. Hendrix.

THE VERTICAL FRUIT OF THE HORIZONTAL TREE

So is every man: he is born in vanity and sin; he comes into the world like morning mushrooms, soon thrusting up their heads into the air, and conversing with their kindred of the same production, and as soon they turn into dust and forgetfulness...to preserve him from rushing into nothing, and at first to draw him up from nothing, were equally the issues of an almighty power.

—Jeremy Taylor,
Holy Dying (1617)

"A very bright student, your brother," said Dr. Manikam, Luke's graduate advisor, as we stepped along over the puddled floor of one of the Missouri Botanical Gardens' orchid greenhouses. "A pity if we've really lost him. We were fairly close, you know—the mentor-student relationship being what it is."

"You knew about his breakdown at Washington U, then?" I asked, fingering the tip of a long, waxy leaf.

"Oh yes," Manikam replied, gazing absently at the peach-colored flower of some obscure epiphyte. A loquacious Sri Lankan-born Tamil with a flashing smile and hair like ringlets of black silk, Manikam seemed exotic for Missouri—though perfectly at home strolling through the humid, color-splashed jungles-under-glass of the Gardens. "Lucas doesn't think like other people, true. His mind runs on a different track. But I

don't think that's necessarily bad. As far as I could tell it never detracted from his abilities as a student—and it almost certainly enhanced his skill as a field man."

"Did he ever mention his, uh, history of substance abuse?"

Manikam nodded.

"He was quite up front about that. I gather he was self-medicating with 'naturals' after his breakdown—nutmeg, dandelion wine, morning glory seeds, datura tea, even smoking toad skin for the bufotenine. Apparently the experience helped him decide on graduate study in ethnobotany." Manikam smiled and shrugged. "I had to remind him more than once that ethnobotany is more than a search for the ultimate high, but...." He stared at a point deep among the orchids. "Ours is still a young and somewhat arcane science, Mr. Larkin. Who knows how many of the best field researchers might not be motivated, at some level, by a quest for the hallucinogenic grail, eh?"

We stepped under a low-hanging purple-flowered liana, pushing our way through heavy steel doors to the blissfully air-conditioned white corridor beyond.

"If he has disappeared or come to some harm," Dr. Manikam sighed as he fumbled through his keys to open Luke's cubicle, "then that would be a great loss. He is a uniquely gifted field researcher."

* * * * * * *

Luke always loved to get out into the field, into any world other than the one he knew. Seven years ago it was the Sierras. Hiking in the mountains, truths got spoken between us—matters we never talked about elsewhere unless we were wired on something. Even in the mountains, though, we rarely thought to ask why it was we went to the mountains.

Luke loved ranging the ranges, climbing the climbs. Almost desperately so. One night as we were bedding down after a long day on the trail, I razzed him about his recurring desire to "head for the hills."

"It's more 'hills for the head,' really," he said, not bothering to explain.

"What do you mean?" I asked after a moment.

"Didn't you ever wonder why it is that so many sacred sites have been mountains, so many mountains have been sacred sites?" he asked. "Why the monasteries in the Himalayas, the old sacred high countries of Nepal and Tibet, the Inca temples up in the Andes?"

"Why?" I said, kidding him along a bit. "Some local 'spirit' of mountain places, maybe?"

"No, not that," he said carefully, as if he's actually thought about it before. "From what I've read of that physics stuff of yours, I think it must be that mountains are the shape of the cosmos, only on a scale we can comprehend. Like the cosmos itself, mountain ranges are fractals. Erosion is the boundary interaction that shapes them, just like it shapes canyons—or caves, for that matter. But I think mountains express the shape best. Anyway, mountains are cosmos-shaped and the cosmos is mountain-shaped, so when we look at mountains we see not only the mountains themselves but also an image of the entire cosmos. Even more than that: we see the noumenal pattern underlying both and everything, at human and non-human scales. The physical and the metaphysical overlap, which is why rugged mountains are supposed to be 'sublime.' That's why the mystics call them sacred."

"You've got mountains on the brain!" I laughed. "That and your 'noumenal' stuff. Noumena this, noumena that! Go to sleep!"

I turned over and tried to rest my trail-weary muscles.

"You know, at the level of some metrics," he said after a moment, "the convolutions in the brain are fractal canyons and mountain ranges too...."

I groaned and threw a head cushion at him. He laughed.

No, Luke didn't think like other people. Before he ever got lost anywhere else, Luke got lost in the mountains inside his head.

* * * * * * *

Inside, Luke's cubicle was a stationary cyclone of notebooks and reports, folders and pamphlets and monographs and papers everywhere. That was always his way. When we shared a room as kids growing up, the walls of Luke's half, besides being covered with full-color posters of birds of prey, were crowded and cluttered with books and magazines—on history mostly, particularly about the indigenous peoples of the western hemisphere. Luke's obsession was largely with the past, mine largely with the future. My walls were far less cluttered but more wide-ranging than his—books and tapes on all aspects of space travel, and physics, and advanced technology, surrounding my aquariums with their exotic fish.

"Did he say anything about where he might be headed?" I asked Manikam, contemplating the mad clutter before me—dreading even the thought of trying to make some sense of that mess.

"I'm afraid not," Luke's mentor replied from the doorway, looking blankly at the floor and shaking his head. "He just... left. Without a word. At first I thought he had just decided to start his break early, but after seven weeks and still no word I began to worry. Always before he contacted us every couple weeks or so, even when he was deep in the field. So last week I began checking around. His landlord said he'd paid off his final month's rent and moved out. When the landlord asked him why he was leaving, Lucas told him, 'It's not good for me to be around people right now.' That's when I called your family—and the police."

I nodded and lifted a sheaf of papers from the desk. Luke's schizophrenia was defined as "long-period." He could seem perfectly normal for years. Now, though, he seemed to be slipping into a bad phase.

* * * * * * *

"But why doesn't he call?" my mother asked. "Paul, why would your brother do this to us?"

I wanted to tell her that no law says you have to call your mother, or your father, or your brother. But Mom gave me no time and I knew she really didn't want to hear it anyway.

"Not a single call in almost two months!" she continued. "Not even on Mothers Day or on our anniversary—the same day as his own birthday! All that time, and not a word. There's something terribly wrong in his not calling us in all this time. Worry from a great distance—that's all he's left for us to do. How can he be so hard-hearted? How could he be so—so insensitive? How could he turn away from us like this? What did I do wrong? What did I do to deserve this?"

I sighed, absently scratching the base of my neck.

"It's not you, Mom," I said flatly, patiently. "It's not anybody. You didn't do anything wrong. Luke's always wanted to cut his ties with everyone and everything, so this time he has. He's probably way out in the bush somewhere. Not many links back to civilization. He's just following his leadings, living the life he wants to live. It's not your fault, it's not my fault. It's nobody's fault at all."

* * * * * * *

"We had him listed as a missing person as soon as you called us," I said, rifling through the papers. "But the police have gone as far as they can go. Luke's an adult, he's got free will. If he wants to drop out of sight, then there's nothing the police can do about it." I dropped the stack of papers back onto the desk, discouraged. "Any ideas?"

"None, really." Manikam shrugged. "He could be anywhere. He's recently accumulated nearly one hundred thousand dollars in grants and loans, you know. His work at Caracamuni tepui has been very well received. Quite a few granting organizations responded favorably to his research proposals."

"What's a 'Caracamuni tepui'?" I asked, staring at a satellite

photo of jungle and mountain on one wall.

"You're looking at it," Manikam replied, venturing a pace or two into the office but touching nothing. "A tepui is a high mesa or plateau. Many of them are found near the headwaters of the Orinoco and Amazon drainages. Rugged, remote places—stone islands rising up to two miles above the surrounding rainforest. Many have never been climbed. Caracamuni was thought to be one, until your brother explored its summit."

"Luke climbed this—?" I gestured at the satellite image.

"Oh yes," Manikam smiled, brightness flashing from his dark face as he stepped further into the office. "He had a very successful expedition. More than half the species on Caracamuni's top are found nowhere else on earth. Speciation in isolation. Lucas collected half a dozen new sundews, a dozen new bromeliads. Some particularly interesting new species of *Cordyceps* fungus, too."

"Really?" I asked, only half interested. I was still trying to detect something—I didn't know what—in the satellite image.

* * * * * * *

Maybe I was trying to see something that wasn't there. That was Luke's way when he went paranoid—hanging at the center of everything, seeing things that no one else could see. Completely enclosed by a sphere of suffering with center everywhere, circumference nowhere. In a way he was one of the world's great unrecognized architects, an artist so impassioned he got lost inside the all-encompassing maze of his own creation. Reality and Luke's personal fiction fused into one, trapping him in that indestructible sphere of his own life-labyrinth. I tried to punch holes in his sphere, point out flaws in his arguments, gaps in the structure of his madness. I didn't know you couldn't argue a paranoid schizophrenic into sanity, so I kept trying.

Once I thought I'd finally broken through. Luke's self-esteem had shrunk down to zero and he kept talking about how he was nothing, how he was nobody—yet at the same time he was

always alluding to this huge paranoid conspiracy of priests and nuns and social workers supposedly following him all the time, keeping him under constant surveillance. So I asked him the obvious question: if you're such a nobody, then why is everybody out to get you?

He looked at me oddly a moment, like the light of logic had broken through for just an instant, but then he was off talking about some other craziness. His sphere repaired itself almost instantly—just flowed in to fill the gap like the surface of a soap bubble.

* * * * * * *

"Yes." Manikam gingerly lifted a large crystal paperweight from atop a pile of papers. "These fungi's microscopic spores penetrate the skin of various animals then germinate explosively in their blood, sending out mycelial threads to digest everything but the skeleton. In a matter of days the fungus spawn has filled the animal's former shape with itself, leaving behind only a mummy—and fungal fruiting bodies jutting out of the corpse like parasol mushrooms. In one of his reports your brother described them as 'ghostly antennas broadcasting more spores at more hosts, endlessly.'"

"Fascinating," I replied, trying to discover some pattern, any pattern, to the books on Luke's shelves. Nodding vigorously, Manikam absently turned the crystal paperweight about in his hands.

"It turned out that he wasn't the first to Caracamuni's top, though. He found an indigenous group up there. Apparently a splinter tribe of the Pemón Indians, separated and isolated from their fellows for many centuries. 'Ghost people,' they're called. Lucas became very fond of them. He didn't want the anthropologists and archeologists to go running all over their tepui, but I'm afraid the word's gotten out. Fash at NIU has an expedition scheduled for the spring."

Manikam placed the paperweight carefully on the desk,

exactly upon the spot he'd picked it up from, then nodded his head toward the satellite image.

"If I were trying to find your brother," the scientist said suddenly, "I think I'd start there."

"Thanks," I replied over my shoulder as I opened one of Luke's notebooks. "I just might."

Dr. Manikam, though, was already gone, and I had a mountain of clutter to sift through that wasn't getting any smaller. I set to work.

* * * * * * *

Can you see a disappearance coming? I don't know. Luke was having his troubles for years. Even in second grade, when we were in parochial school, the nuns found him walking around on the playground with his arms stretched out like Christ on the cross. That disturbed the Brides of Our Lord profoundly. Jesus was a non-repeatable event, after all. It was much easier for them to be his brides if their husband stayed far away from the flesh.

The programming took with Luke, maybe too well. As a kid, he got it into his head that sex was 'dirty' and 'evil.' He was always distressed by his own sexuality after that. In high school he was extremely shy and didn't date. That was okay, though, because he'd skipped grades and was a good deal younger than all the other kids. He put all his energy into his studies anyway.

He received his bachelor's degree in history while he was still in his teens, had nearly completed his master's in anthro when he was twenty. That was when the breakdown came. He'd started trying to 'dumb down' long before that, though, first through heavy drinking and then through drugs. Figured that if he killed enough brain cells maybe he'd fit in better, I guess.

* * * * * * *

Two days later—with the patient understanding of my

station's news director and his expressed hope that my trip might turn into some sort of feature story—I was on a jet to Caracas, Venezuela. Manikam's advice had pointed out a path. Following that path through Luke's papers, I found a journal describing his first ascent of Caracamuni and began paging through it.

Through endless rain and fog we've come at last to the edge of the great stone labyrinth that crowns the tepui. My guide, Juan Carrillo Garza, and his Pemón assistants refuse to travel any further. They cannot explain except to talk of the 'ghost people.' I remind them no people are supposed to live atop Caracamuni. They say no people do, but the ghost people do—creatures who live forever in the rain, eat only what lives on dead things, are able to call back the ancestors and all the departed. If such "ghost people" exist, I am tempted from the description to speculate. An extremely ancient tribe, perhaps? The "dead things" reference—saprophyte totemists? "Calling back the ancestors"—some natural substance that enables them to tap into the collective unconscious?

Hopeful of this, I have decided to push on without my guide and assistants for the final ascent. They have never traversed the labyrinth, so could not be much help to me in any event. If their superstitions and my suspicions prove unfounded, I will still at least be the first to climb Caracamuni summit. If there is truth to any of these "ghost people" supposings, then there's also hope of accomplishing something of far greater importance....

Judging by the tag ends of pages still caught in the spiral notebook's wire binding, whatever entries might have followed had been hastily ripped out.

* * * * * * *

What information had Luke been in such a hurry to destroy that he'd overlooked this entry? The "living on dead things" reference kept coming back to me. I tried to tell myself it was just the simple universal truth: life sustains itself on death. From that vantage, vegetarians are different only in that they eat life-

forms that can't get away—gathered, rather than hunted.

It was more than that, though, and I knew it. The "sapro-phyte totemist" stuff made me think of mushrooms, particu-larly psychedelic ones—the particular "natural" that Luke so much favored but which Manikam had not mentioned in that regard. I remembered that the few times I'd done shrooms with Luke he'd always end up talking about metaphysical commu-nications from the planet—often concerned somehow or other with overpopulation.

"That's the big topic when the mushroom spirit talks to you," Luke said. "Nearly every shroomer I know has experi-enced that voice. Maybe it's like what some of the scientists are talking about, the Earth being a sentient organism and all, with a noösphere. Maybe altered states and hallucinations are one more channel of communication into what the planet is trying to tell us."

I was never one for mystic emanations. For me psychedelics had been recreational, a funkier kind of beer. Not Luke. The anti-drug hysteria of our times seemed almost a religious perse-cution, to him. Did he believe he'd found the cosmic sacrament down there in South America? Was that what he was trying to protect by ripping pages out of his own journals?

* * * * * * *

As the jet began its descent toward the sprawling, densely-populated jumble of Caracas, I pushed the notes aside at last, questions still spinning in my mind. Manikam's phrase, "hallu-cinogenic grail," hovered in my head and would not go away.

Given what I knew of Luke's ways, at least this sort of mad quest fit his pattern. After his breakdown he'd sworn off speed and acid, and moved in with me in my own graduate school digs. In almost no time, though, he began making his first forays into urban ethnobotany. The firemen at the neighborhood station got an afternoon of laughs at his expense from Luke's gath-ering dandelions on the firehouse lawn. He gave the old ladies

peeking from behind their lace curtains some puzzlement too when he began collecting seeds from their autumn-withered morning glories.

No one seemed to care, though, when he gathered leaves from white- trumpeted datura plants growing in a vacant lot at the edge of town. I was the only one who noticed when, hours later, undergoing powerful auditory hallucinations, Luke began charging about from one room of the apartment to the other, talking all night long to people who weren't there. Nutmeg he could buy at any grocery store, gritting it down with dollops of ice cream and staying semi-comatose all weekend. When two of the young kids who lived with their mothers in our apartment complex found a thoroughly desiccated toad corpse, Luke stopped them from throwing it away and, before their astonished eyes, crumbled the papery remains, bones and all, into his pipe and smoked it. The boys' mothers never looked at Luke (or me) quite the same way again, after that.

Becoming a graduate student in ethnobotany was a logical enough next step for him, conferring a certain aura of respectability and academic rigor to what Luke would have probably been doing anyway. It all made sense—except for the bills and receipts, the check stubs and requisition slips I'd found among his office clutter. They didn't fit at all. What did he need with an industrial autoclave? Portable solar and gasoline-fueled electric generators? Diamond saws? Thousands of feet of power cables? Foldout satellite dishes and uplink antennas? Language acquisition and real-time translation programs? Camcorders and optidisk player recorders? Fifty microscreen TV sets—fifty!

That he'd bought such gear was odd enough, but then to have the lot of it shipped to a little nothing outpost in the middle of the rainforest—that seemed a little too strange to be sane.

As the jet came to a halt on the tarmac, I knew that "little nothing outpost" would have to be my next destination. Shouldering my gear, I deplaned and walked through the muggy, crowded terminal to the ticket counter of a regional airline, on which I booked a flight to Amianac.

* * * * * * *

"Lucas Larkin's your brother, yes?" Juan Carrillo Garza asked, not bothering to look up from the figure he was carving from some unidentified dark hardwood. Having eyed me once as I approached him on the long wooden verandah outside his "offices," the bearded, heavy-set man seemed to feel no further desire to observe me. I asked him in my inadequate Spanish how he had recognized me so quickly.

"Family resemblance," Garza shrugged. "Yes, I went with the mushroom god to Caracamuni—both times—but never did I cross through that crazy maze on top!" His smile as he said it was like the blade cutting the dark wood.

"Mushroom god?"

Garza nodded.

"That's what the ghost people call your brother. They don't speak very good Pemón, but I'm pretty sure that's what they said. I saw them this time. They came right out of the rain and the maze, most of them almost naked. I stood as close to them as you're standing to me now. Saw the white threads of fungus lacing their elbows and knees, the centers of their eyes threaded blue and white. My men and I wouldn't go into the labyrinth, so they had to take all the fancy gear your brother had us haul up that tepui."

"Gear?"

Garza smiled his wood-carving smile.

"TVs. Computers. Generators. Antennas. And this thing like a big pressure cooker. Crazy. I've seen some strange things, I tell you, but watching naked little *indígenas* carrying all that shiny new electronics into a foggy maze atop a floating world— that has to be one of the strangest."

I asked him about "floating world." What some Pemóns called the tepuis, he said, particularly when the tops of the high plateaus stood in the sun, above the clouds that blotted out the rest of creation below. I tried to steer the conversation back around to why they called Luke the "mushroom god."

"That I do not know," Garza said, gesturing his palms open slightly. "Unless—" The wood-carver laughed out loud. "Your brother is very pale, right? Always buttoned up and wearing a sun hat on that wispy light brown hair of his, no? Maybe his coloring reminded them of a mushroom!"

He laughed again, great deep belly laughs, until he had to dab at his eyes.

"Is Luke still up there?" I asked. "Is he still alive?" I put the question somewhat fearfully. Luke was my younger brother, after all. I didn't want to have to attend his funeral any time soon.

Garza returned his attention to his carving. It was so long before he answered that I wondered if he was ignoring me—or if he'd even heard me in the first place.

"Whether he's alive or not, I cannot say." Garza worked a particularly long shaving from the wood and sent it corkscrewing to the ground. "But dead or alive, he's still on Caracamuni tepui."

"Can you take me there?"

"Of course." Garza carved. "For a price."

"Name it."

He named a figure. I told him I didn't have quite that much cash on hand. That was okay, he assured me. He took plastic.

* * * * * * *

"Thanksgiving weekend," Luke said, "I was up at the cabin alone. I'd gotten some great shrooms from this guy in Philosophy, super quality Romero strain stuff. I chewed a bunch of caps and stems, downing them with orange juice from the refrigerator. After twenty minutes the headchange still hadn't started to come on, so I drank and chewed a bunch more—maybe too much more.

"The headchange started coming on then. Boy did it ever. The stereo was on, but after a while I couldn't listen to it. The music I thought I knew began to get stranger than I could take.

I had to turn it off. The temperature seemed to be falling inside the cabin, so I kept stoking up the woodstove with pine—real go-fer wood. I flashed on the fact that building a fire is always really only building a stack of ashes. Constructing a building is always really only building a pile of ruins. All the solemn foolery of being alive—thinking, talking, singing, dancing, breathing, breeding, eating, shitting—just to build a mountain of corpses. I started thinking maybe the second law of thermodynamics is the Holocaust that goes on forever, with God as the biggest of all possible Hitlers.

"Things were getting way too intense. All my necessary illusions began breaking down, falling away. Everything shone with aching clarity. I was freaking out. I went in the kitchen, looking for something to eat, something to bring me down. All I could focus on was a bowl of rice and a bottle of meat tenderizer. I sprinkled some of the tenderizer on the rice. I ate it, but as I ate I thought the rice tasted more and more like sand. It occurred to me that that was the future—more people on the rock, more sand in the rice, less food in the belly.

"After I ate, instead of getting better the distortions got worse. The walls began to swell, expanding and contracting, like lungs breathing, like chambers of a beating heart. The wood grain patterns of the wall paneling became these menacing hieroglyphs demanding to be read. It was incredibly more powerful than the best acid I'd ever had. I downed all the orange juice in the house, gulped glass after glass of water, hoping to wash it all out of my system. When I finally began pissing, I was an enormous giant aiming into a tiny toilet bowl far below me in another dimension. I was losing it, scared to death that I'd never come back, never return to what I'd been. I really needed someone to talk me down. I tried to call you, but you weren't home."

* * * * * * *

Water everywhere. Garza, his small Pemón crew and I were

on a river as wide as the world. It stretched from horizon to horizon. The lingering skeletons of newly drowned rainforest trees hung ghostly grey above us. We passed boatloads of brown men with chainsaws burring like angry metal insects, felling the skeletons, clearing wide lanes through the flooded forest, scavengers on a battlefield where some unheard-of war of the elements had recently been fought. Great rafts of logs floated alone or were guided by groups of men. Many of the workers were armed.

When I asked Garza what had killed off the trees he was vague. Something about the rainy season, or a new hydropower dam downriver, or a combination of the two. When I asked about the guns he was even less clear, muttering something about rubber harvesters, as nearly as my inadequate Spanish could make out.

Toward evening we began to see a river with discernible banks, with vast mudflats beyond. Smoke columned into the setting sun. Occasionally, round a bend in the river, we would see groups piling enormous logs and whole flood-killed trees onto great bonfires. It was an eerie sight, the smoky bonfires flaring over the mudflats, the lurid torches of their flames reflected in the surface sheen of the broad plains of muck, broken here and there by the stumps of the forest that once was. When I asked Garza why they were doing this he told me he didn't know and said I asked too many crazy questions.

We spent a night in a no man's land of shattered and sodden trees and treacherous, crawling muds. We never ventured far from camp, for the exact depth of the mud, though usually passable, was never sure. One of Garza's men sank into a pit of the stuff up to his neck. The rest of us, after rescuing him, concluded sagely that the stump of a great tree must have been there once but had since rotted away or been removed. We had know choice but to sit about in camp, listening to the night. We heard only the occasional sounds of distant night birds and bats, the rare creaking of frogs and the plashing of the other unknown things hunting them. The place was far too quiet, mournful

almost, as if the world, hereabouts at least, were stretched upon its deathbed. The deep, pausing quiet made me long for the bustle and night noise I'd always associated with wild places.

The next morning we continued up a river the chocolate grey color of the Ganges when it flows past the great ashen ghats of the burning dead. The further we went the more obvious grew the current in the great river of silt and ashes. Soon we had no choice but to portage through mist forest round vast brown and white curtains of waterfalls that went on for close to a mile, at a place where half the earth seemed to have suddenly subsided several hundred feet, with no regard for the river that flowed above it. The portage was long, muscle tearing work, made all the harder to coordinate by the unending din of the roaring falls, the white noise of which reduced our loudest shouts to nothing. Drenched and bone-weary, we camped far enough from the falls that the sound of the broad cataracts, which had tormented us all day, lulled us to sleep that night.

The portage at least had taken us beyond the land of mud and ashes. The flooding and felling and tree-burning had not come so far as this—at least not yet. We canoed and portaged up river and stream for a further day and a half, past flights of blue and red macaws, past bands of monkeys shrieking green waves through the forest canopy, past the fluttering flashing blue neon of what Garza called "giant morpho butterflies." I brought my hand-held video camera to bear on such sights again and again, yet somehow the very act of framing the exotic creatures in the viewfinder seemed to reduce them to mere targets, cut them out of their natural context, render them isolated, unreal. At some level too I feared that videotaping these exotic places would only contribute to the global déjà vu of everyone back north, their ennui from having electronically "been there and done that"—further reducing any desire they might have to preserve this place in reality, since they had already experienced it on TV.

When at last I saw a young boy with wide brown eyes peering out from the dense leafy greenery, his face painted red and blue

under a yellow headdress, I stopped taping, content to just be a part of the strange beauty going on around me.

Packing through the jungle though, for all its beauty, wasn't quite so pleasant: venomous snakes, brittle scorpions, stinging ants, ever-present mosquitoes. Air so thick with sticky steaming humidity that breathing seemed a waste of effort. Heat and dampness that turned my clothing and pack into a portable sweat lodge. Night came, noisy with the jungle and the particularly dense clouds of bloodsucking wonders that hovered about in the dusk.

For two days more we slogged our way through wet green hell, accompanied by the sound of machetes on brush, of insects and animals and muttered human curses, and always the dripping and drumming of precipitation onto or off of the forest canopy. The trail switchbacked endlessly, frustratingly, wracking knees and legs and lungs. I knew we must be gaining altitude, but still the forest cover did not break. I seemed to walk that twisting green tunnel even in my dreams—when I managed to sleep at all.

Surmounting a ridge, we at last left the rainforest. As the five of us—the three Pemón *indígenas*, Garza, and myself—dropped our packs and made camp, Garza pointed out one of the mountains on the horizon, a high mesa shaped roughly like a giant anvil that had been partially cloven in the middle by some unknown force. Caracamuni tepui, Garza said. A cool wind began to blow against our tents. It blew all night long.

Over the next day and a half we made our way along the backbone of the ridge and onto the tepui itself. It was not an easy passage. At many points the trail turned into a goat scramble up broken talus slopes, round boulder-strewn uplifts. We seemed always to be balancing on logs precariously fording rushing streams, or leaping from rock to rock, or—once—swimming our gear across a fifty yard stretch of unexpectedly frigid water.

Though the switchbacking of the trail increased, if anything, and we always seemed to be walking under leaden skies, at least now the elevation gain became more obvious as we passed from

one biome to the next in increasingly rapid succession, the air growing cooler and cooler. We passed completely above and out of the rainforest canopy, into more and more marginal spaces where hardy plants struggled to survive, punctuated here and there by small copses and other spots favored with protection from the heaviest of the wind and rain. I particularly remember resting from our march in a sheltered swampy glade, a place filled with tree-ferns, club mosses, insane living-fossil plants of a dozen types—all surrounded by the glint of dragonflies, the unending hum and chitter of nameless insects. A spot straight out of the Carboniferous.

I fully expected to hear giant amphibians thrashing about in the bushes, killer scorpions and massive centipedes scurrying toward me out of a time-lost world that I'd somehow managed to stumble upon. The place had no need of human beings whatsoever. Despite its great beauty I was glad to move on—and sooner than I might have expected.

After a morning of goat-footed upslope scrambling, noon of the fourth trail day since the broad falls brought us shivering, at last, to the high mesa's top, to a place of stone black with rains that seemed to have been falling there forever, a place where fog and algae and fungus were shaping, always shaping the stone. Slowly.

I looked about me. Rocks and pinnacles, columns and arches. The sort of city that time and water dream from stone. No streets, no right angles anywhere. Everything rounded— nothing straight could stay. Ancient strata stood before me, always already broken by lopsided eggs of sky, pierced by ellipses of fog, interrupted by ovoids and oblongs of rain. A labyrinth of stone clouds.

"Your brother is out there somewhere," a rain-dripping Garza said, gesturing toward the heart of the maze. "Forty square miles of it. My men and I, we go no further."

I nodded.

"I'm going on. Remember—you've all signed on for another week. I'll keep in radio contact and return within three days at

most."

"We'll wait," Garza muttered. "Three days—that long and no longer. May God go with you."

* * * * * * *

Like a wet ghost I drifted into the forest of rainblack stones. All afternoon I walked there, west to east across Caracamuni tepui, across that island of stone floating among the clouds, rain-desert island above rainforest sea. The more time I spent alone there in the drifting fog and drizzle, the more the place seemed both haunted and holy, sanctified by isolation. Everywhere stood the dark rainsoft contours of the ancient stone: two billion year old geological ruins, nightmare temples, alien cathedrals. Stonehenges and Angkor Wats and Sagrada Familias dribbled like children's slurry castles onto an anvil top two miles up, left to harden, then wash away forgotten. Again and again they drifted up out of the fog, only to disappear back into it. I wondered what Luke had thought of this landscape, mythical and monumental and dreamlike, a maze for a minotaur to feel at home in, and the girl Ariadne with her clue of thread....

For a moment the rain and fog thinned. I thought I saw what looked like a young woman in the distance. Bronze skin, dark breasts, long reddish-brown hair. I blinked and she was gone. A nearly naked woman—in this wet cold? As I walked on, exhausted, my thoughts felt feeble, unreal, the merest shadows cast by the soft tissue inside the stone bubble of my skull. I was losing my senses. Time to stop.

Taking shelter beneath the large overhang of a mushroom-cloud rock, I shed pack and gear and wet clothes and climbed into a merely damp sleeping bag. Under that thundering sky of late afternoon, in a place I feared might vanish like a dream or burst like a bubble, I fell asleep.

* * * * * * *

In the dream I sit in an overstuffed armchair, talking pleasantly to two older people. In the dream I know who they are. Maybe they're my parents. I'm conversing in their pleasant living room, when I happen to glance over my left shoulder. Standing in the archway to the dark room there behind me, half in shadow and half in light, are my Uncle Tim, who's died recently, and my brother Luke, lost and perhaps dead.

I look at Luke's eyes and think, When the mind goes supernova, the eyes become black holes. That's my brother all over: eyes glazed from supersaturation, from seeing too much. The eyes of someone who's dived to the far side of madness and left part of himself "over there."

I begin to see the way those eyes see, their vision devouring everything, nothing falling into them escaping, light least of all. I look at cities and see only fogs of stone clinging to coastlines, mists of metal rolling along river valleys. Through them I see too well how all the living are ghosts in the fog, all institutions unjust shadows in a dream of justice. Through them I see that neither noon nor midnight exists on the surface of the sun, that the fast burn of sunrises and sunsets is only a local illusion, arising from the dizziness of living on the outside of a stone bubble spinning in space. Luke's eyes are forever beyond time, seeing all times, yet all times are peripheral to their vision. They are the eyes of a searching swimmer drowning in the great ocean of truth.

I remember thinking, in my dream, 'Oh, these are the dead, standing behind me, watching and waiting, this is the way they see'—and that thought knocked me right back to consciousness.

* * * * * * *

When I woke the rain had stopped, a subtle miracle. I climbed out of my cocoon to dry naked and new in the orange evening sunlight. Around me still stood the myriad softhard shapes of the maze, a dreamscape refusing to disappear upon waking. The sun was setting behind bars of clouds, smearing slanting light

on ancient stones, suffusing the maze with a melancholy old as the universe, a twilight of men and gods, of worlds and time.

Yet even there in that barren place where rains fell so violently upon the plateau's top as to drive the very nutrients from the earth—even there the gravel was dotted with pocket Edens, swampy rock garden-sized oases. I made my naked and tenderfooted way among them, the first human being returned at evening on the last day. I felt cleansed, free, but also, somehow, watched over.

I put that odd sensation out of my mind and tried to find some contentment amid the stark beauty of the place. When the sun was nearly gone and the long mountain twilight was underway in earnest, I started back toward the sheltering overhang where my empty sleeping bag sprawled. I had not covered much territory that day, it was true, but I held better hopes for the morrow. Remembering that the satellite image had shown the cleft or abyss bisecting the labyrinth top into two neat hemispheres, I convinced myself that most likely there was cloudforest at the bottom of that midline depression. If Luke was to be found anywhere up here, I was sure it would be there.

In the gathering dark I radioed in to Garza and his men. They sounded happy and relieved to hear from me—and more than a little surprised.

* * * * * * *

"They're putting LSD in the cafeteria food here to make me sink uncontrolled telepath into the massmind, the cultural macroorganism," Luke said in a rush over the phone from the university. "But I'm fighting them. I know they're scanning this call, big brother, but I don't care. Their power is growing, but I've gone starburst. Full telepath televisionary. I am your psychopomp, protecting your soul so you can be heard, so your message can get out, so you can communicate. I am a powerful starburst and you are under the silver force field umbrella of my psychic protection, the silver mirrorball that reflects all the

watching eyes, that's reflected in all the watching eyes, and you're inside, infinitely beyond harm."

* * * * * * *

The morning sky when it came hung grey as lead and heavier on my spirits than the damp musty pack and clothes upon my body. Half asleep I renewed my trudge through the foggy senseless maze, the ahumanness of the place working on my imagination. At times I felt as if I were walking through the sleep of some great slow mind, an interloper into eons-long dreams and nightmares I could not even begin to understand. My perpetually fogging glasses began growing some sort of algae or fungi up in the corners near the hinges. As the leaden morning wore on, the rain and fog and algae and fungus which endlessly shaped the convoluted stone of the labyrinth seemed to be shaping me too, slowly covering my runneled face with lichens and mosses....

I stopped abruptly. Ahead, leaning back against a house-sized boulder and warily observing my approach, was the young woman—girl, really, perhaps sixteen at the most—whom I had seen the previous day and written off as a phantasm of my over-tired brain. I stared at her, both of us in that instant motionless as the stones around us. Her presence up here alone was just too improbable—but in this great jumble of rocks always disappearing in and out of fog and cloud, I was sure that there was a human figure clearly discernible at fifty yards, a locus of perspective if nothing else.

We said nothing. I began to walk slowly and steadily toward her. In response she moved on ahead of me, disappearing and reappearing like an apparition, always just ahead, the force of her presence moving me in the direction she wished to go, moving me onward, out of the thickest of the cloud cover.

The young woman stopped where the maze broke off. Above us was a broken sky of high cloud; below us, a cloud-filled gorge came into view. At its edge stood something even more strange and wonderful: a brown-haired, bearded, fishbelly-white man,

clad in tattered shorts and gym shoes and straw sunhat, clip-board in hand on the brink of the abyss, adjusting the angle onto heaven of a small satellite dish.

"Luke!"

Turning startled eyes toward me, my brother jumped back so quickly I was afraid he would plunge over the edge and disappear. He caught himself just this side of catastrophe.

"Wha—yes?"

I strode forward and gave him a strong full hug, thinking how strange it was to see him shirtless, knowing how embarrassed he had always been by his girlish large-nippled pectorals. He stared at me a moment—not recognizing me?—then averted his eyes, just as he always had.

"Paul. This—this is quite a surprise."

"You're telling me! What the hell do you mean, disappearing out here like this?" I found my voice quavering with strong emotion. "What are you doing up here? Have you completely lost it or what, bro?"

"No," his eyes flickered contact for only an instant before turning away toward the gorge. "I think I've found it, actually. If you'll come with me I'll show you."

His work on the satellite dish apparently finished, he called out, "Talitha," and waved the young woman on ahead of us. As she led us swiftly downward into the fine cloudmist that obscured the abyss, I was close enough to see that, though Talitha wore only a loincloth, the garment was masterfully intricate in its design. She followed no path that I could discern, though for a while I thought she seemed to be ranging along the cable from the dish antenna—until that line darted off on its own into the increasingly dense undergrowth. By then I could hear water flowing and falling with almost musical cadence as we made our way into and under the tree canopy, through ever denser cloudforest growth, downward among misted and dripping lianas and orchids and epiphytes of a thousand kinds, the sound of a waterfall growing steadily to a roar then to a thunder blotting out everything else.

Our young guide seemed almost to dance over the slippery downed trees that forded the torrent at the gorge's bottom. Luke crossed them in his game, gangly way and I in my much less surefooted one. Somewhere downstream the torrent turned to waterfall, thundering into empty space, sending back up the gorge to us a twofold sound like an immense echoing heartbeat. Stepping down onto the right-side bank, we continued east along what was more and more obviously a footpath. After following the path for a time we came to a true trail and veered sharply up a small branch canyon, the smoking thunder of the tepui falls at last receding enough to allow the insect and animal sounds of the forest to return.

"Where are we headed?" I asked.

"To introduce you to the people I'm staying with," Luke replied, keeping his eyes focused on the ground in front of him as we hiked along. He seemed a good deal more serene than I'd expected to find him.

"I thought you told your landlord it wasn't good for you to be around people right now."

His eyes flickered over me oddly for an instant, then he shrugged and looked away.

"Maybe I meant white North American people—"

"—who don't think you're a god," I said with a smug and knowing nod. "Who don't think you're some kind of pale mushroom messiah?"

"What do you mean?"

I told him what Garza had said about the "mushroom god"—his speculation as to why the Caracamuni *indígenas* applied that term to Luke, too. Luke laughed a series of breathy smirks.

"That's not it at all," he said, shaking his head. "I'm no fungal Quetzalcoatl. I'm not their savior. If anything, they're mine. These people speak a very old language, a sort of ur-Pemón—when they have to speak at all. What Garza translated 'mushroom god' is more accurately something like 'spawnbroker.'" He smiled slightly, as if at some private joke. "Of course translation's not such a problem anymore. To us and their children they

can speak Spanish and English perfectly well now—French, Russian, and Japanese, too."

"*What?*"

"You'll see."

* * * * * * *

Gradually, as we gained elevation again, the mist cleared around us and the jungle thinned perceptibly. The air had begun to cool again by the time we encountered several foot-trampled pathways converging on an earthen slope beneath a high cliffside. In the cliff face were some half dozen holes or cave entrances from which a brisk breeze issued steadily. Out of the forest on both sides of the gorge power lines and cables snaked—purposeful vines of black, gray, and red, all headed toward the cliff holes. In the wind I thought I heard the muffled sound of motors and smelled...exhaust?

"The gas-powered generators," Luke said, seemingly reading my thoughts. "We don't like to use them, but sometimes we have to. We've got solar generators on the sunniest part of the plateau's top, but even there the sunlight levels are erratic, so we've got the gas ones for backup power."

Talitha came to a stop before the holes. As if at a silent call, heads began to thrust up out of them, then torsos and entire bodies—largely unadorned but for the occasional intricate loin-cloths and, incongruously, electronic headsets.

"Where's Kekchi?" Luke called as we scrambled up the earthen slope.

"In the Cathedral Room," several bronze, gap-toothed faces replied. Nodding, Luke climbed up into that mouth of the cave toward which the greatest number of cables and power lines converged.

Somehow it figured it would be a cave, I thought. Luke was always trying to get back to some cave. When we were teenagers there was that retaining wall with the hole in it beside Clough Creek, the room eroded in the landfill behind it. We could talk

there sometimes. In the dark Luke didn't have to worry about the person he saw in the mirror, didn't have to worry about the way his body hung on him, or his endlessly wide-eyed facial expressions—as if the world were a dream from which he had always, just at that very moment, startled awake.

"Kekchi's the 'wise one,' their psychopomp," Luke explained as he snatched a flashlight from among several resting on a rock ledge in the half-light of the cave mouth. I dropped my pack and, following his lead, grabbed a light source for myself. Proceeding down a slantwise tunnel, we left the muffled thrum of generator motors behind, then passed through rock honeycombed with innumerable small side chambers. Into about a dozen of these alcoves snaked power lines and cables, and from those particular chambers faint light of various colors spilled.

Intent on reaching the Cathedral Room and this Kekchi person, Luke set a good pace, so I caught only glimpses of what was going on in the side chambers. What I saw, though, was strange enough. In one room several *indígena* children watched a Chinese television documentary on Han dynasty artifacts—real-time computer translated into French. In another chamber a young man watched an American news broadcast about an Indian monsoon. In a third chamber a young woman checked an enormous crystal column for flaws as it flowed out of a high-pressure extrusion autoclave and into the long tunnel. Beyond the column's end someone was carving up quartz bricks with a diamond saw. In another alcove a small group of youngsters seemed to be randomly sampling musical forms from various times and places—madrigals and rap, Tibetan temple gongs and rock'n'roll, Sufi chants and Europop and worldbeat.

Other chambers were outside anything in my previous experience. A boy and an oldster sat before computer terminals, running through what looked like extremely complex mathematical equations—at unbelievable speeds—while in the next chamber what might have been star charts and astrogation data darted across screens before a half dozen operators of various ages.

Fascinated by what I was seeing but fearful of what it might mean, I wanted to see more, but by then we were through the holed rock and the tunnel had opened out into an enormous underground space, a deep chamber of unbelievable dimensions, lit vainly here and there by the stars of arc lights and carbides and "tinder bush" fires—but mostly rising away everywhere into cool damp darkness. Somewhere shadowy light glimmered off crystalline rock scattered about the floor of the great space, and water dripped in a symphony of echoes.

"The Cathedral Room," Luke said, staring out into the enclosed vastness.

"Unbelievable," I marveled, gazing about at this immense bubble of open space enclosed by the living rock. "I didn't think there could be this much space underground!"

"It's big for a single cave chamber," Luke agreed. "Not the biggest, though. That one's beneath the jungles of Borneo—530 million cubic feet. This one's only about a fourth that size. Big enough for our purposes, though."

"What purposes?" I asked, starting down the slope after Luke.

"Why, as a resonating chamber, of course."

I was about to ask Resonating for what? but Luke was already down the slope and moving across the faintly sparkling floor, striding toward a grey-headed person stooping among the source of the glimmer—which, as I came closer, I saw to be piles of quartz.

* * * * * * *

"'Lo, Kekchi," Luke called to the greyhead. "My brother Paul's come."

"Hng," the stringy old person grunted, tossing a rock crystal into a bucket. Even as we got closer I could not determine with certainty whether Kekchi was an old man or an old woman. Dressed in a full loose robe of the same intricate weave or knit as the loincloths I'd seen earlier, Kekchi showed only a gender-

less old age—a longhaired, gap-toothed, chin-fuzzed, slack-breasted, bright-eyed ageless age.

"A lost brother come to find a lost brother," Kekchi said, straightening up and turning toward me eyes like white agates rippled with blue and brown. The high raspy voice did nothing to clear up my confusion. If anything, that confusion worsened, for the voice sounded distinctly creaky with neglect, as if its possessor didn't have much use for speaking. "A found brother come to lose a found brother—as one of the lines would have it. Wondering what we're about here, too. Isn't that right?"

"I don't know anything about 'lines,'" I said, fighting down the uncomfortable sensation that for Kekchi our meeting was something that had always already happened, "but yeah, I am trying to make sense of all this."

"Then you'd better learn something about lines!" Kekchi cackled.

"Lines, threads, strings," Luke tried to explain. "Patterns of interconnection and possibility."

Old Kekchi spat and picked up another handful of crystalline rocks to sort through.

"Now how's he going to understand that when he's never been in mindtime, eh?"

"Mindtime?" I said, growing still more confused, admiring what Luke and these people were apparently accomplishing, but uncertain of its source or end.

"Where you go to talk to the ghosts!" said the wise one. "Speak with ancestors!"

"Outside normal spacetime perception," Luke added hopefully.

They looked at me expectantly, but I was blank.

* * * * * * *

"He doesn't understand," Kekchi said sorrowfully, wearily. "Always we must explain." Abruptly the greyhead began to chant—a strange low sound, atonal yet melodious.

"The Story of the Seven Ages," Luke said slowly. "Their cosmic myth. I can only do a very rough translation into English, but I'll try."

The strange chant rose and echoed in the cavernous chamber. Luke translated:

"In the void of endings, the spore of beginnings bursts into spawn. The threads of spawn absorb the voidstuff and knit it into stars. Stars release spores, the spores burst into spawn, the threads of spawn absorb starstuff and knit it into worlds. Worlds release spores, the spores burst into spawn, the threads of spawn absorb worldstuff and knit it into life. Living things release spores, the spores burst into spawn, the threads of spawn absorb lifestuff and knit it into minds. Minds release spores, the spores burst into spawn, the threads of spawn absorb mindstuff and knit it into worldminds. Worldminds release spores, the spores burst into spawn, the threads of spawn absorb worldmindstuff and knit it into starminds. Starminds release spores, the spores burst into spawn, the threads of spawn absorb starmindstuff and knit it into universal mind. Universal mind, the void of endings, the void that has taken all things into itself, releases the spore of beginnings, the fullness that pours all things out of itself."

The chant echoed away into the cave. Kekchi turned back to sorting through the mounds of quartz. Luke's eyes flickered at me an instant, after he'd stopped translating.

"That's a pretty good 'rough translation,'" I said, obscurely embarrassed. "But what's spore? What's spawn? And what's it got to do with anything happening here? The whole thing sounds too pat to me—snake swallowing its own tail."

Luke stared off into the cavernous emptiness, but in the light from the flashlights his eyes seemed to shine with a dark brilliance. A torrent of words, frustrated yet determined, poured forth from him like the waters of the thundering fall we had passed, leaping away into space.

"It's got everything to do with it! Everything for them is spore and spawn and fruiting body—and the darkness or void that comes before and after and always is. Translated into the myth-

language of science, 'void' is the perfectly uniform universe without matter, just time and the enormous blank sheet of space with its potential for gravity. In the first age, spore and spawn and fruiting body are Big Bang and superstrings and first generation stars. In the second age, spore and spawn and fruiting body are the matter of those stars blown off in the bursts of explosions and gravity's configuring of that new matter—some of it condensing into planets. In the third age, spore and spawn and fruiting body are the volcanism of some of those planets spewing out early atmosphere, proto-organics threading out and chaining up, eventually developing into the self-organizing life of the cell. In the fourth age, spore and spawn and fruiting body are reproduction, the threading out of DNA and RNA that make evolution and the panoply of life possible—and eventually the knitting of all that into consciousness, into mind. In the fifth age, spore and spawn and fruiting body are ideas, bedding out into roads, trade, civilization: lines of print and code, railroads and sea lanes and glide paths, power lines and telephone wires, broadcast channels and fiber optic cables, microcircuits and rocket trajectories—some carrying sudden mushrooms, some carrying satellites to move the great invisible threads of information absorbing everything."

He glanced at me as if for some confirmation I could not give, then went on.

"The thick spawn of the world we grew up in, Paul, the world at the end of the fifth age, always on the brink of mushrooming up into cataclysm—or into worldmindfulness. In the sixth age, spore and spawn and fruiting body are interplanetary and interstellar ships, galactic civilization, eventual starmindfulness. In the seventh age, spore and spawn and fruiting body are intergalactic travel and post-corporeal civilization and at last universal mindfulness, the emptiness able to contain the fullness of everything, perfect and uniform, that in the exact instant of its perfection releases the spore that bursts outward again into spawn. Men and universes die, Paul, but the cosmic spawn goes on and on!"

His dark brilliant eyes flickered toward me and away, and in that instant, my instant, I was certain he was insane.

* * * * * * *

"Luke, that's crazy stuff," I said shaking my head, feeling like a very minor actor on the great stage of that enormous underground room. "I don't know how these people have warped you, but we've got to get you out of here."

"He doesn't understand," Kekchi said, looking up from a pile of crystals and speaking to Luke about me as if I weren't there. "Let's show him. Come."

Kekchi took Luke's flashlight and strode away into the quartz-heaped and boulder-strewn immensity of the Cathedral Room. Luke followed, so I did too—reluctantly. We walked over and around and beside mounds of stone slabs, sloughed ages ago from the cavernous room's ceiling, somewhere far up in the darkness above us. We passed onto a broad, more or less level plain from which a great ring of quartz columns rose off into the darkness, each column wreathed at intervals by spike-halos of quartz points floating suspended in the air. Passing into the great ring, I could not help thinking of the columns as pillars in a tremendous airy cathedral, flying buttresses to nowhere, holding up only the dark subterranean sky.

We made our way over a plain of organic muck bordering what looked like a shallow lake, or perhaps a place where a slow-flowing stream broadened out in a wide channel. The muck dragged and sucked at our feet as we squelched over it, weighing us down, turning our footsteps to lead. The water when we waded into it was mercifully shallow, not more than a foot deep at most, and somehow the bottom underneath it seemed firmer.

Kekchi stopped and pointed the flashlight toward what looked to be an island in the center, a raised space like a long low hummock.

"Here!"

Splashing, I hurried forward to the island's edge to get a closer look at whatever it was Kekchi's beam was falling upon.

* * * * * * *

What I saw in the flashlight's beam horrified me. The island was clearly the burial ground of the ghost people, but so crowded with the dead that it seemed made of bodies, corpses preserved by the cave's stable environment. From the heads of the fresher corpses grew fresh fungus—weird mushrooming stalks like vertically stretched convoluted brains, thrusting up like alien phalluses from open mouths, from ears, from eye sockets. Particularly large specimens jutted up from the corpses' abdomens, just below the rib cage, and fine masses of cottony white threads spread and knitted over the surface of each corpse's skin.

While I stood in shock Kekchi reached down and ran a fine white-lined finger inside one of the brain mushroom's convoluted pits. The fingertip he poked at me was covered with a bright bluish dust.

"Spores," he said, blowing the dust carefully from his finger, back onto the island. He reached down and snatched up a plug of the loose, white filamentous threads from where they grew off a body into the surrounding organic muck and humus of the island. "Spawn."

"Vegetative phase mycelium," Luke added, in unnecessary translation. Kekchi reached down a third time, plucking the convoluted ball-stalk fungus from a corpse's eye socket.

"Vertical fruit of the horizontal tree," Kekchi said reverently, thrusting at my face the fleshy thing, pitted and ridged, whitish in color overall but deepening to brown-veined pale blue in the pit areas and crowned by a pale tannish fuzz on top.

"Oh my god," I moaned, the fungus's damp rich smell wafting into my nostrils, stirring a mounting wave of nausea in my guts.

"Ours too," Kekchi said with a crooked smile, biting off a hunk of the thing, chewing and swallowing it, then belching the

breath of death into my face. The wave surged up uncontrollably, dropping me to the mud on my hands and knees, projectile vomiting again and again, my guts heaving and twisting until there was no more to be wrung from me. At last I sat back on my knees in the muck, wiping from my mouth and chin the mucus and filth and bitter bile I had brought up, smearing it heedlessly on my arms above my muck-caked hands.

"They're mushroom cultists!" I blurted at Luke.

"Of course," Luke said matter-of-factly, crouching down beside me, seemingly oblivious to the gastric apocalypse I'd just endured. "These mushrooms and particular quartz crystals are their major totems. They've been collecting fine Brazilian quartz of a particular 'resonance' for nearly a thousand years. Rite of passage for everyone in the tribe—the only time they leave the tepui. By the time I arrived, they had several metric tons of the stuff stored here, waiting. As for the fungus—well, it sort of collected the people."

"Collected them?" I gazed past them to the corpse yard around us. "Killed them, you mean."

"Not at all," Luke said, shaking his head at me, though his eyes were elsewhere, as always. "I've studied the fungus's life-cycle, Paul. Collected dozens of spore prints, analyzed the spawn and the fruiting bodies—and talked to the people, too. For a long time they've been expecting someone who looks like me, so it was easy. The fruiting bodies, the 'mushrooms,' only appear like this after the person dies. The sacred fungus is a myco-neural symbiont. After someone ingests the fruiting body, the spores germinate and the spawn forms a sheath of fungal tissue around the nerve endings of the central nervous system. Some of the fungal cells penetrate between the nerves of the brain and brainstem, without damaging them. I did a radiological study of them up north, before I returned here. I used x-rays generated at a low enough voltage so that the soft tissues, which would otherwise be transparent, cast shadows instead. The densities of the mushroom flesh and human flesh are very nearly the same. The relationship is mutually beneficial: the fungal spawn

obtains moisture, protection and nutrients even in adverse environments, and the human hosts are assured a steady supply of the most potent informational substances imaginable—"

"Drugs," I croaked from my place in the mud. "You mean drugs."

"If you wish," Luke said with a shrug, his eyes darting along the crystal columns that ringed us round in the middle distance, glinting dimly in the light of distant tinder bush fires and carbide gleams. "I prefer to think of them as 'adaptogens.' The 'side effects' are interesting, at least. The DMN, the dorsal and median raphe nuclei in our brains, function as a sort of 'governor' on the level of brain activity, keeping it down to low percentages of total possible activity. It's your body's way of stepping on your mind. The myconeural complex, though, circumvents the raphe nuclei, allowing consistent high-level brain activity without burnout or any apparent ill effects. At such levels of brain activity, parapsychological phenomena become commonplace: clairvoyance, second sight, forays into mindtime, a very clear sense of the patterns of possibility backward and forward in spacetime."

* * * * * * *

Luke sketched complex patterns in the dirt with a finger while at the same time gazing off toward the line of crystalline columns. I felt too queasy and incredulous to say anything. He went on.

"Full development of the myconeural symbiosis takes about twelve years, but once that is achieved human hosts with full networks become natural telepaths with each other—immediate information transfer, mind to mind. Among the ghost people, language is for children, for only children have need of it." He sketched patterns faster and faster, denser and denser, never looking down at them. "Most importantly, though, is that even when I experienced mindtime for the first time, I realized that it tapped into a type of collective unconscious I never suspected.

You see, the spawn *remembers*."

"Remembers what?" I asked. Disheartened and frustrated, I felt the cool muck chilling my legs, the realization slowly sinking in that my brother already had those things growing inside of him.

"Everywhere it's been," Luke said, now drawing great circles again and again in the mud, "and, according to their mythology, it's been just about everywhere. Because it remembers, its hosts remember too. As far as I can tell, it's never been discovered anywhere else on Earth, but what the spawn and the people remember indicates it's not endemic to Caracamuni tepui—or to Earth, for that matter."

"What?" I asked, rubbing my begrimed hands on my pants. I feared that Luke was about to launch into another crazy scenario, and my fear did not prove unfounded.

"Look, this plateau is shield rock, 1.8 billion years old. The spawn remembers how it got here, tens, probably hundreds of millions of years ago. It's a living fossil. Translating the ghost people's shared memory and mythology into our own, I would say the spawn was part of a 'contact ship' from a sixth-age civilization, a craft that ran into trouble near the Oort cloud at the edge of our solar system. The ship was crippled and began falling toward the sun. Its fully myconeuralized crew came from diverse worlds, but for all their experience they couldn't save their vessel. Understanding their situation, they decided to attempt a spore crash on a world that looked as if it might someday harbor intelligent life. In the attempt most of the ship burned up in our atmosphere, but the crew was still successful: they had managed to seed the planet with spores, which germinated and spawned and fruited, to spore again."

"I thought they lived inside people," I said tiredly, sensing that I was losing this wrestling match with my brother's grand delusion.

* * * * * * *

"The fungus can survive without a myconeural association, though it is not nearly so robust as these you see here," Luke says. "Its long-term genetic stability and survival chances are greatly reduced outside a host. But 'long-term' is exactly what happened. A long time passed. Cometary impacts, incident radiation, corresponding mutation rates—all were greater than it would have normally experienced before it found an intelligent host. Throughout most of the world it changed, evolved, became denatured. In some places it adapted by intermixing with indigenous forms, branching off into ascomycetous fungi, the ancestors of morels and truffles—still delicious like the original form, but unable to generate myconeural spawn networks upon ingestion. Elsewhere its spawn networking interbred and evolved into totally parasitic forms, as in a number of *Cordyceps* species. In still other places some of its informational substances survived in much degraded form, particularly in the *Panaeolus* and *Psilocybe*.

"Only in a few marginal, shielded places—particularly caves—did anything like the original strain survive. The truest of the living fossils. Even in caves changes occurred and gradually the pure strain died out nearly everywhere, though I'm prone to believe a moderately pure strain hung on at the great parietal art caves of Franco-Cantabria, the ceremonial centers of Altamira, Lascaux, Tito Bustillo, El Castillo, Cuevo del Juyo and the rest, until about ten thousand years ago—"

"Gone, everywhere but here," Kekchi put in, frustrated with the unwieldyness of language but unable to avoid adding his voice to the tall echoing darkness of the cave. "Many thousands of years ago my people came to live here. What you call refugees. Inside this cave, inside this tepui, we found the sacred mushroom, ate it, joined with it."

"Full myconeural symbiosis," Luke said, nodding, gesturing. "It's their millennia-long familiarity with mindtime that's impressed upon them the importance of collecting quartz of a particular lattice configuration—for that time when they will 'sing their mountain to the stars.' "

"That time has now arrived," Kekchi intoned. "All the signs agree."

* * * * * * *

"So that's what all this is about, then?" I said, smacking my forehead with the palm of my left hand, rising shakily to my feet. "These people have been collecting rocks for millennia because mushrooms told them to? And you believe that? How much of this crap have you eaten? It's pushing you over the edgeless edge, bro. We've got to get you out of here, get this fungus stuff out of your system—"

"No, Paul." Luke shook his head and slowly rose from his squatting position to stand upright. "My mission here is too important to be absorbed into anyone else's—even yours. The work is not yet finished so the tribe can leave."

"What work?"

Luke turned away, looking into the dim reflection of the columns upon the water's surface.

"We must finish fabricating the quartz information drivers. Information is everything—the spawn memory makes that clear. The universe is information, gravity is an expression of it, matter and energy are two states of it—but information underlies and shapes it all. We're pulling as much information down from the satellites as we can and pumping it into our minds wide open, shaping it and casting it from mindtime into the structure of these quartz collecting columns you see around us, the ones we fashioned with the autoclave I brought, columns grown upon the seed crystals with the most appropriate crystalline structure—"

"The rock we have revered for ages," Kekchi interjected, "for its ability to capture and strengthen the subtle energies of mind."

"Impossible!"

"No—real!" Luke said with manic assurance. "I've seen it! A cruder level of it can be found in the piezoelectric effect, by which quartz and similar materials translate mechanical force

into electrical energy, and vice versa. But crystalline quartz of proper lattice configuration and sufficient size can also receive and amplify mental energies and translate them into motive forces. These people *know*, Paul. Their culture is unbelievably ancient. Look around you—everything here is a synergy of two living fossil species, one human, one fungal."

"What do you mean?" I asked, fearing the onset of more weird theorizing.

"Look at the skulls on that hummock," he said, walking over to the low island and crouching down beside the nearest skull. "I'm no forensic anthropologist, but I can see the obvious. The occipital 'rose' or 'bun,' the emphasis on cerebellar development, the large supraorbital ridges, the semi-nocturnal lifeway, the focus on aural over visual, the lack of left-brain dominance. 'Strong archaic *Homo sapiens* traits,' that's what a forensic professional would say, just like they said about the Australian aboriginals. Only more so, here. *Neanderthalensis* traits, *soloensis* traits, troll and wild man traits. They're a people whose universe is bound together by the thread and web of song extending all the way back to Europe and Africa more than a hundred thousand years ago, the same songweb differently echoed in the Aboriginal songlines."

"But that's crazy!" I shot back, trying to puncture the all-encompassing bubble of his paranoid theorizing. "Human beings have been in the New World only thirty thousand years, and the Neanderthals were already dying out by then."

Luke shook his head fervently.

"That's only if you buy the idea that the first humans to cross into the New World were hunters following the herds across Beringia. There's an alternative, you know. Fishing groups began following the coastline out of Asia and into the New World much earlier, long before the inland parts of Beringia were even free of the ice."

"Then why don't we have any proof of their settlement?" I said, still gamely trying to argue him into sanity.

"Preservation bias. Their settlements were primarily along

the coasts. But the oceans have risen four hundred feet since the last ice age. Any artifacts or traces in those settlement areas would have been destroyed when the intertidal zone passed over them. Archaeology is stone-biased as well. For much of the last century, archaeologists believed there were no tool-using cultures in much of Asia during the Paleolithic—because they found no stone implements. Then someone did contemporary ethnographic research among low-tech peoples in those areas and discovered that most of the toolkit there was bamboo—and since bamboo doesn't preserve well, the scientists had erroneously assumed there was no tool use going on.

"It was probably much the same with the fisherfolk who first crossed into the New World, and for most *Homo sapiens neanderthalensis* outside Europe: toolkits centered on the heavy use of plant fiber and wood, less bone, much less stone, if any— just like these people here. Absence of stone evidence is not evidence of human absence, certainly not in this case."

What could I say to that? It had always wrankled me to think that, even in his madness—perhaps because of his madness— my younger brother might be brighter, more intelligent than I am. Before his breakdown he was always the more studious one. Even now I couldn't out-argue him on his own ground, the field of his expertise, no matter how unconventional his theorizing might become. I gave up in disgust, but he kept right on.

"The quartz they've collected is not something you shape into a crude tool—it's something you worship as a totem. Their very existence here is proof of the fisherfolk hypothesis, of *neanderthalensis* in the New World. That's why Fash got so hot to bring a major expedition here once he found out. That's why we have to hurry—before the rest of the world finds them and destroys their uniqueness. Think of it, Paul: these people and their culture are one of the last outposts of a lost empire of wood and song. They're a thread that, on this different continent, in this cave, found its way back to the source of the world songweb. Synergy and co-evolution. For them, every sound has a form; they can read the musical notation of time's signature. According to their

myths, Song, shaped information, makes the world. Once we have sung and thought critical information densities into these collectors, they will translate and amplify it so we can dissociate ourselves from the gravitational bed of local spacetime. Then we can join in the Allesseh, the great Cooperation, the telepathic harmony of all myconeuralized creatures throughout the galaxy—"

* * * * * * *

"No!"

I shook my head in disgust. A swelling rage ignited deep inside my skull, an icy bright pinpoint that exploded outward like a cold Big Bang, a blizzard of invisible light radiating out of my temples, a crown of white thorns working its way to my forehead from the inside to finally storm outward in all directions, away and away. I paced heavily and furiously in the mud, the terrible anger rising in me, bringing with it all the memories of all Luke's strange times.

"I thought you were acting crazy when you said you were getting secret personal messages from commercial radio stations! I thought you were acting crazy when you said you were under surveillance by a secret conspiracy of shadowy agents disguised as nuns and social workers! I thought you were acting crazy when you were convinced They put a secret transmitter in your brain while you were knocked out having your wisdom teeth removed—to monitor your thoughts! I thought you were acting crazy when you said you were a mutant, a victim hero of the evolving human organism like Jesus or Gandhi or Martin Luther King—so you'd have to die the way they did, be killed off. I thought you were acting crazy when you started talking about the dream wars, when you said your fellow grad students were having dreams in which you died but you were using your own dreams to counter them. I thought you were acting crazy before, but this—this is the craziest of all!"

In full fury I ran about on the death island, kicking fiercely at

those mushroom phallus-brains growing up out of their corpse beds. Again and again I kicked, corpse after corpse. The fungal fruiting bodies split apart like tender new flesh against my muddy boot clad feet.

When breathless I at last stopped, I saw Luke had plopped down in the mire and was rubbing tears from his eyes.

"You'll never understand, will you?" he moaned. "Yeah, you're right—out there I am crazy, a freak! Always trapped between what I am and what I'm supposed to be! Always letting people down! No more! This is my world now, these are my people. It's better here! Paul, please, get beyond your demons! Don't you see? We were meant to be telepaths, part of the Great Cooperation, but we went wrong, we developed consciousness and intellect, but not the fullness of empathy we misname telepathy. All the wars and brutality of human history are proof of that wrongness." He turned to me, almost pleading. "The contact ships missed us. We became a preterite planet, but now we have a chance to gain our rightful inheritance, our place in the bliss of the Cooperation! Stay with us! Come with us!"

"Where? Where are you taking them? Where are they taking you? I don't get it, Luke. If you really think they prove your theories right, then why are you trying to help them escape the scrutiny of the anthropologists? If you're really trying to preserve their culture from our civilization, then why'd you bring all the high-tech gear here for them to mess with? Doesn't that already change their ways beyond recovery? And why should I want to stay here? To end up a flipped out fungus-head with a parasite mushroom growing inside my skull? Like these throwbacks? Is that the kind of life you want?"

"They're *happy*!" Luke shouted, turning reddened eyes on me—eyes that would not break contact, would not flicker away this time, no matter how much I might have wished it. "*We're* happy! What kind of life would I have out there? In and out of institutions all my life, dosed up on 'meds,' watched over by high-school dropout 'psychiatric aides' in case I 'go off'— giving them the chance to execute a well-planned 'take down'

so they can strap me into a floor-bolted cot in the 'time out' room? Out there, even freedom is my jail—a prison as big as the world! No thanks. Not while there's even a chance of real freedom, and the stars."

* * * * * * *

I felt like crying. It was all wrong, all so wrong.

"Luke, we've never institutionalized you. All I want to do is take you home."

"This is my home," he said, turning away.

"What about Mom and Dad?" I asked. "What about Professor Manikam and your career?"

"Tell them I quit school," he said without turning around. "Tell them I quit work. Tell them I disappeared into the back-country. Tell them I went native, stopped communicating, fell beyond reach. Tell Mom she only waited on us hand and foot to bind us hand and foot to her. Tell them both they only gave us everything so we would owe everything to them. Tell them it's all been said already. I've got nothing more to say to them, they've got nothing more to say to me."

"What about *me* then, you ungrateful bastard?" I shouted, my sorrow turning once more to anger. "I came all the way down here after you! What about me, huh? What would your mushroom people do if I grabbed one of these long bones here, clubbed you over the head with it, and took you out of here in a fireman's carry? Would they try to stop me?"

"Probably not," he said with a deep sigh, turning slightly toward me, glancing over his shoulder. "But I would. I'll fight you to the last breath. I won't let you sentence me to a life in prison—not even if it's 'for my own good.' Not even if I should be 'grateful' to you for doing it. Leave me here, or you better leave me alone."

The flash of determination in his eyes as he turned away was something too strong for me to challenge. I turned away too then, plodding through the shallow water, squelching back

tiredly through the plain of muck, flashlight flickering before me in the hollow emptiness of the cave. I came onto solid ground again and kept walking, never looking back.

"We must leave soon," the old psychopomp Kekchi said to Luke. I could hear his words echoing through the tall strange darkness of the cave almost too plainly—some weird acoustical effect. "Things don't have to be perfect, they just have to be done."

As I passed between two crystal pillars in the great ring of the same, I wanted to emulate Samson, to send the ghost people's crystal mushroom cathedral crashing down about their heads, then in the chaos and confusion snatch my brother from their embrace. But it could not be. I knew now that Luke would never consent to come back with me, and I would not take him against his will. I could not deny him that much respect for the human being he had been—and still was. Even then.

* * * * * * *

Approaching the exit tunnel through which I'd entered, I saw the people from the side chambers streaming down into the Cathedral Room, their work apparently done for the day, save for the group cheerfully singing as it carried a lengthy crystalline column. The children chattered back and forth with incredible rapidity, while among the adults not a word passed—though I had the distinct impression that they were communicating with each other without at all appearing to do so. Though there couldn't have been more than forty ghost people coming into the deep chamber, somehow I sensed that they represented the total numbers of the tribe.

At the mouth of the exit tunnel, I at last stopped and turned around. Fearing I would never see my brother again, I looked back at him, trying to catch a sense of the way he looked and moved, trying to form a composite lasting impression, something to hold, a living fossil of memory inhabiting the thin stone bubble of my skull. I caught something, but what I held could

never equal what I was losing.

To say that in this last impression Luke's eyes (made more prominent by the thinness of his face, the tightness of the skin on the skull) are brown and soft, something about them suggesting far away vistas from which the seer has never completely returned, the eyes of a vision quester, a sufferer through ordeals, a minddiver who has plummeted to the far depths of madness; to say that Luke's hair (moderately long and unkempt, receding a bit in that shape called a widow's peak) fringes the forehead of a troubled thinker; to say his thick brown mustache and beard frame cheekbones and eyebrows that, for all their prominence, can still add no solidity to the ghostly soft lostness those eyes confer on the entire face, making it the visage of an alcoholic young priest, a gently stoned Rasputin, a shaman who has lain too long in a land of eternal ice and winds that carve canyons in the soul—to say all of that and more, to call to mind even his words, is still to say too little.

The other tribesfolk were moving into the ring of crystal columns, toward Luke and Kekchi on the island of the dead in the center of the slow lake. I watched them as they gathered together in a circle of clasped hands, the living among the dead. They stood motionless for a time, until at last an otherworldly chantsong began to rise from them, unnerving yet hypnotic, reverberating upon the crystal columns and the far away walls of the cave, weaving and knitting and concentrating the echoes, all sounds, my attention, my focus, my very thoughts, until there, far underground, I seemed to see sunset glow pulsing through the pillars, iridescent blues and salmon pinks, fractal image of the universe flickering over their heads like the paraclete, beating in time to that song of piercing sensitivity, of painful beauty, eternal seductive lassitude and the horrible mushrooms in their midst—

When I thought I heard countless more voices begin singing, myriad ghosts joining the people, I turned and fled, fearing for my sanity. *I must stop thinking like this. I've got responsibilities, Luke. A wife, a news director, a career. This is not a good time*

*for me to go crazy. I can't let myself get sucked into the mad
gravity that keeps you here, the grave's black hole devouring
all with its silent meaninglessness. Your story and my story do
not have the same ending. They do not collapse into one. I'm not
an imposter playing myself. I'm still in my right mind, dammit,
and I know what's real. Don't send me your songs—or your
dreams.*

Stumbling and careening up the long slantwise tunnel behind
my flashlight's madly bobbing beam, feet tangling in power
cables leading to chambers where screens bled information
from space into space, I tripped and fell and surged to my feet
again, until brightness shone from around a corner and I found
myself plunging headlong into evening light. Snatching up my
backpack and gear from where I'd left them at the entrance, I
saw the sky above me shimmering—iridescent blues, salmon
pinks. Panting hard, I hastily averted my eyes, focusing my
attention on flat jungle green, afraid to look into the tall strange
chalice of that sky.

In the waning light I forded the flood that thundered away
to falls. I remembered when Luke and I were kids, there was a
stretch of woods not far from home that led down to the Little
Miami River. We'd called the woods "Monster." In that patch of
wildness there was a broad deep spot where two stream branches
flowed together, a place full of frogs and turtles and salaman-
ders and snakes. We'd called it the "Pool of Life." Further downstream there were waterfalls and, up another tributary, a cave
hole some kids had dug high in a sandy cliff a half mile from the
river. Making my way upward now through the drowned world
of jungle twilight, I wondered if that time we shared there in
those woods so long ago was what Luke had been trying to get
back to by coming here.

Finally I surged onto the plateau like a swimmer breaking
surface after a long dive. Wandering only a short exhausted
way through the maze, I shed my gear and radioed in to Garza
and the men. Something in my voice must have confirmed their
fears, and their words seemed smug, condescending.

Collapsing beneath a ledge, I do not know whether I slept or not. The air around me thundered and the earth shook, and through it all I heard the ghost people, singing and singing in the very rocks.

* * * * * * *

That last morning the hollow labyrinth on the tepui's crown was like a maze of inverted cave tunnels, or a brain and all its convolutions turned inside out by some topology-transforming supercomputer. After several hours of numbed walking, I strode free of it. It did not matter. No matter how empty and lost the world became, I was more so.

Garza and his men when I joined them were full of horrified tales of apparitions and earth tremors and streams of lightning leaping up from the highest stones. They were overjoyed at my return—and our leaving—and our descent from the tepui's top was swift, passing me in a blur. The weather cooperated, rains falling only lightly for a few hours, so that by mid-afternoon we had descended the bulk of the tepui's height. By evening we were on the lower ridge, making camp for the night, looking back at that mysterious height from which we had so recently descended.

The sun had just set when it happened. The earth shook with such violence that we were knocked from our feet and the forests below us seemed to toss like waves in a storm. The tremors calmed for a moment and, looking wildly around, I saw it: a great ring of dust about halfway up Caracamuni's height. The tremors gradually stopped and from where I lay sprawled on the ground, I saw something that to this day I can neither explain nor forget.

Caracamuni appeared to be growing taller. As its top continued to rise, though, I saw that it was not growing but separating, top half from bottom half, at that ring of thinning dust. In moments the top half had risen free of the dusty billows and a space of clear sky intervened between the sundered halves

of the ancient mountain.

* * * * * * *

As I got slowly to my feet, I realized Caracamuni was decoupling from the earth, rising smoothly as a mushroom in the night, drifting away like a ship slipping from harbor, heading toward open sea, open sky. Garza stood beside me, seeing it too, crossing himself and murmuring prayers he probably hadn't said since he was a boy. I grabbed my videocam and framed the scene in my viewfinder, but there it looked like trick photography, cinematic special effect. After a moment I stopped taping its ascent and just watched it with my own eyes.

Caracamuni had risen beyond the highest clouds when the sound hit us in a great wave that drove Garza's Pemón assistants to bury their clenched faces against the bosom of the earth. It was a fearful, prodigiously powerful sound—but one which I had heard before, more softly. It was the song of thought strengthened by stone uncountable times.

The sun shone full upon the ascending mountain, now clear of earth's curve, where we lay in darkness below. But the waterfall—the waterfall did not disappear in a long mist to earth. I puzzled over it, until I saw the way the light bent around the mountain, refracting in a great sphere like the shimmer of heat waves from asphalt, from desert and mirage, from the boundary of a soap bubble. Caracamuni was ascending in a bubble of force, its high waterfall plunging down only to spread out again in a broad swirl along the boundary's edge. As the cave's deep chamber had stood ensphered in the stone bubble of its mountain, so too the mountain itself now stood ensphered in the bubble of force.

From the mountain in its sphere a pale fire like inverted alpenglow began to shine, increasing in intensity until, in a brilliant burst of white light, the mountain disappeared, as silently and completely as a soap bubble bursting in a summer sky.

Only after the tremendous blast of thunder rolled over us,

distant and deep, did we hear the silent coda to the song.

* * * * * * *

Another obscure piece of rainforest real estate had disappeared. The seismologists and volcanologists interpreted our tale of the ascent of Caracamuni as an "anomalous volcanic eruption" and filed it away for future reference. My short tape of the tepui rising was written off as a video hoax. Fash's anthropologists and archeologists cancelled their expedition. The controversy over the arrival date for human beings in the New World continued unabated. The idea that a pocket of living fossil *Homo sapiens neanderthalensis* had survived into the present day on an isolated tepui in South America was dismissed out of hand. Those organizations that had granted or loaned Luke funds hassled our family for a time but eventually wrote off both Luke and his failed expedition under something called a "forgiveness clause." After my brief emergency leave to take care of family matters was completed, I was expected to go on with my life as if nothing had happened.

Nothing but flying mountains. Nothing but mushrooms from space. Nothing but incredibly ancient tribes and failed white messiahs gone native. Nothing but forty-odd aboriginal astronauts and a schizophrenic ethnobotanist as humanity's first personal ambassadors to the universe.

I know how crazy all that sounds. Still, in my study, I have a desk drawer filled with memories. Luke has been reduced to text. The only traces of him are lines of print and code—police reports, bills, receipts, and notes, all carefully filed away. The specific details of my brother Luke's life and death recede and fade and vanish, yet the emotions surrounding those memories grow always nearer and more powerful. I cannot resolve the paradox, so I live in it.

I try to fill the empty space with research. In the drawer there are also clippings and notes about quartz: fused from silicon and oxygen, the two most common elements to be found in the

crust of Earth and Earthlike planets; harder than steel, fashioned into weapons for the past fifty thousand years; beloved by ancient Sumerians and Egyptians, Bedouins and crusaders, Oriental craftsmen, electronics manufacturers, New Age spiritualists. I read the notes and sometimes wonder about the source of humanity's long romance with that rock.

Though it's certainly not my field, I read with interest the speculations that the indigenous Tasmanians, extinguished a few hundred years ago, had a Mousterian toolkit, had features that would later be described in terms of *neanderthalensis* and *soloensis*. I keep any notes and clippings I find about living fossils. Darwin coined that term for them—for the sole survivors, the small groups of plants and animals that are the last living representatives of ancient categories of life, creatures frozen in time, still resembling relatives that lived tens or hundreds of millions of years ago, even billions of years ago, as in the case of the stromatolites of Shark Bay. I read of gingkoes and nautiloids, horseshoe crabs and Lingula, coelacanths and cycads, dragonflies and scorpions and tuataras. Such creatures seem to me the undying memories in the mind of Life.

About mushrooms my resources are much sparser, but amongst them is an item that will never leave me. I found it in an envelope deep in my backpack after I emptied the pack on returning home: a carefully folded sheet of white paper, upon which can be seen a dusty blue image like the photo-negative of a brain—a spore print.

Whether the print was planted there while I was in the cave or during that long night on the tepui top, and by whom, I do not know. I only know that I cannot see fit to make public its existence—nor can I bring myself to destroy it, any more than I could destroy any of my information on Luke. Information, as he said, is everything. Even information held in the limbo of the lost.

At the thought of his death, I'm never able to cry—at least not while I'm awake. I have never cried for him, yet I am somehow always on the verge of tears. I tell myself it's all too deep for

tears, yet I fear the tears may be too deep for me—that, once I allow myself to cry, I'll never be able to stop, that it'll break down the dam I've built in my soul and overwhelm my small sanity in the flood of grief.

I do go on, but differently. I go on, each day another mushroom on the mycelium of time. My destiny has gone awry, like a Jesus who wakes up to find he's thirty-four and has somehow missed the crucifixion. Luke would understand about messiahs gone awry, I think.

I don't know if there's quite enough of me left over to cover up the hole in the universe Luke's going left behind. I have since returned to Caracamuni hoping to find a spot in space and time for mourning my loss, but the mountain I knew is gone, vanished. Space and time can't fill the void. I feel so full of emptiness. I do not know if I go on rushing into nothing, or if nothing goes on rushing into me. I do know, though, that all that stands against the dark tide is the memories, the bright shadows cast inside a stone bubble, by soft-tissued fossils which refuse to die.

THE HOLLOW
EARTHLINGS
1948: Game of Ant and Spider

"'Krakatoa comes from the Malay word *kelakatu*, meaning 'white-winged ant.' After Krakatoa erupted in 1883, however, the first macroscopic creatures to return to the devastated island were not ants but ballooning spiders'. Gentlemen, that statement is why I brought you here."

Admiral Cortright looked up from the folder on his desk. The three young men with their crew-cut hair and crisp uniforms—Logan Ladner, Chase Whitley, and Wyatt Bailey—glanced at each other, puzzled. Cortright smiled to himself. For a moment the three of them struck him as almost interchangeable, somehow—the best and the brightest of the officer cadre shaped and machined by the Second World War—but Cortright suspected this mission would test their mettle to the limit.

"Sir, I'm sure that's a fascinating bit of information," said Whitley, "but I don't quite see what it has to do with us."

"What it has to do with you and your compadres, Captain Whitley," said the Admiral, "also has to do with what the three of you examined in Roswell last year—and the fact that you were the only three Naval aviators granted that access. What you're here for today is part of the first top-secret case to be looked into by the United States Air Force Office of Special Investigations."

"I've never heard of such an office, sir," said Bailey.

"That's because it didn't formally exist until very recently, Commander. It's even newer than the creation of the Air Force as a separate service, though not by all that much."

The three aviators nodded. Each of them knew the old brown-shoe air force of the Army Air Corps was being revamped into the boys in blue, but the junior officers still had many questions.

"If this is an Air Force investigation, sir, why bring us into it?" asked Whitley.

"General Marsden, my opposite number at USAF-OSI, insisted we be involved," Admiral Cortright replied. "Our current best information concerns objects originating in the western Pacific. That's a big area to cover, and we're in the best position to cover it. Off the record, I can also say that Marsden is concerned by the fact that that the Air Force's top man in Japan is Curtis LeMay—a great wartime general, but perhaps not the best candidate for a minimum warfare operation."

Ladner, Whitley, and Bailey nodded. LeMay had a reputation for going big. B-29s and atomic bombs, however, might not always be the appropriate response to a perceived threat.

"But what do ants and spiders have to do with what we examined at Roswell, sir?" asked Ladner.

"Despite thorough examination by yourselves and others, Lieutenant Commander, many questions remain about those recovered materials. Externally, in the popular press, what you examined was rumored to be the wreckage of some sort of 'flying disc' or 'flying saucer.' We've been saying it was the wreckage of a weather balloon. Internally, and more quietly, we've put out the word that it's the wreckage of high altitude balloons used to eavesdrop on Soviet atomic bomb and ballistic missile testing—as part of the highly classsified Project Mogul effort. All of those stories have some truth to them. All of them are right, and all of them are wrong."

"Balloon *and* saucer?" asked Bailey.

The admiral nodded.

"What you examined are indeed the remains of a 'balloon', of a sort, but not one of ours, and not one of the Russians'. Not

one made by any nation on Earth, for that matter."

"From beyond the Earth, then?" Whitley asked skeptically.

"No, Captain. From *inside* the earth."

"I don't understand, sir," Ladner said.

"Any of you gentlemen ever hear of something called the 'Hollow Earth'?"

"I have, sir," said Bailey, sheepishly. "Product of a misspent youth."

The admiral smiled.

"What understanding of the concept did your 'misspent youth' leave you with, Commander?"

"Basically, the idea is that the Earth is in fact not solid, but hollow. Some fairly impressive people have believed in the notion: Edmund Halley, John Cleves Symmes, Jr., William Reed, Stanton A. Coblentz, among many others. The concept has largely been discredited. About the only places you'll find mention of it these days is in the same kind of pulp magazines where I first read about it, when I was a kid."

"Why discredited?" asked the Admiral.

"If the Earth were truly hollow, sir, then gravity wouldn't work the way it does. Neither would magnetism, presumably. Seismic waves from earthquakes wouldn't show the same profile they do, either."

"Discredited—yet not disproved."

"No, sir. We know less about the interior of the earth than we do about the surface of the moon. No one has drilled down far enough into it to fully prove—or disprove—any theory about the planet's interior. But the magnetic, gravitational, and seismic evidence are all against it."

"Yes. Which is why we now believe that any actual subterranean space is less like a 'hollow world' and more like the tunnels of a vast ant colony permeating sections of the Earth's crust. We also believe that the 'saucer-balloon' materials from the Roswell crash site, and the 'white-winged ants' of Krakatoa, are one and the same."

"I don't understand," said Whitley.

"And I'd better not be the one to explain it," said the admiral, thumbing a switch on his intercom. "Martha, please send in Professor Garberlein."

A moment later, the door to the General's office opened and a bespectacled man in a mortician's black suit and tie, with his hair combed back severely from his forehead, stepped into the office. Admiral Cortright rose to his feet, as did Bailey, Whitney, and Ladner.

"Gentlemen, let me introduce to you the man from whose report that ant-and-spider statement comes. This is Professor Paul Garberlein. During the war he was one of our top linguists and mathematical codebreakers at OSS. He's working for us on this project."

Garberlein shook hands perfunctorily with each of the three young men, then began to fiddle with setting up a stand and a slide projector. Admiral Cortright pressed a button that caused a projection screen to slowly descend from the ceiling.

"If you'd be so kind, Professor, as to explain to these gentlemen the discovery of the Trilith and your translation of its inscriptions, we'd be much obliged."

"Certainly. If you'll dim the lights...Yes, good. About the time of the events in Roswell, an unidentified but very powerful radio source began broadcasting some eighty miles west of the crash site. When searchers were able to triangulate on it, they found this object."

On the screen appeared something like a cross between a three-sided pyramid and a spear point. Each side of the pyramid seemed to be made of a different stony material—one side white, one black, one grey. A yardstick positioned nearby for scale showed the object's length to be approximately three feet.

"This object is what has been somewhat erroneously named the Trilith. This next slide is a close-up of the black side of the object. Note the arrays of bumps."

"Like something made by one of those braille-writing machines," Ladner suggested.

"Similar, yes—but it's a good deal more complex than that.

The sections separated by lines alternate between substitution and transposition ciphers. Not tremendously difficult for dedicated codebreakers to decipher, but to someone not already involved in codebreaking the bumps would appear to be no more meaningful than any purely aesthetic decoration. Mere decoration was, in fact, what these bumps were first thought to be. What you're looking at now is the side of the object for which we have the best translation of the object's inscriptions, at least so far."

"And it says—what?" asked Whitley

"Something very odd," said Garberlein, flashing up the text of the translation on the screen and reading it:

Inside your world's hollows dwells a race alien to your planet. They have been named Tuans by those of your species who have encountered them. They are descendants of criminal psychopaths exiled from a dozen homeworlds. We are the Warders who exiled them to the prison we constructed inside your world.

We, the Tuans, and you are all seeds born of the same cosmic ancestry. The imprisoned Tuans are very similar, genetically, both to us and to yourselves.

We hoped the prisoners' offspring might not suffer from the predispositions of their parents and, if that proved to be the case, that they might someday be allowed to colonize the surface.

We also very much doubted, however, that these incurably narcissistic and destructive individuals could ever make common cause and establish social order among themselves. Such pariahs,we reasoned, would be more likely to attack each other endlessly and viciously, descend into barbarism, and die out, long before their offspring could prove or not prove to be substantially different from their forebears. So we thought.

We blasted an entrance and an extensive network of tunnels into the depths of your world at a place you call Toba. This act of excavation produced a vast volcanic eruption as one of its secondary effects. Inside the great warren of tunnels thus

created we imprisoned the ancestors of those whom some among you would later call Tuans.

Our initial survey of your world failed to note your own existence. As the prison project began, however, we became aware that there were already on your world several smallish populations of autochtonous sapient species with rudimentary tools. Among them was also your kind—Founder genestock like ourselves—who, as a sort of experiment, seemed to have been planted on your world, despite its already possessing indigenous protosapients.

By the time we discovered your existence, you were already engaged in eliminating all other sapient species in your world, either through interbreeding, resource competition, or outright violence.

Despite your success against the other sapients of your world, the Founder experiment was nonetheless failing. Our best estimates indicated that, after destroying your local competitors, you would yourselves become extinct within seven thousand of your years—with or without the impact of the worldwide winter that would result from our excavating the tunnel system and completing prison construction.

Our hastening of your demise was something we lamented as a most unfortunate consequence of our efforts, but at least your extinction would mean that, should any of the prisoners manage to escape, we would not have to concern ourselves with the possibility that Tuan criminals might interbreed with your kind.

Although your species very nearly died out during our excavation and construction work, and in fact genetically drifted from its previous makeup because its numbers were so extremely reduced, you did not become extinct. We also didn't foresee that, long before the prisoners could kill each other off, a spontaneous mutation arose among them, an alteration in the structure of what you call the pineal gland or "third eye."

Those who possessed the mutation were not only increasingly neotenized—retaining several of the pineal functions of

childhood—but also developed biomagnetic sensitivity in their pineals which, like those in some of your world's migratory birds, allowed the prisoners to orient themselves to your planet's magnetic field.

In their underground prison world, such an orientation capability seems to have conferred a strong survival advantage. The mutation for altered pineals spread with astonishing rapidity throughout the prison population. Within a relatively few generations, all the descendants of the original criminals possessed the change.

The alteration didn't stop there. The Tuans' biomagnetically-orienting pineals went on to become the basis for a new sense through which every Tuan possesses, in his or her head, the equivalent of what you would define as a hyperbolic VLF radio-navigation transmitter/receiver, operating in a spectrum from 10 to 14 kilocycles. The Tuans are thus not only able to communicate with and triangulate on each other almost instantaneously over vast distances but, more importantly, this change has enabled them to develop a group mind.

A small percentage of Tuans, however, did not become part of that hive consciousness. In them, the pineal mutation allowed not for radio-facilitated group-mindedness but for the deeper empathy you misname telepathy.

As a result, the Tuans have split into two variants, the Instinctives and the Creatives. The hive consciousness of the Instinctives has allowed them to channel their destructive narcissism away from each other and toward anyone and anything that doesn't share in their group mind. Inside their hive-mind, nothing is forgotten. The memories of one are the memories of all; the memories of all are the memories of one.

The Tuan Creatives have neither the access to, nor the burden of, vast instant species memory. The hive-mind memory of the Instinctives is the amber in which they are both socially preserved—and trapped. The Creatives, in contrast, have retained far more of that older individual consciousness and innovating imagination which the Tuan Instinctives have long

since lost.

The hive-mindedness of the Instinctives has, however, allowed them to find common ground and create a common hated enemy. At first that enemy was us, the Warders, whose satellites continue to invisibly orbit above your world and monitor all that happens there. Over time, the Instinctives' hatred focused on the Creative minority already in their midst. The Instinctives persecuted the Creatives nearly to the point of extinction.

From examination of your genetic material, we estimate that some six hundred Creatives managed to escape to the surface at a time when populations of your own species were critically small. On your world's surface, the Creatives apparently made contact and successfully interbred with your kind—a species which has since gone on to develop civilizations of its own.

The Tuan Instinctives' hatred has continued to fester and grow until everyone and everything aboveground now comes within its scope—including yourselves.

Remembering old knowledge of geology, metallurgy, and engineering, the Instinctives have again and again built great lighter-than-air flying machines, which have periodically burst from fissures at several places throughout your world, most prominently at the place you call Krakatoa.

Our satellites, detecting the presence of Tuan technology, have destroyed their escape sites and lighter-than-air flying machines again and again. These assaults have had repeated volcanic consequences—among them the eruption chronicled in the Javanese Book of Kings for your year 535, and in your year 1883, chronicled in many other of your records.

Aware that you have developed higher technologies, however, we have of late ordered our satellites to refrain from hunting and destroying. With your recent development and use of atomic weaponry, the situation has become still more complex.

The Tuan Instinctives remain implacably committed to conquering your upper world and eradicating all who dwell there. They desperately seek to capture and "turn" humans and

their technologies. The Instinctives hope to use those technolo-
gies to destroy our sentient machines watching in your skies.
Doing so, they believe, will allow them to escape their long
imprisonment and spread again into the greater universe.

We suspect that, in very small numbers, the Tuan Instinctives
have long infiltrated your upper world and influenced your
history. Our watchers in orbit—both unsleeping machines
and three sleeping Warders—find it increasingly difficult to
distinguish between Tuan and Terran technologies. Whether
that difficulty in distinguishing between the two technological
complexes arises from the Tuan Creative contribution to your
lineage, or perhaps from the ongoing small-scale intervention
of Tuan Instinctives in your history as well, we cannot say.

Your recent worldwide war has provided cover for the activi-
ties of the Tuan Instinctives. Our scenarios all suggest that they
have rebuilt their underground bases and await enough world
disorder to cover their re-emergence. We can circumvent the
lightspeed limit in our communications and in our monitoring
of your planet, but we dwell too distant from your world to
intervene physically in any timely fashion in your affairs. Be
vigilant!

"It's a hoax, isn't it?" Whitley asked.

"That was my first inclination too," said Garberlein. "The more I thought about it, though, the more the relative ease of the decipherment and the 'hoaxy' feel of it struck me. I now believe that the 'feel' of their message arises from their attempt to convey some sense of the real story to us, in ways and in forms we can understand at our current stage of development. You wouldn't expect a six year old to understand James Joyce's *Ulysses*, after all."

"You've got to take people where they already are," the Admiral said with a nod, "before you can take them where you want them to go. Fifty or sixty years from now, the story would probably be told differently, to a different world."

"Exactly. What made me consider the possibility that it all

might be real was ultimately the hard, cold, physical fact of the Trilith. As I said, it's misnamed. It's not actually made of stone at all. One face of it is made of a form of carbon never before seen. Another face is actually a previously undiscovered ceramic compound—one with some very interesting electrical properties. The last face is a metallic alloy, again previously unknown to science."

"Wait a minute," Ladner said. "Are you suggesting that what we examined in New Mexico is the remains of some kind of zeppelin built by these underworlders?"

"That's right."

"And you believe the hole in the ground it came out of might be located somewhere in the western Pacific?" Bailey asked.

"That's correct."

"And travelled undetected all the way to the American Southwest, before some kind of skywatcher machine shot it down?" Whitley asked, unable to keep the skepticism out of his voice.

"And that skywatcher machine left this Trilith as a calling card?" Ladner suggested.

"Yes," Garberlein replied calmly. "I know it sounds like riddles wraped in enigmas, but the very difficulty of such unde-tected travel seems to be yet another proof that we're dealing with things not created by any known human culture. The three of you have examined the material recovered from the Roswell crash site. You may already be aware that the material recov-ered there is extremely radar absorbent. It produces almost no detectable signature in the infrared, either."

"But such an airship would still show up in broad daylight," said Bailey.

"Perhaps not as it actually appears. Members of our team think the shiny material found at the Roswell crash site might function like a sort of television-skin camouflage. Viewed from below, this electronic skin would match the colors and features of the sky. Viewed from above, it would match the colors and features of the ground."

"There's a precedent for that?"

"Many of them, in the natural world. The bellies of many fish are pale-colored, to help them blend in with the light color of the ocean's surface when viewed from below. The backs of those same fish are dark colored to help them blend in with the color of the depths of the sea, when viewed from above. Think of this skin as something capable of responding to altered surroundings the way a chameleon does, only much faster."

"Okay," said Bailey. "I think I see where you got the ant reference the General spoke about. Malay natives, spotting these Tuan lighter-than-air craft, swarming up near what's now called Krakatoa?"

"Yes. Presumably they described the Tuan craft in terms of something already familiar in their environment, which they thought those craft looked like: white-winged ants."

"But what about the ballooning-spiders stuff?"

"That's related to something we've translated from another face of the Trilith. Of course, it's always possible that, with our talk of television chameleon skin camouflage and ballooning spiders, we are actually no closer to what we're trying to describe than the Malays were, with their white winged ants. Like them, we can only describe the unfamiliar in terms of the familiar."

"Ballooning spiders are not something I'm all that familiar with," said Whitley. "What exactly are they?"

"Ballooning spiders are the highest flying animals other than humans. They use long silken lines to loft themselves into breezes all over our world. A dragline that's long enough will function as a sort of one-dimensional sail or parachute. Instead of having to unfold, it simply unreels—a much easier operation, geometrically."

"But what does that have to do with the whole history you've already given us?" asked Ladner.

"The ciphertext we've managed to translate from the grey face of the Trilith suggests that the skywatchers who made the Trilith are also capable of making superlong, superstrong fibers,

rather like an artificial spidersilk, only far stronger, The grey face suggests those fibers have been used to steer even a comet, by catching all of the pressure of light and other radiation from the sun or any star."

"Is that possible?"

Garberlein shrugged.

"Archimedes once said that, given a lever long enough and a place to stand, he could move the earth. Make such a gossamer 'lever' sufficiently long and I suppose one might not even need a place to stand."

"Gossamer?"

"Yes. If our translation's at all accurate, it suggests that these 'cables'—each about the thickness of a human hair, but many thousands of miles long—can be grown from the stuff of a comet's head. At the very least it makes a new sort of sense from the old meaning of comet as 'hairy star'."

"What's the inscription say on the third face of this Trilith?" Whitley asked.

"Ah yes. The white face. That's the one we've had least luck translating, so far. What we *can* make of it is that whoever or whatever sent us the Trilith message seems to at last have gotten quite good at running scenarios concerning our world. Wisdom is a long base-line, I suppose. At any rate, the message on the third face seems to underline the 'vigilance' theme we translated from the black face of the object."

"Even if all that is true," said Whitley, "why here? Why now?"

"We're not sure. Within the last few years we have detonated the first atomic weapons, as the translation on the black face of the trilith notes. We stand poised at the edge of space. More immediately, the world situation has changed a good deal in the fourteen months, since the event at Roswell—perhaps enough to merit the idea that we have entered a period of increased political instability worldwide."

"We've put together a timeline," said Admiral Cortright. "Just since the beginning of the year, we've had British Foreign

Secretary Bevin propose the formation of a union of Western countries to stand up to the Soviet Union. Indian independence leader Mahatma Gandhi has been assassinated by Nathuram Godse. The Soviet Union has begun to jam Voice of America broadcasts. The Communist Party has seized control of Czechoslovakia. B-29 Superfortresses have undergone aerial refueling tests, extending the range of our strategic bombers. We've seen the establishment of the State of Israel, and the Declaration of a State of Emergency in Malaysia, in response to the Communist insurgency. The Berlin Airlift is underway. A major earthquake has hit Fukui, Japan, killing 3895...."

"A quake possibly opening the door from the lower to the upper worlds," Garberlein added, "if our translation of the white face of the stone is correct."

"But what are we supposed to do about it?" Whitley asked.

"That's what we want you to find out," the Admiral said "The three of you depart for Fukui, Japan in the morning, then to Carrier *USS Antietam*, CV-36. Some final modifications to the aircraft you'll be using are still being made. You'll be briefed on our most recent Malaysian findings on your way."

* * * * * * *

"I'm still not clear about this," Ladner said on their comm channel as he piloted Blackbeard Three, his Vought F6U Pirate, over the Sea of Japan. "These Warders travel through space like ballooning spiders, but ballooning spiders don't travel by balloon?"

"Right," said Bailey, at the controls of Blackbeard Two, his own specially modified Pirate prototype. "They use strands to keep them from getting stranded...."

"And these Instinctives who live underground are the source of the Malays' 'white winged ants'," said Whitley, enjoying the feel of piloting Blackbeard One which, like the other two Pirates, had been outfitted with a Westinghouse J34-WE-30 afterburning engine, the first US Navy fighters with such a

power plant. "Only what the natives saw weren't white wings, but things more like balloons!"

"No wonder I'm confused. Well, at least these Pirates are fun to fly.

"Yeah—even with these wingtip fuel tanks slowing us down."

"Time to cut back on the chatter," said Whitley as they flew into the evening light. "We're coming up on the coordinates Garberlein gave us."

"Where the 'lights under the ocean' have been reported?" Bailey asked.

"Ever since the Fukui quake," Whitley replied. "At least according to the professor. Blackbeard Two, I'm as skeptical as you are, but we need to look sharp anyway."

As they went into a search pattern of concentric circles, they looked sharply but saw nothing. During their briefings on the way to Japan and aboard the *Antietam*, they learned that several carriers had been positioned in the western Pacific in response to the findings of Garberlein's group. The cover story was that they were all engaged in searching for a Nazi sub which appeared to have sunk while carrying top-secret material to Japan in the waning days of the Second World War. There was precedent for that, since the Germans had sent at least two submarines carrying jet aircraft prototypes and atomic material to Japan during those last days.

Anomalies associated with the Fukui event soon brought the *Antietam* into the area, as well as three submarines positioned at what was presumed to be a safe distance, though safe from what wasn't entirely clear. Long-range carrier-based F4U Corsairs conducted photo-reconnaissance missions over the Sea of Japan at fifteen to twenty thousand feet. The "lights" had been detected when, viewing the photo-recon runs, photo interpreters aboard ship spotted what appeared to be bright spots beneath the ocean's surface.

Once the undersea lights were confirmed, the fleet moved to stand-by positions—ready reserve, on the off-chance that

things might go wrong in the worst way. One target-location sub was kept within fifty miles, but that wouldn't be much help to the pilots in their Pirates, once they were committed.

Whitley, Bailey, and Ladner knew their job was to locate the anomalous lights, determine their source, and destroy that source if it went airborne and proved hostile—and to do it all in greatest secrecy. Both to prevent the loss of scientifically valuable material and to avoid the creation of a Roswell of the Far East, the fleet would collect all flotsam from any action, including the remains of the pilots and their downed or obliterated aircraft, if it came to that.

All three of them were keenly aware, too, that all they had in the way of weapons against the unknown were their skills as pilots, a 4 x 20 mm M3 cannon mounted under each jet's nose—and one section of the Trilith per plane too, also in under-nose mount, but recessed more toward the cockpit.

"If we're close to our targets, shouldn't my chunk of the Trilith start to glow, or something?" Bailey asked.

"You've got me there," said Whitley. "All I know is that something from the Malaysian reports helped Garberlein's people finish more of their translating—enough to figure out how to pop the thing into three separate pieces."

"What are those sections supposed to do, though?" asked Ladner.

"That I don't know, but the Professor and the Admiral insisted we each get one face of the thing. They must do something—otherwise, why go to the trouble of mounting them to our aircraft?"

"Right," said Bailey. "Or to sealing the butt of each section into the cockpit of the aircraft around it. Seems like a lot of work for nothing, if you ask me."

"Chatter again, Pirates. Let's stay focused."

The sun was nearly down when Whitley noticed something very much out of the ordinary.

"This is Blackbeard One. I don't believe it, but I think I just saw a flash over here. And not from my piece of the Trilith

spear-thing, either."

"A flash?" asked Ladner. "From under the water?"

"I think so, Blackbeard Three. Here are the coordinates."

Ladner and Bailey joined Whitley in a tightening spiral above the undersea flash point. As they watched, the flashes increased in number and intensity until the ocean bubbled and roiled into maelstrom. A moment later the sea below them assumed the shape of a vortex. Out of the heart of that vortex, oddly shaped craft soon began to rise.

Ladner thought that the fat, horizontal discs of the crafts' lifting surfaces might indeed have passed for white-winged ants, at least from a distance. Bailey was reminded that the first unidentified flying objects reported in the nineteenth century were thought to be cigar-shaped dirigibles. Whitley, however, simply couldn't believe what his eyes were showing him.

"Blackbeard One, shouldn't we maybe try to contact them?" Ladner suggested. "See if they might be friendlies?"

Before either of his comrades could answer, bolts of light like tracer bullets began arcing toward them.

"So much for that," Ladner muttered.

"Evasive action," said Whitley. "Return fire."

They peeled away from each other and dove toward the disk-balloons rising swiftly out of the vortex.

"One rising on your left, Logan! Eight o'clock low!" Bailey said.

"I see it," Ladner said. His Pirate rained down lead at the disk from his M3 cannon—to no apparent effect.

"Hitting the lifting surface is no good!"

"Go in close," Whitley said. "Look for an undercarriage, some place where pilot or crew might be, and target that."

"Roger."

In a moment Ladner was joined by Bailey and together they dove toward the underside of the nearest disk balloon. The lightning bolt tracers danced up around them. Bailey felt a jolt.

"I'm hit! Not too serious, I think. Melted the top of the tail boom a bit."

"Roger that, Blackbeard Two," said Ladner. "Looks like they're shooting molten metal at us."

Ladner and Bailey spotted the small undercarriage of the craft and dove toward it, guns thumping. They came in close enough to see their opponents—pale red-pink, hairless, a barred horizontal headpiece covering that part of their faces where their eyes should have been. There was something both vulnerable and malign about them, at once beautiful and horrific—and recognizably human—before the undercarriage bubble smeared over completely with bursts of red.

"Got 'em!" said Ladner. "They bleed standard-issue, anyway."

In his Pirate, through the thicket of bright molten slabs slamming his way, Whitley was boring in toward his own target.

"A kill!" he said, static crackling over his voice. "Wait! They're trying to jam our communications. Go to channel three."

Ladner watched as the motion of the first disk balloon he and Bailey had hit began to drift and become erratic before dropping toward the sea.

"It's working! They have to be actively controlling the lift—especially if we hit the lift-surface first!"

For a brief while they had it down to a system: lay in a few dozen rounds across the disk of the lifting surface, then dive under and go in for the kill at the undercarriage. Soon, however, the sheer number of alien craft began to overwhelm them. The thickets of barred molten light grew denser and denser.

"Too many! Too many!" said Whitley. "Break off—ascend five thousand and regroup."

As they began to climb, voices suddenly said "No!" into each of their heads. They were all plunged into the same dream—a thick fast outpouring of information flooding into their minds—sent by the same Sleepers. Each Sleeper (they felt as much as saw) dreamed away inside an ice-cave thawed into an "iceteroid"—one or another of the relatively few cometary bodies found in the main asteroid belt.

The information flooding into the pilots' heads informed

them that, through the use of gossamer sunstreamers, robotically grown from the stuff of the cometary nuclei themselves, the sleeping Warders had long ago repositioned the iceteroids to near-translunar orbit. There they slept away the ages in a deep freeze of their own. In turn, the frozen thickness of the icy dirtball (or dirty ice ball) completely protected them against the cancer-inducing cosmic ray bombardment that would have otherwise killed them early on.

Whitley, Ladner, and Bailey felt and understood all of that in a flash. Stranger still, they knew—without knowing how they knew—that the release of the Tuan-made lighter-than-air gas from their damaged craft had alerted the Warders' satellite monitoring systems.

Strangest of all, in an instant each of the three pilots also felt how he should use his piece of the Trilith—as if the knowledge had been dropped directly into his head.

As one, they turned back toward the myriad disk-balloon craft now columning up out of the watery vortex. The Sleepers seemed almost to be dreaming *through* the three of them. Whitley, Bailey, and Ladner each placed a hand on the cockpit-end of their particular trilith piece, in the patterns they saw in their dream-visions. A protective shield of force sprang out at the nose and swirled completely around each of their jet fighters.

Fierce and brilliant—but harmless—the slabs of molten metal fired at them splashed against their shields as their jets screamed into the midst of their foes. The only harm the winged-ant craft could do was block the pilots' radio transmissions among themselves. An odd silence prevailed among the three pilots as they made their way through the enemy, toward locations they understood already, as if remembered from a dream.

Or as if, for a brief moment, Bailey, Whitley, and Ladner thought in each other's heads, as the sleeping Warders had dreamed in theirs.

In their jets, the three screamed through the swarm of ant-craft, toward the surface of the ocean. They swung far out from the center of the battle, then turned, each separated by one

hundred twenty degrees of arc from his comrades. Flying just above wave-top height, they flew toward the vortex that had opened in the sea's surface.

On his piece of the trilith, each of them placed his hand in a new pattern.

From the black trilith section in Bailey's jet fighter sprang a red beam of fire-bright light. From the white trilith section in Ladner's fighter sprang a beam of ice-blue radiance. From the grey trilith section in Whitley's fighter sprang a beam of light green as a backlit leaf of early Spring. Where the beams met, an explosion of white light burst like a column of vast lightning above the sea.

In an instant, all the disk-balloon ant craft were destroyed. The roiling of the vortex in the sea slowed and came to a stop. As Ladner, Whitley, and Bailey turned their aircraft away from the sunset—toward the *Antietam*, the western coast of Japan, and the devastated city of Fukui—the sea grew calm beneath them.

Above that placid sea and beneath the early stars, the three exhausted pilots watched as three points of light fell toward them from the sky like slow-motion shooting stars. The points of light fell unerringly in their direction, one toward each craft.

At last each point resolved itself into a figure surrounded by countless gossamer streamers lofting and drifting, a human form divine cradled in evanescent bright wings against the deepening twilight.

The sleeping Warders had awakened. One wakened Warder stood before each of the jet fighters, only a few feet in front of each pilot, staring each man hard in the eye. The Warders stood before the nose of each jet as if hovering motionless, though all were moving at hundreds of miles per hour. A neat trick, Ladner, Whitley, and Bailey would later agree—but only after each of their Warders vanished like the wind back into the night.

* * * * * * *

"And you remember nothing else about how to activate the Trilith section?" Professor Garberlein asked, yet again, as part of another debriefing that was anything but brief.

"Gentlemen, I urge you to do everything you can to recall," Admiral Cortright said. "I'm sure you must realize how frustrating it is for all of us that you three have operated a weapon of tremendous power, but now have no idea how you did so. Think of how valuable such information might be, in our competition with the Soviets."

"I'm sorry, sir," Whitley said, "but I just can't remember. It's like that memory's been completely erased."

Ladner and Bailey shook their heads in sad agreement.

"Maybe we can only do it with the Warders' help," Bailey suggested. "Any idea where they might have disappeared to?"

"Your description of their icy 'homes' suggested a possibility," Garberlein said. "We checked back through photographic plates and astronomical observations for that night and the days and nights immediately following. There is some indication that three celestial objects left the Earth's orbit that night. Where they might be headed—the asteroid belt, or cometary clouds, or belts further out in the solar system—we cannot say."

"About all of this, too, you must remain silent," the General said, "The F6U Pirates you flew will be mothballed, and the program that created them will itself be cancelled within two years. The *Antietam* will be deactivated shortly. The Air Force has demanded that all flotsam recovered by our submarines and surface ships be sent to Wright-Patterson. That material is already on its way, labeled 'high-altitude weather balloon debris' to confound the curious. This episode—the history of the Warders, of the hollow earthlings both Instinctives and Creatives, and of everything you experienced—all must remain shrouded by utmost secrecy."

"Absolutely," said Garberlein. "I don't doubt it will someday weigh upon you as heavily as the albatross about the neck of the Ancient Mariner, but you must never reveal what happened. It simply raises too many questions."

Whitley looked at his two comrades.

"Agreed. No one would believe us anyway."

By the time Cortright and Garberlein at last released them, the day was nearly through.

"So, we're supposed to consign it all to oblivion," Whitley said, as they walked across the grounds of an airbase that wasn't supposed to exist—but which pilots had already begun referring to as Dreamland.

"Easier said than done," Ladner said with a nod.

"True," Bailey said, looking up into the evening sky, "but I don't think those folks above the air or below the ground will forget us. And I don't think this is the last we'll hear from them, either."

STAGES OF NIGHT AND TWILIGHT

Momentarily disoriented, Martin stared at the holes in the metal plate for Lalande 21185, tonight's target star. Had he come back too soon? Believing that work would take his mind off what had happened, Martin Merrill had eagerly returned to his research at the Allegheny Observatory. Now, however, he wondered if he hadn't been *too* eager.

All day long he had felt out of phase and out of focus. From the moment his alarm clock went off that morning, the world had played on him like two radio stations of widely different formats interfering with each other on the same broadcasting frequency and switching unpredictably back and forth between them.

Shaking his head and smiling crookedly, Martin tried to think only of well-behaved quanta as he plugged the last of the fiber-optic leads into the pre-drilled holes of the Lalande plate. Finished, he let his gaze drift upward, along the barrel of the Thaw Memorial Telescope. The Thaw's thirty-inch lens and its focal length of 561 inches gave it an overall f-number of about nineteen—ample enough for gathering the photons which the fiber-optic leads piped to MAPS, the Multichannel Astrometric Photometer and Spectrometer.

As his gaze continued upward, Martin's crooked smile broadened. An awful lot of equipment, just to discern a tiny wobble in one of innumerable stars. Wobbles, phases, and shifts—proofs of the invisible tugging at the visible—were what it was all about

in the search for extra-solar planets, or ESPs, as some of his less sympathetic colleagues called them. Lalande 21185 apparently wobbled in tune to not one but two invisible objects of near-Jovian mass. At only eight light years out, tonight's target was right in the neighborhood, too.

Above him, beyond the end of the telescope, the bent blue monolith of twilight sky shone down through the open-shuttered observatory dome. Soon, the Earth would spin the observatory down the stages of twilight and that bright-dark rectangle above him would fill with stars. Tonight, however, the tall rectangular slit seemed at once two, three, and n-dimensional—as if, in the bend of that plank of twilight, he saw the curvature of spacetime itself. Rationally he knew that bend to be merely the product of the observatory dome's own curvature, but twilight was always a good time for illusions.

Another of his favorite romanticisms (as he preferred to call such twilight illusions) was that the Thaw telescope, which had gathered first light in August of 1914, partook somehow of the character of those other guns of that August, those whose voices had signalled the start of the First World War. The Thaw resembled, for him, a cannon of particularly large bore and length—a howitzer pointed at the heavens, trained upon its celestial target. Sometimes he mused that, just as the sound of the cannonball or shell, moving as a coherent wave, always paradoxically arrives at the target zone in reverse order, before the order to "Fire!", so too at twilight it seemed to him that the role of the big telescope was also reversed: Rather than gathering light, it was instead a cannon, firing stars into the heavens like single photons in classic light-slit experiments, each visible photon interfered with by its counterparts in invisible and innumerable parallel universes...

"Martin," his red-headed colleague Joy Turnshek called over the loudspeaker, laughing from the control booth, "you're spacing out again!"

"I know, I know," Martin said, returning his gaze to the floor of the dome, glancing away in embarassment. "Time to take a

break. Everything's hooked up and on line. I'll be back in an hour or so."

"No rush," Joy said. "It probably won't be dark enough for good observations until then. Catch you later."

"Use a big net," Martin said, barking a short laugh as he saw Joy grimace at his small joke. A genuine grimace, which was good to see. After what had happened, everyone had been acting quite tender toward his time and feelings. Martin appreciated their concern, but sometimes he felt as if he were being swaddled in cotton candy.

He made his way up and down steps. As he walked the Observatory's too-familiar maze of stairs and corridors, Martin's thoughts darkened. "Civil twilight"—the formal name for this time of evening—took on a forbidding resonance: the twilight of citizens and cities and nations, things falling apart in an apocalyptic epoch of collapse and ruin. He shivered, though the evening was warm enough.

Without quite knowing how he got there, Martin found himself standing behind the glass doors of the Observatory's main entrance. Etched in the glass of both doors was "AO," for Allegheny Observatory—letters delicately linked, like a gracefully Classical preconfiguration of the much later and cruder Anarchy symbol.

Turning away from the doors, Martin shook his head, thinking that maybe he was not yet ready to face what had happened. Perhaps he did need to be swathed about in sentimental cotton candy and romantic moonbeams, at least a while longer. The Observatory was perfect for that. Built in 1901, it was a sublime confection of late Classical astronomy, right down to the spiraling ram's horn Ionic capitals of its false pillars. Beneath its three-domed, three-telescoped roof, the building seemed at least as much a temple as an institution of science—an effect not lessened by the heavy use of marble and rich cherry wood throughout its interior public spaces.

Walking slowly away from the marble and cherry environs, Martin let his wandering steps lead him groundward, spiraling

down and around the cold, whitewashed-brick drum of the Keeler telescope's support pier. Inside the Keeler's pier was the *sanctum sanctorum* of this temple to the heavens: a small, windowless, low-domed white chamber with strange acoustics.

The crypt.

When Martin had first learned of the chamber's existence, he had been more than a little surprised. A crypt was not something that he usually associated with an observatory, but here it was—death at the heart of the search through the stars, mortality the dark core of astronomy's bright quest. Looking about him, he read on the walls the inscriptions naming the astronomers and benefactors of the Allegheny Observatory who were buried here: John and Phoebe Brashear, and the Keelers, both father and son.

Martin shivered again, and not just because the chamber was the coldest place in the observatory. Yet, in this room cut off from all access to sunlight, moonlight, or star shine—where the only light that could shine would be either artificial or divine— there was also a strange solace. The oddly comforting aspect of the crypt lay in its sole memorial inscription that went beyond names and dates, the quote on the Brashears' plaque which had apparently been taken from a poem:

We have loved the stars too fondly
To be fearful of the night.

After seeing that quote this morning, Martin had returned to it in his mind throughout the day. He even sent an e-mail query to Art Glaser, the Observatory historian, seeking a source for those lines. Until he heard back from Art, however, he could only speculate on the context out of which those lines had come—and why they should so resonate with him today.

He slid down the cool white wall opposite the inscription until he sat on the floor looking up at it. Martin read the quote again, and thought of his father's recent death.

* * * * * * *

On an achingly beautiful Spring day he drove through the western Alleghenies, across the tip of West Virginia at Wheeling, then through rolling Ohio farm country. Near Columbus the landscape leveled out, where thousands of years earlier enormous glaciers had scraped the countryside flat from here to the Arctic. Martin turned south then, past the old glacier's terminal moraine, into the hilly landscape of the Ohio Valley.

Driving through the outskirts of the city, it seemed to him that Cincinnati had been transformed into one gigantic flower show. In the green-gold woods, redbud trees fountained pink hallucinations to the heavens. Dogwoods blossomed in snowstorms suspended motionless above the ground, each tree holding its whorled blooming self with a grace so thoughtlessly perfect any Zen mystic or Chinese landscape painter might envy it. The lilac- and wisteria-scented air was a drug, beneath a sky more blissful blue than an opium addict's dreams. In the yards innumerable tulips burst like low, slow fireworks.

The world growing and renewing itself all around him. And his father was dying. *April, the cruelest month*, Martin thought.

His mother had not changed much in appearance since he'd seen her the previous summer. Perhaps a bit more silver among the gold, but still shockingly blonde for a woman of seventy. Her demeanor, however, had changed markedly. Her husband's sudden illness had shaken her with a sense of impending loss too deep to measure, a great quake beneath an unfathomable sea of grief, upon which shock and bewilderment moved now like tidal waves that had not yet reached the shallows.

With his mother, Martin made his way to the hospital room his father shared with another dying man. Nothing his mother and brother had said could prepare him for the decline he saw in his father's condition. It wasn't the IV dripping into his father's arm, or the oxygen tube running to his nose across his face, or the whiteness of his hair, or the way he lay motionless on the bed, curled in almost fetal position. No, not even that. It was the haziness in his father's eyes that struck him most.

Martin tried to make small talk. Since his father was groggy

and could not respond well verbally, even such minimal conversation proved to be a challenge. Martin talked about his research with Lalande at the Observatory. About his recent long but unsuccessful sojourn in England, trying to get the British and Commonwealth scientists to use their outmoded telescopes in the search for ESPs. About returning in nautical twilight up the Thames to London from the Royal Observatory in Greenwich. About seeing *Hamlet* and Frayn's *Copenhagen* and the British Museum. As he spoke, it seemed to him that the father he had known—the gentle, open-hearted man with a childlike curiosity about everything—was already far away.

Almost in desperation, Martin described working with the Thaw telescope. He talked about the bent blue monolith of twilight sky shining down into the dome, darkening and slowly filling with stars like bright grains of sand falling upward in a movie of an hourglass run backwards. His father's former smile and the ready twinkle in his eyes, however, seemed more lost and distant now than the stars and invisible planets Martin was trying to tell him about. He wondered if his father understood anything he was saying.

Martin took his mother, his brother Derek, his sister-in-law Rena and their two-year-old daughter Lauren out to dinner. Having the little girl there was good for all of them, especially his mother. The two-year-old almost kept their minds off the man dying in a hospital room a few miles away. Thinking of Gertrude's words to Hamlet—"Thou know'st 'tis common: all that lives must die, passing through nature to eternity"—Martin at last understood Hamlet's irritation at the "commonness" of it. Watching his little niece, it occured to Martin that neither the common miracle of birth nor the common catastrophe of death was rendered any less catastrophic or miraculous by how commonly each occurred.

After dinner, Martin returned to the hospital with his mother. Derek soon joined them. His father seemed slightly more alert, or at least more responsive to Derek's approach, which involved direct questions spoken in a clear, loud voice—Is there anything

you want? Are you in any pain?

The three of them were eventually able to put together, from his father's grunted sounds in response to the first question, that he wanted "pear juice" and "vanilla ice cream." He even made them laugh when they had so much trouble understanding his way of saying "water" that he began spelling it out—"W-A-T...."

When they had given him the water he wanted from a child's sippy cup, his father grunted out a sound that Martin's mother and brother translated as "Flag it," a Korean War-era phrase they said his father used when he wanted to say he was finished with something. To the question of whether he was in pain, however, Martin's father could only nod his head slightly. Derek called in a nurse and saw to it that Dad would be given more pain killers.

On the drive home, Martin's mother disillusioned him as to the course of his father's stroke therapy. In contrast to what Martin had envisioned while away in England—the image of his father sweating on treadmills and exercise tables—Dad had in fact been so weak that he'd been essentially bedridden for the last five weeks.

"I should have known something was wrong," his mother said as they pulled into the driveway. "His appetite kept declining. He stopped eating almost two weeks ago. He hasn't laughed or smiled once since his first big stroke, and you know how unlike Dad that is. The nurses kept commenting on how his stomach was distended, but he was always a big man, that way. The doctors said the X-rays were clear, until that last doctor, the Pakistani woman at Good Samaritan Hospital—she ordered the CT scan. That's when they found the cancer."

"No way you could have known, Mom," Martin told her before he went to bed. "No way anyone could have known about the cancer. Even the doctors didn't know—and he was hospitalized for over a month before they found it."

That night, Martin dreamed a strange dream. He and his mother were on either side of his father's hospital bed. That hospital tableau gradually overlaid itself on computer simulations of Lalande 21185 that Martin remembered from the obser-

vatory. His father's face became Lalande, Martin himself and his mother the star's hypothesized dark companions in orbit around it.

The scene shifted again: his father was orbited and encircled by the dark invisible worlds of stroke and cancer, was tugged at by their hidden presence. Then it was if a tall narrow gateway opened and Martin suddenly found himself falling toward one of those dark worlds, coming to rest beside a high, arid city of dark towers and domes behind an immense bleak wall, all deeply blackened and dulled by time. The city's buildings and ramparts, cut into and from the ancient stone of the surrounding mountains, now seemed almost imperceptibly to be sinking back into the rock and rubble from which they'd come.

Around the dull black city stood enormous white glaciers and jagged black peaks. Above them, the sun of that world stood occulted by one of three moons visible in the cloudless, violet sky. Below the eclipsed sun and scimitar moons, the ancient city stood utterly abandoned and lifeless—until a great gong or bell began to toll loudly and persistently. From everywhere in the city, dark birds erupted, as if they had always been there, hidden, waiting....

Martin awoke to the sound of his travel alarm clock ticking away on the night table beside his bed. To the mind in twilight, in hypnagogic sleep, he supposed the ticking of an alarm clock could sound like the blows of a mighty hammer, the stroke of a stroke, the tolling of a black bell called cancer. According to the clock face in the lightening room, his alarm was due to go off in ten minutes. He turned off the alarm before it could sound and sat up at the edge of his bed.

Beginning his day, he thought about parallel universes and slit experiments, about dream life and waking life, appearances and realities, things latent and blatant. Before he could shake his initial depression, however, Martin in his mind saw oceans of cold dark matter, everywhere tugging at island galaxies of light, threatening to overwhelm them.

Later that morning Martin returned to the hospital with his

mother. His father could not speak at all, now. The most he could manage was to squeeze Martin's hand when Martin asked him to. That was the only way Martin could tell there was someone still inside the body on the bed.

Leaving his mother in the room with his father, Martin walked to a private consulting room with Doctor Goyal, one of his father's attending physicians. Goyal informed him that a cytological workup had confirmed the CT scan findings of metastatic pancreatic carcinoma. The presence of nodules in the lungs as well as the abdomen had also been confirmed. The words came thick and fast: Occulted blood. Inoperable. Incurable.

The doctor refused to speculate on whether there might be any link between the pancreatic cancer Martin's father was now dying from and the late-onset diabetes he had been diagnosed with six years earlier. As to whether the cancer might have somehow caused the stroke—invisible tumors throwing clots of cells through his father's blood, manifesting visibly in the brain attack—or whether the stroke might have somehow caused the cancer—the brain attack knocking down his father's immune system to the point that the cancer, lurking invisibly in him, now was unleashed to rampage through his body—on those possibilities too the doctor remained noncommittal.

About all the doctor would speculate on was how much longer he thought Martin's father had to live. Given his father's age of seventy one, and his stroke-weakened condition, the doctor estimated Martin's father had two weeks to a month left. He informed Martin that the staff would be discontinuing intravenous nutrition. Since there was nothing more they could do for Martin's father in the hospital, Goyal recommended that they begin discharge proceedings—preferably transferring the patient to a hospice, where the staff could try to make his last days as comfortable as possible.

Martin agreed. When he returned to his father's room, Martin thought that, just as his father's body was failing him, just as the doctors had failed his father too, so too was even science itself

failing his family as a source for final causes and explanations. The science that used to resolve paradoxes, Martin thought, now seemed to resolve itself only in paradoxes. Which came first—the cancer or the stroke? The projectile's impact, the sound of the firing of the gun, the order to fire? What did it matter, when you never hear the one that gets you anyway?

Martin and his mother returned home for lunch while an ambulance transferred his father to the VistaCare Hospice. Over lunch he and his mother discussed her future finances for that time after Dad was gone.

"Your father never made much money," his mother said, "but that never much bothered him." Somehow her voice managed to be resigned, proud, yet a bit worried as she said it—all at the same time.

He and his mother went to visit his father again that afternoon and evening, this time in his room at the hospice. The facility, with its carefully color-coordinated reception area rather like the lobby of a pleasant resort hotel, was "very nice," as his mother put it. His father's room, too, done up in subtle rose patterns against dark blue backgrounds, reminded Martin of a comfortable hotel room—except for the hospital-style bed, the catheter tube discreetly covered by the bedclothes, the quiet thrumming of the oxygen system and the thin, clear plastic tubing hooked to the septum of his father's nose. It was, at any rate, covered by the hospice care provision of his father's insurance—though only for a week.

The hospice nurse who met and talked with them was a kind and sympathetic woman of middle years. While his mother remained behind with his father, Martin spoke with the nurse, who gave him a brochure on "The Ethics of Artificial Hydration and Nourishment," which seemed to be mainly about the removal of those things, in his father's case. The nurse informed him that his father was receiving via dermalgesic patch twenty-five micrograms per hour of a synthetic opiate, equivalent to fifty milliliters per hour of morphine. His father might be less responsive now, but it was also much less likely that he would

be feeling any pain.

Although his father could not respond and Martin could not be sure whether his father understood or even heard him, he still felt the need to talk to Dad. That evening Martin reminded him of the first time his father took him out of the city to see the meteor showers and count shooting stars. Martin could only retell it the way he recalled it, trying to reawaken that long-ago time in both their memories.

"I remember you saying 'Look! There! Did you see it?' when the first star shot past overhead," Martin told his father. "Thanks, Dad. I owe a lot of what I've done, and who I am, to you. I'm still counting starlight—all the way down to individual photons, now. I wish we could have seen more meteor showers together over the years, but thanks for the ones we did see."

Over the next few days, Martin and his mother fell into the strange routine of visiting his dying father in shifts—first in the latter part of the morning, then again in the late afternoon and evening. On Sunday morning they met the hospice medical director, Doctor Bletcher, when he came in to examine Martin's father. The doctor too had lost a parent to pancreatic cancer—his mother, also at age seventy one.

"We're not talking about weeks or months here," Bletcher said, gently but straightforwardly, when he had finished his examination of Martin's father. "We're talking about hours or days. You do understand that?"

Martin and his mother understood. They thanked the doctor before he left, and soon afterward they left too. When they returned again in the afternoon, his father drank slowly from the child's sippy cup Martin or his mother held to the dying man's lips. Martin told his father the story of how he remembered that summer evening on vacation in Kentucky all those years ago, when the odometer turned over in the old Rambler from "99999" to "00000"—all together and all at once, "and you watching me, saying 'Look! There! Did you see it?'"

The skies had not opened, nor the New Jerusalem descended from the clouds, but Martin remembered it anyway as an

epiphany, a small apocalypse, at least in the sense of "revelation." His father, however, now seemed farther away than ever, completely unable to speak, unable even to squeeze Martin's hand—as if he had already stepped through the sky to somewhere else.

"This is what they mean by a deathbed watch, isn't it?" his mother asked Martin on the drive home. "I've never done this before. God, I didn't expect to be doing this with your father—never so soon, anyway."

Martin nodded. They all had expectations. His mother had hoped and expected that she and his father would both live to celebrate their fiftieth wedding anniversary. Martin had at least hoped his father would live some ways into the new millennium. It was not to be, no matter how much they might have desired it.

That night he dreamed strange dreams again, first of time-dilating space flights and equally miraculous suspensions of death in life, then of his father, trapped in a limbo entirely composed of vicious, paradoxical dilemmas played out in innumerable worlds great and small, virtualities to his dying daylight reality, interference from other universes flashing out of the tall slit doorway toward which he was moving.

Breathing hard, waking bolt-upright in bed, Martin disappeared from dark dreamed worlds. What horrible nightmares. What did it all mean? Did it mean anything? Martin shook his head, but he could not shake the dream out of his mind. If existence is a dream and the dream has no meaning, then meaning has no existence. Life, Reality itself—all just a waste of time. Better never to have been born, as the ancient Greeks said.

Later that morning when they returned to the hospice, Martin's father, still silent and motionless but for the pursing of his lips when they gave him water or juice, nonetheless seemed unusually alert, awake, clear-eyed. Martin talked and talked.

"Thanks for all the things you've done for me, Dad," he said, sitting beside his father's raised bed, holding his father's right hand. "I love you, Dad. Always have, even if I never really

appreciated you enough. Sorry for being such an ungrateful little thug when I was a teenager...."

His mother gave an embarrassed laugh.

"You weren't so bad," she said. But Martin remembered it differently.

"You know, Dad," he continued, remembering what had come into his mind that night in England when his mother called to tell him of his father's stroke. "Sometimes I'm afraid one lifetime is never enough time to learn all the things we really need to learn. But you—you always kept learning. You've always been open and curious about everything, just for the pleasure of knowing about it. Thanks for that. Thanks for showing me that."

When the nurses eventually came in to turn his father on the bed, Martin and his mother said their morning shift good-byes. Martin was surprised to feel his father squeeze his hand and try to say his name before they left. His father hadn't been able to manage that much in days.

Driving home, Martin felt a bit embarrassed by all his chattering at his father. "That I must like a whore unpack my heart with words." That was how Hamlet put it. Words unpack the heart, Martin thought, but also make trivial what they unpack. If each of his words to his father were itself an ocean of newly-minted salt tears, all of those oceans could not empty the emptiness that filled him at the prospect of his father's death. Perhaps, he thought, I allow myself to talk only because I cannot allow myself to cry.

Over a late lunch, Martin's mother wondered if Dr. Bletcher might be wrong. Dad had seemed so awake and aware this morning. She thought he might linger on, beyond the seven days of hospice care his insurance covered. What would they do then? Should they transfer him to a less expensive hospice? Should they bring him home?

They had come to no resolution when they returned to the hospice late in the afternoon for the final shift of the day. Dad's eyes were wide open when they walked into the room. Through many sips, he drank the full container of apple juice Martin's

mother gave him, as if to please her—and it did, very much.

A few minutes later, Martin's father began to make a bruffing sound. Was he trying to say something? Was he aspirating the apple juice and choking? Martin's mother walked hurriedly into the hall to get the nurse. The nurse came in and checked his pulse, then said she needed to get a blood pressure cuff.

"I guess we need to be more careful giving him fluids," Martin's mother said to the nurse when she returned and continued to examine Martin's father. "So he doesn't choke like this."

"That's not what this is," the nurse said to Martin and his mother, simply but with the force of urgency. "He is dying. He's going. Come up on either side of him: Now. Hug him and pray for him and say good-bye to him as he goes."

Martin and his mother hurried forward. They hugged him and held his head. Across the bed Martin's mother cried, "We love you! We love you!" Martin said, "Love you, Dad." The nurse muttered a steady stream of words, prayers in which "Jesus" was the most often repeated sound. As they prayed their good-byes to his father, Martin closed his eyes and pressed his head to his father's.

The image of the bent blue monolith of sky shining into the dome above the Thaw telescope filled his head. Upward, into the warped plank of twilight sky darkening too rapidly toward night, the telescope softly fired stars, heavenly fire shining anew again with the glint his own father's eyes had gathered from the light of 26,000 days. Now, passing upward into that single tall slit of twilight sky, that light was given back, the stars the slit filled with always and only each star's innumerable versions of itself in innumerable parallel universes. In the aching clarity of that light, Martin at last understood that reality is much bigger than it seems. The whole of the universe all the world's telescopes peered out toward was only a tiny microcosm amid a tremendous ensemble of invisible universes, a vast metaspace made visible now in an instant of unbearable brightness.

Then it was done. Martin and his mother stepped back in

silence. When the last breath was gone, there was only open-mouthed, slack-jawed death. His father was there, yet he was gone.

* * * * * * *

In the observatory crypt, Martin rubbed his eyes and checked his watch. Time to go, he thought as he stood up. Full astronomical twilight now, as dark as it gets.

The darkness, when it comes, always comes too soon, Martin thought as walked out of the crypt and upstairs. Making his way through the familiar maze of the observatory once more, it occured to him too that the speed of death always outruns all preparations for the event, no matter how hastily those might be undertaken.

Over the ten days following his father's death, Martin had moved numbly through the worlds of funeral homes and headstone carvers and obituaries and memorial services. For the epitaph on his father' stone, Martin chose the words Hamlet to Horatio said of his father, Old Hamlet: "He was a man, take him for all in all; I shall not look upon his like again."

The words helped him, through his own grief and loss, and his mother's and his brother's. Death must be rightly weighed, but who knew what scales to balance it in? Events, like unexpected music, like numbers in new equations, took on a life of their own. Grief, like time, was universal, yet always also painfully local.

When he had come back to work today, and all day long, his waking life was that disconcerting music playing from the radio in a car being driven through hilly terrain at the overlapping edge of two broadcasting territories. Or at least it had been, until a few moments ago. His time in the crypt had helped, somehow, to make that strange duality collapse back to unity again.

Rejoining Joy where she was processing tonight's Lalande data in the control room of the Thaw, he checked e-mail on his computer. He found a message from Art Glaser:

Hi, Martin—

Here's the source you wanted to know about, the context for that Brashear quote in the crypt:

> *Reach me down my Tycho Brahe,*
> *I would know him when we meet...*
> *Though my soul may sit in darkness,*
> *It will rise in perfect light.*
> *I have loved the stars too fondly*
> *To be fearful of the night.*
> —*Sarah Williams*

Best,

Art

Martin leaned forward, against the glass of the control room window. His eyes passed along the barrel of the Thaw 'scope, rising upward, to the star-filled slit of night sky, to the light of Lalande 21185. Yes, he thought. Perfect light. Invisible things tug at visible things. Words unspoken tug at words spoken. Hope tugs at memory. The future tugs at the past, across that standing wave and traveling catastrophe called the present.

Look! There! Did you see it?

Yeah, Dad, he thought. I saw it.

KNOT YOUR
GRANDFATHER'S KNOT

Mike Sakler knew about chaos. In the 1950s his doctoral work in turbulent airflow dynamics eventually led to a job with a major aerospace contractor in Southern California. He'd dabbled in nonlinear dynamics throughout his career, then chaos and complexity theory in the 1980s and '90s. Since his retirement and his wife Ginny's death of lung cancer, in 1989, he'd had lots of time for dabbling.

With the kids grown and gone, he sold the family house in Southern California and moved to the central Sierra Nevada near Alder Springs, an hour outside Fresno, among tall pines and old oaks and tree-sized manzanita. He spent his days working and playing on his twenty-acre spread and in his great barracks-like, 12,000 square foot retirement "party house." Solar powered and off the grid, he built the house with his own hands, out of wood from his own land's trees.

Once the house was up, he found himself playing more than working: tossing horseshoes, bowing his fiddle, strumming his banjo, jamming with young friends, endlessly tinkering with his home sound-studio's electronics.

His fascination with the Cord 810 Beverly was much more than just play or dabbling, however. Mike considered the mothballed green 1936 Cord to be the strange attractor underlying his increasingly chaotic life.

Part of it was personal history. His own grandfather had owned a Cord exactly like the piece of automotive sculpture

previously owned by Donald and Rita Batchelder: same make, model, and year. When Mike was twelve and his Grandfather Sakler about the same age as Mike himself now was, the old man took him in that very car to the 1939 World's Fair, for the first of a dozen visits.

The Batchelder Cord had a long and complex history of its own, going back to Rita's late husband Donald and his purchase of it at an estate sale in New York, years before. Time had pretty much blown the original paint job—a sort of silvery grey-green, like a spruce forest seen at high speed—but that was typical of Cords. Aside from that, the only further damage was the small scratch and dent made by Rita herself in 1955, for which crime Donald had forever after mothballed the car.

So it was that in all other respects the 810 looked the way it did the day it left the factory. The Cord emblem with its art-deco wings, still shining. The eyes of the hidden headlights bliss-fully sleeping away the years in the big pontoon fenders. The coffin-lid hood fronted by futuristic grillwork—still giving off an impression of blunt velocity, even though the car had been parked and motionless for more than forty years when Mike found it in Rita's garage and had to have it.

Unfortunately, Mike's relationship with Rita didn't continue very long once the sale of the Cord was consummated. What with her calling him a "mercenary, self-centered, heartless old bastard," he couldn't say the affair had ended well.

Still, he reassured himself that, if he wasn't too busy, he could always find another girlfriend through either his martial arts or folk-dancing classes—"ai-ki-do, tae-kwon-do, and do-si-do," as he liked to think of them. He'd been doing all of them for so many years that he'd have blackbelts in all three if they handed out blackbelts in folkdance.

Widow Batchelder may have called him heartless, but his heart was fine—or at least as fine as years of exercise, the latest heart meds, and the occasional angioplasty could make it. Oddly, though, he took the fiasco of his break-up with Rita worse than he would have thought. Funneling all his energy

into restoring the Cord had the virtue of diverting his attention to what seemed to be more tractable problems, at least at first.

He started with the car's aesthetics—smoothing out the dent and scratch, lifting off all the chrome pieces, getting them and the bare-steel bumpers all shined up again. He redid the paint job in its original green, working on all the detailing that would return the car to absolutely mint condition.

The body work went well. Rita claimed her husband had drained the gas and thoroughly changed the oil when he moth-balled the car in 1955, so Mike felt his odds of restoring the engine should at least be even, too.

He removed all the plugs and mystery-oiled the holes. The car wouldn't start.

He removed and cleaned the fuel system. It wouldn't start.

He rebuilt the carburetor, did a leak-down test for the rings, and checked the valves. It wouldn't start.

He hooked the pulleys to an external electric motor and cranked things around a bit to check the compression. It wouldn't start.

He adjusted what didn't need replacing, brought up the fuel, water, and electrical levels, put the key in the ignition, said a fervent prayer, and still—it wouldn't start.

He would have loved to give up, but he couldn't. When he neglected to work on it, he felt guilty, as if shirking some responsibility he didn't fully understand. He returned to it again and again, often reluctantly.

He put less effort into keeping up his own health. Where before he had been more than willing to "keep active," now he avoided trips down to the valley for martial arts classes and dance performances.

He'd be damned if he'd let the sawbones put him on one of those bland rabbit-food diets. He would eat the way he wanted to, thank you. If you couldn't enjoy life while trying to stay alive, you might as well already be dead.

The same was true of his drinking—which, after long hiatus, he took up again in a big way. His young party-people friends

kept visiting for a while, some even helping him with his automotive restoration work, but gradually his "drinkering and tinkering" drove them away.

A year and a half into the Cord project, after the endless big failures and small successes, Mike Sakler finally hit bottom.

He drank heavily the first part of the night, then fell asleep. Toward morning, Mike knew he was starting to wake up again when he dreamed he was drunk—and had tied a noose to hang himself.

He had hoped for months and months the drinking would turn up the stage machinery that made the fog in his brain, until it filled the theatre of his consciousness, obscuring his memory uniformly. It hadn't worked out that way.

Instead, as the months had passed, his memory had become more and more like the Tule fog that came up out of the ground in the valley below—fog thick yet low, so that it was easier to look straight up through it and see a star shining down out of all those long lost lightyears than see the streetlamp just passed a block and a moment before.

The star that shone down on him in his foggiest darkness now was a perfect image of the Perisphere and Trylon, with the Helicline ramping down around them: the "Egg, Spike, and Ramp," the prime symbols of the 1939 World's Fair and its "World of Tomorrow" theme.

His childhood attempts with the Build-Your-Own New York World's Fair kits never got much beyond building scale models of the 610-foot-tall Trylon obelisk, its 188 foot tall Perisphere globe companion, and the Helicline ramp linking them, but that had been all right with him. Those three were what really mattered.

How much Grandpa had loved that fair was a surprise to everyone in the family. Patriarch of a large New York Jewish clan, all the relations thought him old-fashioned, with his banjo and fiddle-playing, the same instruments he'd taught Mike to play before Mike was ten. Mike knew his grandfather wasn't old-fashioned, though. The old man had been picking up

Amazing This and *Popular That* at the newsstand for years and sharing them with his precocious, frenetic, problem-child of a grandson.

After that first trip to the Fair, Grandpa was a quiet visionary no more—a result of the same run-in with Yorkville street toughs that had altered the old man's physiognomy, or so some in the family theorized. From whatever cause, in his last two years of life Grandfather Sakler experienced a personal Indian Summer, a blaze of fierce, bright, quirky creativity in his closing days. He began keeping a journal and corresponding with world leaders and thinkers, especially Albert Einstein, with whom he met once (by accident) at the Fair and, later, by appointment at Princeton—twice.

Now, amid his deepest fog, Mike remembered the trunk load of Fair memorabilia he inherited from the old man. Rummaging with sudden furious energy through closets and drawers in the eight empty bedrooms and the enormous party room on the top floor of his cavernous house, he found he couldn't remember where he'd stored the trunk.

He staggered down his house's great spiral staircase to the main floor and pillaged more storage spaces. Fear and frustration gnawing at him, he stumbled down one last circuit of the turning stairway. In a spare basement room he finally found it: the musty sealed steamer-trunk that was his legacy from an old man dead more than fifty years.

Inside, he found journals and correspondence and other writings, an intriguing but inexplicable device apparently hand-crafted by the old man, even a full suit of what appeared to be his grandfather's clothes, smelling slightly of smoke, with fine shoes and shirts and underwear too, wrapped in a garment bag that had grown brittle with age.

All the Fair memorabilia was still there. The Trylon and Perisphere-adorned orange and blue high-modern Official Souvenir Book. Democracity clocks. Fair plates and puzzles and radios. Heinz pickle pins, and a crop of GM-Futurama "I Have Seen The Future" buttons—of which the old man had

been particularly fond.

Mike hadn't looked at any of this stuff since the early Fifties and had looked at none of it thoroughly at any time. What he remembered from his previous glances through it was embarrassment and fear that, in his final years, his grandfather had become a slightly crazed technobabbler, his notebooks full of inexplicable terms, diagrams, and equations.

What caught his eye now were the photos. In the shots taken before May 1939, the family resemblance that was always there was never so striking as it was in those images taken after that first trip to the World's Fair.

He stared at a fading color picture of himself as a boy. Beside him stood a thin, mostly bald man whose remaining hair and beard were a mix of white and grey and yellow—his grandfather, on one of their later trips to the World's Fair, with the Trylon and Perisphere in the distance behind them.

Mike knew his own visage well enough to see how close the resemblance was between the way the old man looked then and the way he himself looked now. It was almost as if the boy had grown up to become his own grandfather.

Grabbing the trunk by both handles, he hauled it upstairs. Its weight forced him to pause and lean against the railings or wall of the stairwell every few feet. When he reached his office, he set the trunk down beside his 8 x 20-foot worktable.

Clearing his Cord-related stuff from the workspace, he removed the trunk's contents and spread them out over the table's broad top. Up came the suit of clothes and other garments. The sharp leather shoes, too.

Next came all the memorabilia, the flyers, the brochures, the programs. The oxymoronic prose of the captions describing GM's futurama, "a vast miniature cross-section of America as it may conceivably appear two decades hence...."

He sat down slowly in the chair at the worktable. Looking more carefully through the correspondence and the writings again after all these years, Mike thought that the notes now seemed less demented than eerily prescient. Here, paperclipped

to a page of typed notes in a binder, was a letter apparently sent from Einstein himself:

Matter can be made to 'degrade' into energy more readily than energy can be made to 'upgrade' into matter. I do not, however, believe matter and energy are just types of information, as you have suggested, or that there is a spectrum linking them such that consciousness is just a more complex form of information than matter or energy. Nor do I believe that consciousness can be made to 'degrade' more readily into matter and energy than matter and energy can be made to 'upgrade' into consciousness. Although the distinction between past, present and future is an illusion, the distinction between energy, matter, and consciousness is not.

Indeed the notes from that page on were most curious. "Planck energy for opening gap in spacetime fabric = 10^{19} billion electron volts," read one, but then that was crossed out with a large X as the writer of the notes took a different tack.

"At each bifurcation point," read the next, "flux occurs in which many potential futures are present. Iteration and amplification mean one future is chosen and others disappear. In bifurcations the past is continually recycled, held timeless in eddies or closed time-like curves, stabilized through feedback. Time is turbulently recurrent, expressing self-similarity across different scales."

After a flurry of equations came an underlined conclusion: "Human nervous system both classical and quantum, exploits quantum scale processes to accomplish macroscale ends—solution lies in phase-locking feedback!"

Mike picked up a page with a meticulously hand-plotted diagram, hauntingly beautiful in its elegant simplicity. When he looked at it more closely, he found the diagram was labeled with questions: "Closed Timelike Rössler Attractor? Temporal Möbius in Phase Space?" Below the question was the note, "Always incompleteness and missing information at the center. The shape of uncertainty shapes certainty."

What pushed Mike back in his chair, however, was how much

the "Temporal Möbius in Phase Space" resembled an idealized, abstract image of Perisphere, Trylon, and Helicline. Looking away from the image, he realized that the sun was up, that his head hurt with hangover, and—something else. Bifurcations? Self-similarity? Phase-locking feedback? Phase space? That was the language of chaos theory!

His hand trembled as he flipped through more and more pages of detailed notes, until he reached the inside back cover of the notebook-binder. Taped to it was an ancient envelope, with the words MICHAEL SAKLER written on it. With a shaky hand he pulled the envelope loose from the notebook and opened it.

LETTER TO MYSELF:

If Professor Einstein is right about what he calls a "temporal Möbius" and I am right about the role consciousness plays on the information spectrum, then reading this letter is about to stop you from drinking yourself to slow suicide. Perhaps you have by now realized that these notes are memories of the future, not only mine in 1939, but also yours. In 1997 you have not written these notes yet, but you will—in 1939.

As a boy, we first traveled with Grandfather Sakler to the Fair on May 28, 1939, to witness the opening of the Jewish Palestine Pavilion. Albert Einstein speaks there, and that day you—I—meet him for the first time. The old man whom the boy returns home with is not his grandfather. It is himself from sixty years into that boy's future.

Why must "we" go through such temporal acrobatics? I'm glad I asked. If we don't, our grandfather will be brutally murdered after running out of gas in Yorkville on the night of May 28. The very fact that this temporal Möbius exists proves that possibility.

On one timeline, embittered by our grandfather's death, one of the many possible "us" devotes his life to inventing a time-travel device and uses it to return to 1939 to save our already severely injured Grandfather by sending him into the future.

*He—we—I—remain in 1939, taking over the role of that grand-
father. The boy is spared the suffering and grief of seeing his
grandfather die from his injuries.*

*In creating the device and using it to alter his own timeline,
however, our other self on that line creates a temporal paradox.
On that timeline, Grandfather Sakler is killed and as a result
one of us grows up to create the device that will allow him to
travel back to 1939 to prevent Grandfather Sakler's murder.
Preventing Grandpa's murder, however, means none of us ever
grows up to become the man who invents the device to prevent
Grandpa's murder. Therefore Grandfather Sakler is killed and
one of us grows up to create the device that will allow him to...
et cetera, et cetera.*

*Professor Einstein tells me the structure of the universe will
not tolerate such an endless conundrum. Instead it conserves
its own integrity by melding the two timelines together into "the
temporal equivalent of a Möbius strip"—something both and
neither loop and intersection. On such a dimension-collapsing
Möbius, "either/or" (either Grandpa is saved or the device is
created) becomes "not only/but also" (not only is Grandpa
saved but the device is also created).*

*We have, in some sense, been "grandfathered into" this
temporal loop-hole, but at a cost. The price of this shift to "not
only/but also" is the energy of our eternal vigilance. If we want
his murder to never again recur, we must ever again prevent its
recurrence.*

*I know this is difficult for you to understand at first, but if you
choose to perpetuate this recurrence, you will learn that time
travel is less like running a particle accelerator and more like
experiencing a lucid dream or particularly vivid memory.*

*Utilizing the chaotic effects always present in consciousness,
we can exploit time's turbulent and strange-attractive properties to burst the surface tension of spacetime at far, far less than
Planck energy. I know we can, because we already have.*

*For us, it's not only the dream of the doing that's grandfather
to the memory of the accomplishment, but also the reverse: The*

memory of the accomplishment is grandfather to the dream of the doing.

The device in the steamer trunk is only partially complete. I have done as much as I can with technology available before mid-century. The system can only be completed with technology from your era. I have enclosed a list of what you'll need. You'll have to search it out and make it all work together, if you choose to perpetuate our responsibility in this and knot your grandfather's knot in that old Cord.

I hope you will do so, and will find it both a loophole that binds and a knot that frees, as I have. At all events, good luck!
—Michael Sakler

P.S.: That Cord's no hot rod, but it's crucial to the set and setting of the mental state required for this time travel experience. It also works well enough for hauling batteries and getting around New York in 1939, so treat it kindly!

Mike slowly folded the letter. Lost in thought, he stroked his beard absently for a while. Well, it's better than the other option for a loophole that binds and a knot that frees, he told himself, remembering his hungover dream of a hangman's noose.

He got up from the table and the chair, and stretched. Then he went downstairs, down to the garage/workshop where the Cord sat with its hood up. The sun was shining brightly just beyond the shadows. He got to work.

* * * * * * *

Focused on his work, Mike's days flew by. A certain balance had returned to his life, too: his obsession was no longer a mad one. He returned, at least sporadically, to his ai-ki-do, tae-kwon-do, do-si-do classes. He sent a card of apology to the widow, who unfortunately was not interested in re-establishing contact. During 1998 and early 1999 he even went to Temple a

few times—something he hadn't done in years.

Maybe the prayers paid off. In June of 1998, he was able to start and run the Cord's engine for the first time—and the completed restoration cost him less than he'd expected. Such was not the case with completing the "Temporal Möbius Generator", however.

The interface synching his mind up to the machine and capable of inducing the mind-chaos needed for his time trip required state-of-the-art neuro-hookups so expensive he had to take out a second mortgage on his property. They were on the 1939 list, however, so he purchased top-of-the-line units from a "mindware" dealer operating out of a software storefront in a Marin County strip mall.

Using the system he put together, Mike experimented with low voltages to create a map of his own mind's functioning. Taking as his guide the 1939 notes—with their jargon of "ekstasis points," "temporal dissipation vortices," and "eschaton particles"—he located regions of his brain that, when stimulated, produced both "out of body experience" and vivid strange-attractor memories of the World's Fair. These, the notes indicated, were vital to the temporal voyage he was to undertake.

By May of 1999 all was in final readiness. A couple of days before his planned time-jaunt, he took the now operational and fully-equipped Cord on one lengthy test drive—but only one.

That test drive in itself narrowly missed becoming a disaster. Driving the Cord down to the Valley to see his doctor for his routine physical, he felt fine and the car was running fine, but he still almost didn't make it. Pulling off of Herndon Avenue and into the rat's maze of private medical offices surrounding St. Agnes Hospital, he blanked out at the wheel. Only in the last second did he catch himself—and catch the hard left turn he very nearly missed.

When he finally pulled into a parking spot, he was both shaken and relieved. He had narrowly escaped smashing into the cinderblock wall separating the parking lot of his doctor's building from the Hospital's parking lot.

Well, he reminded himself as he walked to his appointment, *if I'd smashed through the wall, at least I would have practically landed in the Emergency Room!*

The only sign of Mike's brush with Fate was a slightly elevated pulse rate. No trace of a mini-stroke or any other brain glitch that might explain his blanking out just moments earlier. His doctor declared him to be in fine shape, outside of the pulse spike—especially considering his cholesterol, and his plaqued arteries, and everything else the doctor deigned to lecture him on.

Given Mike's failure to change his diet to save his ticker, the doctor warned him that he would have to remain absolutely faithful in taking his heart pills and would likely still need to have surgery within the year to remove his blood mud. Mike agreed politely but planned on changing nothing because, two days later, he was ready to go.

Into his winged chariot's trunk Mike loaded the big Exide storage batteries which had, until then, provided electrical storage for the solar panels atop the roof of his off-the-grid party house. Despite the fact that his house would soon be going dark, he was in a celebratory mood.

He decided to dress appropriately for the occasion. From the closet in his office Mike removed the full suit of clothes and shoes he'd taken from the trunk, so long before, and tried them on. All the clothes fit perfectly, as he somehow knew they would.

He looked at himself in the mirror, a man of not inconsiderable years, dressed in a dark suit and tie of a rather conservative cut, topped by a snapbrim hat. Yes, just what the well-dressed time traveler would be wearing in 1939.

He locked up his home. Walking toward the Cord in the driveway, he twice glanced back wistfully toward his huge handmade house. Starting up the Cord, he drove it through evening light along the deserted Forest Service gravel road until it passed directly beneath the hydroelectric power lines, where he stopped.

Rigging up a coupling and converter, he linked power from an overhead line to the battery array in the trunk. From the system of dams and turbines on the upper San Joaquin River, he swiped enough of that "clean, safe" Democracity energy to bring the device and the storage batteries up to maximum.

As he decoupled his power tap, he doubted the power company would much notice. A little free juice was the least they owed him, after he'd put up with this power line eyesore all these years.

The fully restored Cord spun gravel on the last stretch of switchbacks before fishtailing up onto the blacktop of Alder Springs Road. Einstein had once contended that imagination was more important than knowledge. At this moment, Mike felt like a living embodiment of that premise.

No machine alone could do what he was going to do. The chaos of brain, the individuality of mind, the singularity of memory: all were indispensable to the reality of travel in time.

Over the blacktop he drove to the summit of the ridge, then stopped the Cord. Its engine thrummed along placidly, idling, as he watched the sun go down. Slowly, the rim of the turning world obscured the light of day. Soon the first stars began to come out.

Mike took off his hat and put on his temples the circlets containing the neuro-hookups. Checking everything one last time, he threw the switches to activate the timers and all the memory systems of all the computers on board, revved the engine as high as it would go, put the Cord in gear, then took his foot off the brake.

He was overcome by a euphoric sensation of floating upward, not unlike what he had sometimes experienced just as he drifted off to sleep and the bed beneath him seemed to fall away. This time, however, there was no hard jerk of ordinary consciousness striking to reassert control.

This time he just kept drifting, a full-blown out of body experience bringing his body and the car with it. Faintly he heard the engine sounds breaking up, digitizing, becoming discrete,

then wildly dilated, then sounding almost as if they were being played backwards.

Through the windshield and windows he saw a fog rising—a type of Bose condensate. Mike seemed to have seen it before: thick yet low, the Tule fog of memory.

He looked up through the windshield and saw a star perched atop a great curving skybridge, like a diamond ring effect seen during a total eclipse of the sun. The bridge was a vast, slightly rainbow-shimmering catenary Möbius curve. From this angle, it looked rather like the St. Louis Gateway Arch, only countless miles high—and it wasn't so much "in" the sky as it somehow *was* the sky.

The Cord was moving in and through the skybridge, in the ultimate daredevil stunt loop. His own memories ran like cords of fog through the suspended and suspending bridge and tunnel. Particular events in his life possessed their own unique gravity, curving and warping his memoryspace in ways he could not have foretold—

—until the fogbridge did its Möbius fillip and he sat outside the 1939 World's Fair, in sunshine, in the Cord, in the parking lot that would one day become Shea Stadium. Through the windshield he saw the Trylon and Perisphere surrounded by the whole of the Fair, a candied confection of the Future to be consumed by the present.

Putting on his hat as he stepped out of the car, Mike was man inside his own dream.

* * * * * * *

Might as well enjoy myself, he thought. He grabbed a frankfurter with everything at Swift & Company's streamlined superairliner building, then some ice cream over by Sealtest's triple shark-finned edifice. He paid for them with the antique liberty coins the notes had suggested he bring.

Strolling about the Fair grounds, he saw again how windshaped so many of the structures appeared. Buildings that

looked as if they'd been designed in wind tunnels. Frank R. Paul mélanges of fins and keels and flanges. Spirals, helices, and domes, their towers topped with zeppelin-mast spires. An airstream wonderland, waiting for the inevitable arrival of Northrop flying-wings and Bel Geddes tear-drop cars.

Stopping at the base of the Trylon and examining it closely, Mike rediscovered the Fair's secret. Like everything else, the Trylon was intended to look smoothly mass-produced, machine-precise and slipstream-slick. Up close, however, he saw that its surface was rough, stuccoed with all the "smoothness" of jesso over burlap. Beneath its assembly-line dreams of aerodynamic cowls and zero-drag farings, the great exhibition felt hand-crafted—a prototype of the shape of things to come, not a production model.

The Future is best viewed from a distance, Mike thought as he approached the Chrysler Motors Building in the Transportation Zone. Remembering its "Rocketport" display, he went inside.

Where he literally bumped into Albert Einstein.

"Pardon me, professor," Mike said quickly.

"Not a problem, not a problem," the Nobel laureate said with a distracted smile, turning back to lean on a railing. Together they watched the Rocketgun simulate another blastoff into tomorrow, with full noise-and-light special effects.

"They'll probably use it for shooting atomic bombs at each other," Mike remarked, "long before they use it for passengers."

Einstein gave him a startled look, then smiled wryly and shrugged.

This was the hard part. The only way Mike had been able to come up with to get the great man's attention was the way Klaatu had gotten Professor Barnhart's attention in *The Day the Earth Stood Still*. Mike couldn't remember how fluent Einstein's English was, but he pressed on quickly nonetheless.

"I know you've been working on unified field theory," Mike said, pulling a folded sheaf of papers and a card from his coat pocket, "so I thought you might be interested in this."

Unfolding the papers, Mike presented the sheaf to the

Professor. On the pages he had diagrammed, with explanatory captions, a particularly interesting variant of what would someday be called the Einstein-Podolsky-Rosen theorem.

Einstein glanced at the pages, perfunctorily at first, just humoring him. Then the physicist's eyes grew wide as he realized the importance of what he was looking at.

"Wo—Where—?"

"I knew you'd see their merit," Mike said, gesturing toward the thin sheaf, then handing Einstein the card with his grandfather's name, address and phone number. "It's been a pleasure meeting you in person, Professor. I can be reached at this address. Let's keep in touch."

"Ja—er, yes!" Einstein said, shuffling papers and card about in his hands so he could shake the hand Mike offered him. Tipping his hat and turning before he melted away into the crowd, Mike was pleased he'd made his Einstein contact already.

Deciding to treat himself to as much of the Fair as possible before he made his way to the Jewish Palestine Pavilion, he toured the Town of Tomorrow. Then it was on to the Immortal Well and its streamlined Time Capsule, scheduled to be opened in 6939 A.D. Next he saw the robots Elektro the Moto-Man and his Moto-Dog, Sparko, perform in the Westinghouse Building.

He felt a childlike awe at General Electric's ten-million volt indoor lightning-bolt show, and Consolidated Edison's block-long "City of Light" diorama. The line for the GM Futurama was far too long, however. His rendezvous with that tech triumph could wait for another visit.

He made his way through what felt more and more like a planetary county fair, until he at last reached the Jewish Palestine Pavilion. During the day the numbers of spectators for the pavilion's official opening ceremonies had swelled past 50,000. On the fringes of the crowd, entrepreneurs sold Jewish Palestine flags, as well as armbands and yarmulkes adorned with the Star of David.

Recalling that his grandfather—though neither Orthodox

nor Conservative—had on a lark bought such a yarmulke at the World's Fair today and all those years ago, Mike now bought one as well and put it on, in hope and remembrance.

In his accented English, Einstein himself at last pronounced the words "I am here entrusted with the high privilege of officially dedicating the building which my Palestine brethren have erected." Amid the great crowd, Mike despaired of finding the old man and boy he was seeking, but he kept looking.

By the time the ceremonies ended, however, Mike still hadn't found the boy and the old man he sought—not even after the crowd broke up.

Worry, frustration, and anxiety warred within him as he drifted like a lost ghost through the great squares and avenues of the Fair, alongside the Lagoon of Nations, past the pavilions of states and governments. He wandered beneath the closing fireworks, his hope fading like blown starshells. He came to the reflecting pool beneath the Perisphere, at just the moment the great Voice of that globe began to sound its eerie tocsin over the emptying Fair.

With other stragglers he made his way toward the parking lots, panic rising in his mind. He'd lost them somewhere in the Fair! They were no longer on the grounds anywhere! He banged his forehead with palmed fists. How to find them? How to find them?

Getting into the Cord, he sat and stared through the windshield. He felt forlorn and powerless as a lost child. Not even the play of faerie lights over the Trylon and Perisphere could alter his despondent mood. He leaned his head against the steering wheel and mourned inconsolably.

Yorkville.

The word drifted into his consciousness like a boon from a merciful god. Yes! New York's German-American section, where his grandfather had had his run-in with the street gangsters. Only a hunch, but as he left the parking lot for the streets he could think of nowhere else to go.

He had maps, but the maps were not the city. He got lost,

again and again. By memory he had successfully navigated across sixty years of time and thousands of miles of space, but now he was having difficulty finding his way around New York City!

When at last he made his way into Yorkville, streets and landmarks began to take on the faintest aura of *déjà-vu* familiarity. He began to remember. They'd run out of gas, yes. He had waited in the car while his grandfather had gone to fill up the gas can. His grandfather had been gone a long time—

At the far edge of a streetlight, in a vacant lot, Mike saw and heard it, before he was ready for it. Four young men yelling "Jude! Unflätig Jude! Verderber! Teufel-Jude!" as they pummeled and kicked an old man.

Mike skidded to a stop beside the nightmare tableau and got out of the car.

At the sound of the Cord screeching to a halt, the young men stopped their heavy-booted work. Hearing the car door opening and slamming, one of the men, the smallest, took to his heels. The other three stood their ground, fists clenched.

Mike walked steadily across the lot toward them. When he was perhaps fifteen feet away, one of the three abruptly broke away toward something off to one side—a gasoline can. Mike saw the youth take matches and handkerchief rag from his pockets. He knew immediately what the boy intended to do.

While the fire maker fumbled about his work, Mike in battle dance kata waded into the remaining two, punching and kicking.

An elderly avenging angel, he felt strangely detached, as if in a minor trance. His only barely-conscious thought was an odd little mantra—*ai-ki-do, tae-kwon-do, do-si-do*, again and again.

He knew he took many blows and strikes, but he gave far more, stomping insteps, roundhouse-kicking ribs, smashing noses, snapping collar bones, shattering kneecaps. Even Yorkville street toughs had never encountered such a fighting style. They fled at last, but they had done their damage.

His grandfather, doused about the neck and chest with a

slosh of gasoline, was going up in slow immolation. It was all Mike could do to put out the fire with his suit coat. The old man's pulse was thready, but the pain of his burns roused him to consciousness.

"Thank you," he whispered, coughing blood.

"Grandpa," Mike said, cradling the old man's head, "it's me, Michael."

"Michael?" asked his grandfather, confused. "How?"

"I know—I'm old," Mike said, picking his grandfather up awkwardly in a fireman's carry. He headed toward the Cord, heart pounding, talking all the while, adrenalin-delirious, trying to explain. "I know it doesn't seem to make sense. But listen, you've got to believe me. I'm sending you into the future. You'll die of your wounds and burns, here. I've come from the future to help you. Having you to save saves me, both as the boy I was, and the old man I'll be."

Mike opened the passenger side door of the Cord and propped his grandfather in the seat. Dazedly his grandfather watched him. Taking Grandpa Sakler's keys and money clip, Mike tossed his own wallet onto the seat beside his grandfather.

"All the ID you'll need to pass for me in 1999 is in that wallet and in the car," Mike told him. His grandfather nodded weakly, or perhaps he passed out. Coming around past the back of the car, Mike opened up the driver's side door. Slotting his own key on its key chain into the Cord's ignition, he started the car and turned on the temporal Möbius generator.

The car was equipped with enough computer power for a full memory of his trip here, as per the notes he had written, the notes he would write. Now, though, he would have to change its return destination.

Putting on the neuro-hookups, he fast-reversed the memory guidance record to a bifurcation point two days before he left 1999—to his last trip to the doctor's office near St. Agnes Hospital, for his physical.

This time, the Cord would miss the turn, and not miss the cinderblock retaining wall. He remembered all he could, then

imagined the car through wall and total smashup, into the hospital parking lot—right in front of Emergency, where an old-fashioned man with a secret desire to see the future would finally get his wish.

Turning to his unconscious grandfather, he kissed the old man lightly atop his bloodied head.

"I love you, Grandpa."

He stood on the brake, revving the engine while in gear. At the same instant he flipped the Möbius generator's last switch, dropped his foot off the brake, and threw himself from the car, the circlets tearing free of his head.

Around him he felt the chill of death. He was every place and no place at all, every time and no time, and he was falling....

He landed heavily on his hip. Around him a thin mist dissipated as a breeze blew along the street. He propped himself up on his forearm, feeling old and very tired. Something had happened to his memory. His recall of the last several hours was as hazy as a dream or nightmare dissolving on waking.

"Grandpa?" A boy's voice said, coming toward him. The boy peered into his face with evident concern. "Grandpa, is that you? You don't look right. Are you okay?"

"Just tripped and fell down, is all," Mike said, getting slowly to his feet. At last he began remembering something of the role he was supposed to play.

"Grandpa? Where's the gas can?"

For a moment Mike had no idea what the boy was talking about. The boy looked around.

"Oh, here it is," the boy said, running to pick it up from the vacant lot, then coming back, still looking at Mike. "Here. Your yarmulke fell off too."

"I'm a bit discombobulated from the fall, is all," Mike said, trying painfully to smile and joke as he took the yarmulke with its Star of David from the boy's hand. "Thank you. Lead the way back to the car. I'll follow you."

The short walk returned Mike partway to his senses. His chest hurt. He realized that, here in 1939, without medications

or surgical techniques yet to be invented, he would not live very long.

So be it. Until he died he would lead a very full life. Here, in this time when the Future was beautiful and distant as Heaven, he would spend his remaining days remembering—and planning.

"Hey Grandpa!" the boy called when he'd reached his Grandfather's Cord automobile. "Gimme the keys."

"What?" Mike said. He looked quizzically at the kid as he took the gas can from the boy. The can was still close to half full. Pouring its remaining contents into the fuel tank, he hoped it would be enough to restart the car.

"You know," the boy said. "Lemme drive."

"No, no," Mike said, waving his hand in a light gesture of dismissal. He put the empty gas can in the trunk, then opened the doors to let them both in. He slipped the key into the ignition and looked at the smiling boy sitting on the other side of the front seat.

"You may just be driving this road too, someday," the old man said quietly. "Maybe sooner than you think."

After a time, the engine caught and they drove away.

ABOUT THE AUTHOR

HOWARD V. HENDRIX's first four published novels appeared from Ace Books (Penguin Putnam): *Lightpaths* (1997), *Standing Wave* (1998), *Better Angels* (1999), and *Empty Cities of the Full Moon* (2001). His fifth novel, *The Labyrinth Key*, appeared from Ballantine Del Rey in April 2004. His sixth novel, *Spears of God*, was published by Del Rey in December 2006.

His most widely available works of shorter science fiction can be found in his "double" short story collection *Human in the Circuit/Depth of Perception* (Borgo Press 2011), *Möbius Highway* (Scorpius Digital Books, 2001), the *Full Spectrum* original anthology series, Vols. 1, 4, and 5 (Bantam Books), and in *The Outer Limits*, Volume 1 (Prima).

He has also published numerous poems, political essays, book reviews, and works of literary criticism, including his book-length study of apocalyptic elements in English literature from Langland to Milton, *The Ecstasy of Catastrophe* (1990). An avid gardener, his book on landscape irrigation, *Reliable Rain* (co-authored with Stuart Straw), appeared in March 1998 from Taunton Press.

His degrees range from a B.S. in Biology to an M.A. and Ph.D. in English Literature. He and his wife Laurel both teach at California State University, Fresno, and live near Shaver Lake, California, where they enjoy backpacking and snowshoeing in the Sierra Nevada.